D0820812

TOMBSTONE BLUES

TOMBSTONE BLUES

A NOVEL

KEN HODGSON

FIVE STAR

A part of Gale, Cengage Learning

GALE
CENGAGE Learning®

Detroit • New York • San Francisco • New Haven, Conn • Waterville, Maine • London

GALE
CENGAGE Learning

LIBRARY OF CONGRESS CATALOGING-IN-PUBLICATION DATA

Hodgson, Ken.
    Tombstone blues : a novel / by Ken Hodgson. — 1st ed.
    p. cm.
    ISBN 978-1-4328-2603-1 (hardcover) — ISBN 1-4328-2603-4
(hardcover) 1. Murder for hire—Fiction. 2. Tombstone (Ariz.)—
Fiction. I. Title.
PS3558.O34346T66 2012
813'.54—dc23   2012013199

First Edition. First Printing: August 2012
Published in conjunction with Tekno Books and Ed Gorman
Find us on Facebook–https://www.facebook.com/FiveStarCengage
Visit our Web site–http://www.gale.cengage.com/fivestar/
Contact Five Star™ Publishing at FiveStar@cengage.com

Printed in Mexico
1 2 3 4 5 6 7 16 15 14 13 12

This book is for my wife, Rita, along with
Curt and Dana Kockx, for all of the right reasons.

CHAPTER ONE

As Samantha Sterling drove her shiny new red Jeep Liberty out of Houston heading west, her heart was happy. She had no intentions whatsoever of killing anyone. If Samantha had had any inkling of the twists and turns her starting anew in life would entail, she would have shot off the nearest exit ramp and sped right back to Houston.

Driving through the monotonous expanse of bleakness that comprises West Texas, Samantha (Sam to her friends) began trying to cast off a bitter memory at every milepost she passed. There were a lot of mileposts in Texas, but Sam worried if there were enough.

At the age of thirty-six, she was on her own for the first time in fifteen years, fourteen of which had been wasted on her ex-husband, a weasel of a man by the name of Arnold Wilkins.

Samantha had met Arnold in college. For some reason she could no longer remember, the two had fallen madly in love. After graduation they'd gotten married. Arnold went on to law school while Samantha worked two jobs to pay his tuition and their bills.

It was after Arnold had passed the bar and joined a prestigious Houston law firm specializing in personal injury law that she realized an appalling reality: All lawyer jokes are based on solid truth.

Her husband became a changed man. Arnold loved money and he loved winning—by any means. Samantha was shocked at first when he bragged that "the truth doesn't matter a whit in court, it's what you make the jury believe that counts."

Then, Samantha became a castoff from Arnold's life, just as he had forsaken what was honest and true in this world. A man who loves success and power more than his devoted wife eventually finds himself with only the ashes of what used to be flames of love.

Milepost 351. There goes the memory of catching Arnie in bed with a blonde bimbo. Splat!

The Enron debacle had been the straw that broke the camel's back of their marriage. Samantha had drifted into the slipstream of passionless existence so often found by women after love grows cold.

Arnold's greed and living life by "the deal," as he was so fond of saying, blinded him to the fact that he was swimming in a sea filled with sharks. And many of these sharks were far more accomplished predators than he.

Arnold had gleefully invested most of their joint savings of nearly a million dollars into Enron stock. Samantha had actually begged him to take out at least half of the money once their brokerage account had swollen to over ten million.

But her husband always knew best. He lambasted her for being a wife who held him back, called her a wimpy bitch from the sticks who was devoid of class and culture.

Milepost 350. Splat, there goes the memory of losing ten million dollars.

They filed for divorce only a week after the collapse of Enron. She found that hiring a lawyer to fight another lawyer who happened to be her husband quickly became another bitter and expensive lesson.

After the legal dogs had quit snarling and fighting over what scraps remained, Samantha Sterling (she had reclaimed her maiden name, one of the few things her lawyer had actually managed to accomplish) found herself living in a one-bedroom apartment with not quite fifty thousand dollars in the bank. The only thing she felt grateful for was the fact they had no children. The future loomed black and threatening as a Texas tornado. It would have been cruel to subject a child to its throes.

Milepost 349. Splat, there goes the memory of a lawyer. Any lawyer. The nearest one will do nicely.

For a year after the divorce Samantha kept working at her job managing a chain restaurant. She became a recluse, ignoring entreaties from old friends and co-workers to join them for a drink or to enjoy some of Houston's plentiful nightlife.

To help stifle the empty loneliness, she adopted a cat from the local animal shelter. The black tom was six months old, having obviously been a stray, fighting for scraps of food just to stay alive. A good-sized piece of the cat's left ear was missing, along with the tip of its tail.

"We have a lot of nice kittens," the lady at the shelter had said when she noticed Samantha staring at the soft-eyed tom. "That one won't be adopted by anyone. He'll be put down tomorrow."

The second the cage door opened, the cat jumped into her arms, snuggled in deep, and began purring loudly. It was as if the tom had understood every word of his intended fate and realized this was his last chance to snag a human companion.

And snag Samantha's heart he did. She adopted the cat, naming him Shakespeare for that wonderful line the Bard wrote in *Henry the Sixth,* "The first thing we do, let's kill all the lawyers."

She'd never had a cat before. It surprised her just how fast Shakespeare had claimed her apartment for his own. The skinny feline Samantha had brought home was now a sleek, though chunky, tomcat weighing over twenty pounds. When he stretched out on the floor he was more than three feet long and enjoyed irritating her by sleeping on top of her head at night.

"We're both castaways, aren't we buddy?" Samantha said, tapping the carrier on the seat beside her. "No one wants us, but we've got each other."

A loud purring from the carrier told her Shakespeare agreed.

Milepost 348. There goes the memory of Arnold Wilkins. Splat!

Last month Samantha had taken a personal inventory. Everything and every place in Houston reminded her of past hurts and failures. Even the hot, humid weather had become oppressive. It was time to move on to some place fresh and start life anew.

She had undressed and examined herself in a mirror on the bathroom door. Not bad, not bad at all. The visits to a health club had kept her figure trim. She had fluffed out her shoulder-length auburn hair, wet her ruby lips, turned to the left and then the right, while fluttering her emerald eyes seductively. She could still entice a man, that was for certain. Only this time she would be much more careful to check him out before handing over her heart.

A job search on the Internet had produced hundreds of possibilities. There were restaurants and inns in every state looking for managers. The problem was, they were all in large, faceless cities along with the usual traffic jams, smog, and crime. Aside from the weather, she doubted her life would be much different in Denver or Seattle.

Then, it had happened: a small ad seeking a manager for a "small and exclusive bed and breakfast with only select clientele in the historic town of Tombstone, Arizona."

A few e-mails and faxes later, Samantha Sterling gave notice to her boss along with the apartment manager and began poking through closets and drawers, trying to decide what to take and what to donate to the Salvation Army.

Milepost 347. Here goes the memory of the time Arnold sold my Lexus and invested the money in Enron stock. Splat!

Living in a Western town founded on legends and history, a girl needed transportation to fit the area. All her life she had driven nothing but cars. This needed to change just like everything else in her life.

Samantha loved her brand-new Jeep. It was four-wheel drive and the only vehicle she'd ever bought all by herself. Sure it cost more money than she should have spent, but starting over wasn't a cheap thing to do. Then again, being married to the likes of Arnold Wilkins had been terribly costly.

Milepost 346. Splat. There goes another memory of my ex. I wonder how many more there are left?

Now, driving west to a new job and a new life, Samantha's heart and spirits were high. Tombstone simply had to be a fascinating place in which to live. She had never even been in Arizona or west of San Angelo, Texas, for that matter. Everything would be new and wonderful.

The die had been cast. Samantha patted the animal carrier, sending up purrs to blend with the whine of tires on blacktop as she headed west.

The buoyant young lady drove on, toward a brilliant desert sunset that shimmered on the horizon, red as a pool of fresh blood.

CHAPTER TWO

Tombstone, Arizona, the historical silver boomtown that had given birth to so many legends, clung to the sides and valleys of rolling, treeless hills like a broken promise. Much of the strange vegetation that lay low and omnipresent appeared dead. Samantha thought the plants had taken a close look at their surroundings and decided giving up the ghost was preferable to hanging on in such an inhospitable place.

Driving through the town of St. David, only a few miles hence, she'd been hopeful. There were lush trees, ponds, and fertile fields. Then, as the road climbed to the south, it was as if she had crossed an invisible line that separated the living from the barely alive.

Get over it.

This was not Houston with all its greenery, hustle, bustle, and traffic jams, Sam reminded herself. Tombstone is a frontier mining town. History has been preserved here.

"It's like we're going back in time a hundred years, Shakespeare."

The tomcat had either dozed off or the glimpses of the countryside he could see through the slots in his carrier had put him into shock. In any event, Shakespeare remained silent.

Rounding a slow curve, carefully adhering to the thirty-five-miles-per-hour posted speed limit, Samantha began to feel a flicker of hope. There were a few trees and quaint old buildings interspersed among gaudy convenience stores and billboards hawking everything from gunfights to Vincent Price narrating the town's history.

Samantha was fairly certain Vincent Price had been dead for a number of years. She shook her head and decided any narrating the grand old actor was doing, came from really old tape recordings.

From studying a map her new employers had mailed, Samantha turned to the right, drove for one block, then turned left onto Allen Street. This was where the most famous gunfight in the West took place. Wyatt Earp and Doc Holliday had thoroughly trounced the Hatfields and McCoys here back in 1881.

Samantha tilted her head in thought. *No, it was the Clantons and McLaurys that got shot on that fateful day.* Now that she was soon to be a resident of Tombstone, it was imperative she get her history straight.

A few books on the area would be helpful. A glance at the dash clock told her she had a couple of hours to do some shopping. For some inexplicable reason, her new employers had made it quite plain she was to show up at five o'clock sharp.

Samantha shrugged as she pulled into a parking space. A lot of small, exclusive resorts were owned by somewhat eccentric people. And the salary her new job would pay was twice what she had earned in Houston. Being punctual simply gave her time to get acquainted with the town.

Having to wait until a horse-drawn stagecoach clattered by before she could open the door of her Jeep was a totally new experience. The sharp cracking of gunfire in the distance told Samantha that quite a few new experiences were in store for her.

CHAPTER THREE

Sidney Munson ambled into the kitchen of the Sunset Bed and Breakfast to see how his best friend and life mate, Michael, was coming along with pressing the oleander leaves and flowers.

"This is slow going," Michael complained, looking over the tops of small, gold-rimmed eyeglasses. "We really do need to shop about and find something larger than a garlic press for this grueling task."

"We shall do just that on our next trip to Tucson," Sidney replied. "Then you can cease straining your poor hands."

Michael backed off and stared at the glass measuring cup with Sidney. Both men were in their fifties and reading the graduation marks on the side required them to use their bifocals.

"I'm going to squeeze another ounce or so of juice," Michael said. "I want to mix it with a dab of flour and place it in the pantry."

"Are those pesky cockroaches back again?"

"Yes. I am afraid it is so. They do have a way of coming back no matter what we try."

"Ummm," Sidney mumbled, a trait he had had for many years when he thought hard on any subject. "I believe you may be on to something here, Michael. None of the commercial roach poisons we have purchased seem strong enough to do the trick. A dab of oleander may very well solve our cockroach problem."

"I really don't know if it will kill bugs or not. While it works very well for our normal use, only a test will tell for certain. Goats, as we well know, are quite immune to oleander."

"It is worth a try." Sidney stepped up to the long oak countertop and grabbed the garlic press. "Let me do this while you see to the rest of our guests' dinner arrangements."

"I am preparing your favorite: grilled sole almondine with just that slight hint of wild sage you enjoy."

"You work so hard. I have great hopes that we can eventually hire some help to relieve us both from such stress. The Company has kept us very busy of late."

"Quite profitably so, I must add." Michael opened the door to a huge stainless steel refrigerator and began poking around. "Business has doubled from a year ago."

Sidney put on a pair of rubber gloves and began stuffing the press with white oleander blooms. "We could well do with a vacation. That Alaskan cruise we looked into sounded *so* relaxing. The country up there is simply gorgeous compared to the local desert."

"Tut-tut, my friend. I have no doubts that one of the young ladies will work out."

"Hopefully better than the girl last week. Her screaming unnerved me terribly."

"She did have a shrill voice. I have always held that blondes are somewhat flighty creatures. It was a shame, really, having to put her down, she was quite a lovely dear."

"We must simply look on the matter as the cost of doing business."

"I know," Sidney said with a push on the handle. "And we must remember to keep a happy attitude. There will be another applicant here at five."

"Yes." Michael glanced at the wall clock. "This one has auburn hair, I believe. I'm betting she will do just fine. Then, after few months of training her, we can schedule that cruise."

"I hope you're right." Sidney nodded to a Bose CD player sitting at the end of the counter. "Please put on Mozart, I am in the mood for something soothing, and I dare not risk getting a drop of oleander on anything we may touch later."

"Of course, my friend. Then I shall put some fresh flowers on the dining room table and tidy up a bit in the parlor. Our guest may return from visiting Tombstone at any moment now."

"You are so thoughtful, Michael. I do hope you are correct about this new girl working out. What did you tell me her name was again?"

Michael smiled as he slid a CD into the player. "Samantha Sterling. She's coming all the way from Houston, Texas."

"That's a goodly distance should any relatives start poking their noses into our business."

"Only if she fails, my friend."

"We shall know the answer to that question soon enough." Sidney eyed the milky liquid in the cup. "I do believe we have enough for a good-sized cherry pie."

CHAPTER FOUR

Samantha had never seen horses wearing diapers before. She was fairly certain this wasn't historically accurate, but every horse pulling a stagecoach had a bag draped beneath the appropriate area. While almost undoubtedly a modern addition, she had to agree it improved the quality of air and shopping conditions in Tombstone while keeping to the Western flavor.

A new black cowboy hat with a sparkling silver band was the prize of her shopping spree. She moved the rearview mirror to check her appearance.

I've heard a lot of men say that a girl wearing a hat is sexy as hell. I think they're right.

She gave a devilish grin, reached over to the backseat and stowed the two sacks containing a half dozen books, each declaring to be the only one that told the absolute truth about Tombstone's wild and woolly past.

While the town may have had a lot going for it over a hundred years ago, Samantha was shocked to find there were no supermarkets, theaters, or any of the usual conveniences closer than Sierra Vista. A clerk had told her the town was sixteen miles to the west over what he described as a "somewhat twisty" road. "But it *is* paved," he quickly added with pride.

We are no longer in Kansas, Toto.

An urgent meow from the carrier gave notice that Shakespeare was in dire need of attention. Samantha had parked under one of the few shade trees to be found in Tombstone, kept the windows partially open, and checked on him twice. The weather was surprisingly cool for the desert, possibly only into the sixties. This dispelled her theory that it was always hot in Arizona, even in March. Heat was certainly not Shakespeare's problem.

"Poor little guy, I've kept you locked up since we stopped for lunch, haven't I?"

A mix of purring and meowing from the white carrier.

"Hang on for a few minutes, I'll drive outside town a little ways, then we'll take a walk."

Samantha kept a harness on Shakespeare after she found how much the tom loved to be put on a leash and taken for an outing. In Houston this presented problems from other people walking their dogs. Samantha was deathly afraid for Shakespeare's safety. Then one sunny afternoon in the park a large mongrel had jerked free of its owner and attacked. She was shocked when the big tom, which she'd refused to have declawed, not only held his ground but sent the dog yelping off after a few quick and bloody swats from his razor-sharp claws.

It was twenty minutes to five, there was no reason to rush. Following the map she drove south on the main street, disclosing that aside from a few blocks of preserved history, Tombstone differed little from any small town.

She drove past a school, several homes, and an attractive adobe saloon that almost certainly catered to the locals. A turn to the right took her past huge mounds of rusty-looking rocks that she supposed were left over from past mining operations. Considering the size of the piles, half of a mountain was missing somewhere.

The road turned to gravel and dropped into a broad, gentle dry wash the map called Emerald Gulch. Samantha pulled off to one side and shut off the engine. A long look around caused her to doubt the sobriety of any cartographer who saw anything emerald-colored in this wasteland.

The moment she opened the door, Shakespeare tried to bolt from his cage. Samantha grabbed the tom, snapped on his leash, and set him down in the sand. The cat instantly jumped a few feet to grab a passing lizard. To Samantha's surprise, Shakespeare was left with a wiggling tail while the rest of the lizard scampered to safety. Then she remembered reading that lizards can lose their tail as a defense mechanism against predators. It certainly worked for cats.

"Come on big guy, quit fooling around. Mommy's got to show up at her new job in a few minutes."

As if he understood every word, Shakespeare pulled and tugged her until he found a scraggly bush to hide behind. It still amazed Samantha that any animal could be embarrassed, but her cat insisted on privacy for bathroom duties.

After a moment of scratching sounds, Shakespeare emerged from behind the odd-looking bush, grabbed the still twitching lizard tail in his mouth, and hopped back in the carrier.

"Good boy," Samantha said, taking off the leash and latching the cage door shut. Then, as she walked around the Jeep to the driver's side, she caught a glimpse of something in the distance that caused her to stop and stare in awe. She was totally amazed she had not seen it earlier.

No more than a mile to the south, at the base of a low and gray range of steep hills, stood a yellow, three-story Victorian mansion surrounded by greenery. An oasis in the middle of a barren desert. It was stunning how the mansion's grandeur contrasted so starkly against the desolation.

The roar of an approaching engine drew Samantha's attention. A huge, platinum-colored Hummer with chrome light bars came shooting past. Whoever the driver was, they didn't have enough courtesy to even slow down, leaving her coughing in a cloud of powder dust.

"Asshole," she grumbled, then watched as the vehicle continued on to the imposing estate. Samantha sighed. For all she knew that could have been her employers. It would not be pleasant working for tactless people, but from the map and descriptions there was no doubt; the distant mansion was her new workplace, the Sunset Bed and Breakfast.

CHAPTER FIVE

There was no doubt about it now, whoever the jerk happened to be speeding around in that big Hummer, they were headed for the B&B. Samantha sighed and kept well behind the idiot to allow dust to settle as she slowly drove to her appointment.

Most likely it's a customer from Houston. Everyone drives like hell over there.

No matter, she'd find out soon enough. From all appearances, the estate covered a solid three acres. Rows of towering oleander bushes formed an elliptical circle around the mansion. It reminded her of a moat surrounding a medieval castle. As she drove closer, Samantha saw the reason for the odd shape: deep natural rocky ravines, invisible from afar, limited the areas where vegetation could grow.

About a quarter-mile from the house, a massive steel gate hung open. It was surrounded on both sides by numerous threatening "No Trespassing" and "Private Property" signs. A lone wooden sign announced: "Only guests of the Sunset Bed and Breakfast allowed past this point."

Samantha swallowed. "Shakespeare, I'm really beginning to wonder what we've gotten ourselves into."

A deep purr was her only answer.

"Well, I suppose there's no choice except to go ahead and see who or what shows up." She hesitated. "You know, I believe those could have been General Custer's last words." Then she drove on into the immaculately landscaped courtyard.

The enormous Hummer had parked beneath a carport. This was when she noticed gold lettering on its front doors. *SUNSET BED AND BREAKFAST, TOMBSTONE, ARIZONA.*

"Uh oh, Shakespeare, mommy might have made a boo-boo."

More purring as she opened the door and stood looking about anxiously. A pack of snarling pit bulls seemed a distinct possibility, but only the soothing call of a Gamble's quail could be heard over the lonely, keening wind. The speed demon who had driven the Hummer had disappeared without a trace.

Staying close to her Jeep for safety, Samantha began studying her surroundings. The imposing yellow mansion would have fit perfectly in New England. On a rocky hillside overlooking Tombstone, Arizona, however, the huge house seemed out of place as a flashing neon sign on a hearse.

From the size of some of the huge cactus, oleander bushes, and what passed for trees, the grand house had been built many years ago.

Some lucky prospector struck it rich here back in the boom days and decided to build a mansion on the ground that made him wealthy.

Whoever had built it and for whatever reason, a closer inspection showed it was meticulously maintained, as were the grounds. Not a weed grew anywhere. Rocks had been set around numerous cactus and various odd plants Samantha was unfamiliar with. The one central theme of Arizona horticulture seemed to be *if it was green, it had stickers.* Also, she added with a thin smile, *if it's green, don't kill it because there's none to spare.*

Over her left shoulder, a blinding orange sun was lowering in the West in an azure sky. The few high clouds on the horizon were waiting to be set afire and display the grandeur of another of Arizona's brilliantly beautiful sunsets.

A glance to the north and the town of Tombstone showed that half of a mountain *was* missing. Numerous piles of gray and black rock scattered haphazardly on every hill and into the valley told of determined efforts by long-dead prospectors to find another mother lode.

It struck her as odd that the bed and breakfast appeared to be the only habitation since leaving town. For a solid mile in any direction there were only cactus-studded plains or jagged, gray hills.

If someone really wanted to get away from it all, this is a great place to do it.

"Why hello, dearie," a pleasant though somewhat high-pitched man's voice coming from the shade of a huge oleander on the side of the entranceway took her back to the business at hand. "You must be Samantha. We have been *so* looking forward to your arrival."

CHAPTER SIX

Fern Birdsong stuck closed fists to her hips and spun to her husband of forty-six years. "Tex, I am not going to keep putting up with that old bat driving past our home so fast. She's a menace to society."

"Yes, dear," Tex replied by rote. After being married to a shrew for all those years, it was the only safe reply. "Esther Munson is not only a danger to tourists, but also the bus that brought them here. After they got that big Hummer to drive, she thinks she owns the road."

"She flattened the Johnson's cat last week. No one saw it happen, but there's no doubt in my mind she ran it over."

"Dear," Tex gently reminded her, "that cat takes off every once in a while for a few days. No one's found him run over; he's not neutered, you know."

"I'm going to call Bumps Turner and file a complaint."

Tex sighed. Whenever his wife got on a tirade, which seemed to happen with distressing regularity since they'd retired and bought this house on the outskirts of Tombstone, there was nothing to be done but nod and agree with her. But he *had* finally made up his mind to subscribe to the Sierra Vista newspaper. That would require putting a box on the opposite side of the road. Tex had rheumatism, which would be a grand excuse not to fetch the paper, leaving his wife to do the task. Having Esther quit speeding past wasn't something he wanted to have happen.

"Now dear," Tex said soothingly, "you shouldn't get yourself all dithered up. We both know Bumps and his deputies aren't going to even give her a ticket." He hesitated. "At least not until she actually causes a wreck or hits someone. That bed and breakfast of theirs spends more money on local elections than the rest of the town put together."

"There's something fishy going on out there," Fern's mind fastened to a thought like a bear trap. "I just know it. That's why they pay the cops to leave them alone."

"Dear," Tex shot a quick glance to the clock. He felt better when he saw it was time to go to the saloon for happy hour. "It's only a resort for rich people who want to get away and have some privacy."

"Used to be a whorehouse. Everyone knows it. I can only shudder at all the sinning that happened out there."

"Dear, that was a hundred years ago."

"I'm of the mind there's still decadence going on in that place. They have mighty few customers to go throwing money around like they do."

"Yes, dear." Tex headed for his pipe and straw hat. Fern refused to let him smoke in the house. Briefly, he wondered just when it was he had lost control of his life. At his age, it didn't matter much anymore. He thought about the Johnson's cat and wished it the best. "I'm certain you're right."

"You're going to Johnny Ringo's again, aren't you? That place is the Devil's playground."

You should know. You and the Devil are well acquainted. "Yes dear, I'm going to catch up on the latest goings-on, and I can smoke my pipe there."

"Don't spend a lot of money, we're on a tight budget these days."

Tex Birdsong didn't reply, her harping was tattooed on his brain. He stopped outside the door for a moment to survey the best place for the paper box, a site that would require his wife to angle across the road. He noticed a wonderfully remote spot near a cluster of catclaw bushes that could also conceal a nice coiled and deadly rattlesnake. Perfect.

Whistling now, Tex ambled off down the road for a few hours of respite from a woman who had turned meaner than a grizzly bear with boils.

CHAPTER SEVEN

Samantha was duly impressed with the interior of the Sunset Bed and Breakfast. The decor varied from a scattering of Victorian furniture that looked old enough to have come over on the *Mayflower* to a modern widescreen plasma television along with plush leather sofas and recliners.

"We are so glad you made it to our home without suffering an accident," the thin man said, ushering her inside. "The way some people drive these days is distressing."

The only close call I had was when your Hummer nearly ran over me.

"I am glad to be here, and I must say this house is beautiful—far beyond my expectations." Samantha smiled dutifully as she extended her hand. "Mister . . . ?"

"Please excuse my tasteless display of bad manners, I am Sidney Munson." He bent and pecked a kiss on the back of her hand. "My partner, Michael Herod, shall be out momentarily. He is baking a scrumptious cherry pie, which requires the utmost attention at this elevation. You do know we are nearly a mile high here?"

"No, I did not." Samantha said, her eyes adjusting from the outside brightness. Sidney was probably around fifty years old, with short, silver hair and a well-trimmed salt and pepper beard. Piercing blue eyes gleamed mischievously behind gold-rimmed glasses. He stood only slightly taller than she, possibly five feet eight or so. Dressed in an open-necked silk shirt, black leather pants, and alligator hide cowboy boots, the gold chain around his neck only added to his out-of-place image. All told, however, Sidney seemed quite likeable.

"Most people are unaware of that fact. Nearly everyone is under the impression all of Arizona is flat and hot, when in fact our summers here are quite delightful. Occasionally, we even have a mild snowfall in the wintertime to put us in a festive mood for the holidays." Sidney turned to the sound of an opening door. "And here comes my partner now."

"Why Sidney, you did not tell me we hired a goddess to ease our burdens." A large, muscular man, also about fifty, clean-shaven, with shoulder-length black hair who stood well over six feet tall, came smiling at her. "I'm Michael Herod. I am a partner in the Sunset B&B, but apparently Sidney has chosen to keep a few tidbits from me, such as hiring the loveliest lady to ever grace my presence."

Samantha extended her hand to receive another peck. Her two employers were expressing such delightful manners there was no doubt in her mind: *they're both as gay as a tree full of monkeys on laughing gas.* It was a shame so-called straight men couldn't express the same courtesies.

"How unspeakably crass of us," Sidney said contritely. "We must retrieve your baggage and park your splendid vehicle from out of the blazing sun. I also believe your communications mentioned you have a pet cat. That will be delightful for us all, as we simply *love* cats, especially my dear mother."

Samantha blinked. "Your mother lives here, too?"

"Yes, her name is Esther. She is seeing to the comfort of our sole guest at the moment. Mother drives the motorcar to town and back as a courtesy for our clients who wish to enjoy the history of Tombstone."

"They often enjoy it a tad too much," Michael said. His dark eyes sparkled like flint. "We would be terribly distressed if one of our valued clients were to suffer an accident. This is the reason we pick them up at the airport in Tucson free of charge, to discourage the use of private vehicles."

Now I know who drives the Hummer. Considering Sidney's age, Esther has to be close to eighty. Riding with her will give the clients a good reason to remember their visit to Tombstone. "That's very caring of you," Samantha said.

"Let us retrieve your belongings," Michael said. "Then after you and your pet are settled into your new quarters, we must show you around. I notice the shadow is over the yardarm, perhaps a drink may also be in order."

Samantha wasn't at all sure what a yardarm was, but the owners were far nicer than she had feared. A nearly blind old woman attempting to still drive was allowed to speed a little. Even her own grandmother in San Angelo, Texas, looked upon speed limit signs as simply a suggestion. She smiled, then followed the gentlemen outside to gather all that remained of her past life.

CHAPTER EIGHT

Samantha stood alongside Sidney in the parlor inspecting old framed pictures. "This must have been the mansion shortly after it was built."

Michael had returned to the kitchen after helping stow her belongings in an immaculate upstairs room with a private bath. Shakespeare had planted himself on a windowsill with a view of lizards and quail scampering about in the courtyard below, and showed no interest in leaving the show.

"Yes," Sidney said. "That picture was taken in 1881, shortly after the famous gunfight at the OK Corral. The longer a person lives in Tombstone, the more you realize everything is dated from either that event or the lives of Wyatt Earp and Doc Holliday when they were residents. It seems odd that the killing of a mere three reprobates in the Old West caused such a stir, but it did."

Samantha kept her gaze on the picture. "What a grand home. It must have been the fanciest one in town at the time."

"Oh, indeed it was, and still is. There are also many legends attached to the Sunset House. One of the more famous is that Doc Holliday's woman, Big-Nose Kate, once worked here."

"I'm surprised to hear that. I would think a doctor could have made enough of a good living to keep his girl from working as a domestic."

Sidney chuckled, his laugh like the peal of tiny silver bells. "Big-Nose Kate was a prostitute. A madam by the name of An-

30

nie York built this mansion to be the classiest brothel in Arizona. It was too bad the mines flooded and closed only a few years later, otherwise she would have reaped a tidy fortune from all of those wonderful rough and tumble miners."

Samantha blinked in astonishment. She decided it would be a good idea to leave the fact she was managing a whorehouse, even one that closed a hundred years ago, off her resumé. Her ex-husband would have a stroke if he knew. Samantha grinned and decided to send him a postcard someday.

A clumping of feet coming down the wooden stairs brought an end to the history lesson.

"Ah, my dear," Sidney said, sweeping an arm to the approaching couple. "This is my dear mother, Esther, and our only guest at the moment, Crossman Speaks from California."

"Delighted." Samantha extended a hand to the skinny old woman who wore a beehive of purple hair over a coke-bottle-thick pair of pink cat's-eye glasses sequined with rhinestones. Esther Munson had enough makeup plastered on her wrinkled face to cover a wall. Adding in the abundance of rings, bracelets, and three pearl necklaces, she gave the appearance of an undertaker's failure.

"You're the new manager my son hired." Esther had a loud voice that sounded like a cross between a hiss and a growl.

"Yes, Mother, this is Samantha Sterling. You really should accept her hand and attempt to be civil."

"I just hope she works out better'n the last one," Esther snapped as she strode past Samantha without another glance. "I'm gonna fix myself a drink."

"Mother can be a smidgen testy at times," Sidney said contritely. "Please accept my apologies for her. She *is* seventy-five years old."

Samantha painted a business smile on her face and turned to their client. "Mr. Speaks, I am very pleased to meet you. My name is Samantha, but my friends call me Sam. I hope your stay here has been pleasant so far."

"The food's okay, Sam." Crossman was in his early forties, overweight and dressed far too nattily, down to his wearing designer glasses with a green string to hold them on his head. "But Tombstone sucks. I don't know what's supposed to be so special about the dumpy old town anyway. I'm just glad I didn't pay to see the place."

"Mr. Speaks won a free trip here," Sidney said happily. "We are often selected by companies as a destination resort for some of their most *qualified* employees."

"Well, I'm leaving tomorrow, and can't get back to Los Angeles fast enough. At least there's things happening in that town." Crossman Speaks shook Samantha's hand, his grip limp and sweaty. "I'm going to have a drink before dinner, will you join me?"

"I would be honored," Samantha kept her business smile on full wattage and allowed the obnoxious client to slip his clammy hand around her waist for the short walk to the bar.

An hour later, Michael announced dinner was ready, relieving Samantha from the pain of listening to Crossman complain about Arizona and brag about how wonderful California was along with how much money he made at whatever it was he did for a living. All she'd done for the entire time was nod and refill the man's glass with Ballantine's scotch on numerous occasions. He reminded her terribly of Arnold.

"This evening we are, as our guest had requested, serving grilled fish along with a pilaf of rice and organic steamed vegetables." Michael began setting out salads in frosty cold plates. "And for dessert I have baked a most memorable cherry pie."

"And it smells delicious," Samantha said quickly, choosing a chair next to Sidney across the table from Crossman's groping hands. "I believe we're all in for a treat. Michael, I am told, used to be a chef at a four-star hotel in New York."

"That was a *five*-star hotel," Michael beamed with pride. "I left my position there many years ago, but I assure you I have only gotten more skilled at the culinary arts since then."

"Let's eat," Crossman said, grabbing his salad fork. "I'll let you know what *I* think after I've partaken."

Michael Herod's broad smile remained as he said on the way to the kitchen, "I assure you, Mr. Speaks, that you will never have a better dinner than this one."

"I must say, the sole almondine was quite good, but the vegetables were of inferior quality and fairly tasteless." Crossman Speaks refilled his glass with white wine. "The five-star hotels I've eaten at were . . ." He tilted his head to Samantha, a thin smile on his face, ". . . quite comparable, considering the utter remoteness of Tombstone."

"I'm so glad you are enjoying your last night with us," Michael said, taking away the plates and sparing Samantha a reply. "I commend you on your astuteness, Mr. Speaks. The quality of produce I am forced to deal with is atrocious. Every supermarket in Arizona is substandard in that area. I did, however, manage to purchase some excellent fresh cherries for this evening's desert. May I serve your pie now?"

Crossman kept his watery eyes glued to Samantha. "Yes, please and add a scoop of vanilla ice cream on top. Then later, perhaps the young lady and I could take an evening stroll in the courtyard."

"Of course," Samantha groaned inwardly, having slapped away many hands at her ex-husband's numerous drinking parties. "I would be delighted to join you."

A moment later, a loud crash echoed from the kitchen. "Oh,

this is simply terrible," Michael's voice was distraught when he came out carrying a single piece of cherry pie a la mode. "I must sincerely apologize for my inexcusable clumsiness. After cutting the pie I only managed to remove one piece when the oven dinged to tell me the bread for tomorrow's brunch was done. Then for some reason I accidentally knocked that wonderful pie I was so proud of on the floor, spoiling it."

Sidney shook his head sadly. "We are totally embarrassed by this unfortunate mishap." He turned to Samantha, "As Mr. Speaks is our guest, I do believe the reserved dessert must go to him."

"Pie gives me gas anyway," Esther barked.

Samantha kept her plastic smile. "It would be rude to do otherwise. I suggest we all go enjoy a breath of fresh air while our guest finishes his dinner."

Sidney's beard folded into a grin. "An excellent display of good manners, my dear. When you are ready, Mr. Speaks, we shall be on the patio. I believe our new manager has yet to see the splendid display of stars we enjoy here in the Sonoran desert."

"I'll be along shortly," Crossman Speaks droned as he cut into the thick cherry pie with his fork and stuffed a large bite into his mouth.

They'd only been in the courtyard long enough for Sidney and Michael to point out the North Star, along with a couple more obvious constellations, when a loud *thump* echoed from the dining room.

Esther stood off to one side, puffing away on a Marlboro. "Well, I'm glad that's over. He was a real asshole."

Samantha ran into the dining room, her eyes wide with trepidation. Crossman Speaks lay face-up on the saltillo tile floor. An occasional twitch accompanied by a gurgling noise that sounded like a plugged-up sink trying to drain were the only indications that life remained.

"My God," Samantha yelled, "he's dying, call 911."

"Now why in the world would we want to do something like that?" Sidney's grin now appeared vulpine. "He has ingested a quite lethal dose of oleander. It's a painless death. Really, my dear, it's the best way to dispose of clients that we have come across so far."

Samantha did not know what to do. She felt like screaming, crying, and running away all at the same time. Something in the depths of her mind told her if she did any of those, she would join Speaks on the floor. These people were straight out of a horror movie. Only a cool head could save her.

"You *intended* to kill him," Samantha said hoarsely.

"That's what we are in business to do here at the Sunset B&B," Sidney said. "And with you being our new manager, I would venture a nice chat might put things on a clean slate."

Samantha nodded, feeling numb all over. Then she noticed Michael standing only a few feet away from her, casually holding an ice pick. "I think that sounds like a good idea."

CHAPTER NINE

Michael slipped the gleaming silver ice pick into a leather sheath on his belt. "See, Sidney, I told you darker-haired girls aren't as easily upset." He nodded to Samantha. "A good hard jab upward at the base of the skull is a painless way to silence someone. As you learn more about your new profession, we will teach you all the easiest ways to dispose of clients."

A stunned Samantha Sterling could only manage a nod. *This can't be real. It's all a big practical joke that's played on everyone who comes to work here.*

Crossman Speaks twitched one last time, then grew stone still. Wide, unseeing eyes stared blankly at the ceiling, a gray cast forming over his face.

This is no joke. That man is dead as he can get. Samantha swallowed. "Everyone who stays here gets killed?"

Sidney opened his hands. "Why, of course not. That type of behavior would be far too obvious. We occasionally entertain a few people who choose to pay our five hundred dollars a day fee. The persons we dispose of . . . a word we much prefer over the 'K' word . . . are contracted for by an organization we refer to as 'The Company.' "

Esther piped up, "Well, if you're not gonna whack her, at least have the courtesy to offer her a drink. I know I'm having one. The worst part of a hit is the clean-up afterwards. No one ever thinks of all that work."

"He is a heavy one," Michael said, motioning toward the bar.

"I am certain that after a soothing drink and a nice frank discussion, our little lady will begin to understand the wonderful door of opportunity that has been opened for her."

Samantha followed as if she were a zombie. Thoughts bounced around inside of her head like ricocheting bullets, and just as focused. *Play it cool, these people are dangerous as rattlesnakes. Tell them what they want to hear, then run away and call the police. No, just run as far and fast as you can. They'll kill me if I say the least thing wrong. Be a chameleon, live through this, after all, I've done nothing wrong.*

Sidney's melodic voice seemed terribly out of place with a dead man lying on the dining room floor. "I know just the drink to perk up our little lady's spirits, a Tombstone Blues."

Samantha took a seat at the bar and heard herself ask, "A what?"

"It is a drink of my own invention. We always celebrate the successful conclusion of a contract with one of these delightful concoctions. I can't divulge all of my secret ingredients, but blue Tarantula tequila is the mainstay."

After a few moments of fiddling with rattling ice and pouring various liquors into a blender, Sidney began setting out blue-colored drinks served in frosty margarita glasses in front of everyone. There was even a pink plastic umbrella added for a cheerful appearance.

Samantha really needed this drink. She took a healthy sip. "Not bad . . . I like it."

"Well, get to jawing with her." Esther had already downed her drink and was refilling her glass from the blender. "I'm an old woman and don't have time for a lot of lollygagging. If we're getting rid of *two* bodies, I wanna know sooner, not later. I need my sleep."

Michael Herod sat down beside Samantha. "You must understand, my dear, you are going into a profession where loyalty and silence are paramount."

His words were pleasantly spoken, but Samantha felt as if each were as real of a warning as the buzzing of a rattlesnake coiled to strike.

"*My* new profession?" Samantha's voice was raspy.

"That's why we hired you, sweetie," Sidney said after removing the umbrella and taking a dainty sip of his drink. "Michael and I are not as young as we used to be, and business has been so demanding of late that we decided taking in a partner was the thing to do."

"We want to travel, take a cruise together, and get some much-needed rest," Michael said. "But The Company is not an organization that will tolerate being tardy on fulfilling contracts. You can trust me on this."

Samantha sipped her drink. She noticed her hands had finally quit shaking. "You want me to poison people for money?"

"See," Sidney beamed. "She is taking to being a hit-lady like a duck takes to water. Why in simply no time we'll have her whacking clients on a regular basis all by herself."

"She can clean up afterwards, too. I'm gettin' too old for this shit." Esther was on her third drink.

"You see, sweetie," Sidney extended his pinkie finger when he tilted his glass to drink, "there is a great deal of money to be made, and the work is actually quite easy."

"It's inside work too. Warm in winter and nice and cool in the summer." Michael shook his black, shoulder-length hair. It glistened like a starless night. "We also have a very dependable and easy to use tractor with a front-end loader to do all of the heavy moving."

Samantha sipped the last of her Tombstone Blues. "I have a feeling this is one of those offers a person can't refuse."

Sidney's eyes flashed dully, like old ice. "Only once, dearie, only once." Then he brightened. "But we *did* go to great lengths to make your first hit more enjoyable."

"We did a *very* thorough background search on you before accepting your application." Michael said. "First blood, as we say in the business, is always very important. That is why we strove *so* hard to find a suitable client that would be . . . *easier* for you to dispose of."

"The bastard was a lawyer," Esther croaked. "Think of the money as a bounty."

"I was *paid* to kill Crossman Speaks?" Samantha's hands were shaking again.

"Of course you were, sweetie," Sidney began making another pitcher of drinks. "If you should entertain doing something so foolish as going to the law, not only would they laugh at your story, it will be terribly difficult to explain the twenty-five thousand dollars in your new Tombstone checking account, deposited there yesterday."

"Even harder to explain," Michael added. "Will be all of that money you made on Enron stock and paid no taxes on. I do believe there will be severe criminal penalties involved."

Samantha was outraged. "We *lost* ten million dollars!"

"Of course you did, sweetie, but the records will show otherwise. The Company has some very effective methods of persuasion. Compared to you, Martha Stewart will seem like Mother Teresa . . . unless you give us your loyalty."

"And the sooner the better," Esther growled. "I hate pussyfooting around. Now back in my day—"

"That's enough, Mother," Sidney said politely. "The little dear has to make the decision of a lifetime. Don't rush her."

Samantha Sterling blinked building tears from her eyes and slid her glass over to be refilled. "From now on, please call me Sam and I just have one question. Do we get a *lot* of lawyers?"

CHAPTER TEN

Shooting rays of red fire from an Arizona sunrise came unimpeded through a window and jolted Samantha awake. She'd forgotten to lower the blinds. Considering the way things had gone last night, that came as no great surprise. Blinking the residue of stale tears from her eyes, Sam was startled to realize she'd actually slept for several hours.

The heavy, furry lump on the top of her head began to purr, then stretched and sauntered from his bed on the pillow to sit on his haunches and stare at her with soft gray eyes.

"Shakespeare, mommy made a bad boo-boo."

The black tomcat placed a paw on Samantha's arm, and tilted his head sideways, as if he understood her plight.

"I thought we were going to manage a quaint bed and breakfast in Arizona, not be a night clerk for the Bates Motel. Little guy, mommy doesn't know what to do. I don't want to spend the rest of my life killing people for money." She hesitated to rub a palm down the cat's back. "Not even lawyers, but if I don't, you'll likely become an orphan. These folks are stone cold when it comes to disposing of clients, as they call it. Michael had an ice pick out to do me in if I'd said the wrong thing or become hysterical."

Shakespeare tilted his head to the other side, hanging on to every word, then he came and nuzzled her cheek.

"All I can think to do, little guy, is pretend to go along with them, stay alive, then we'll run."

The Enron stock fraud will send you to prison, a small voice whispered in her mind.

"They're bluffing on everything, Shakespeare. Once we're gone from here, we'll tell the police. Then they'll be the ones who go to jail."

These people don't bluff. They have money and connections you don't begin to understand. If you run, someone will kill you for sure, maybe even the police. They're professional hit-men. Be afraid of them. Be very afraid.

Sam reconsidered her options. "Then again, Shakespeare . . . mommy just might have found a new line of work."

She lay in bed for several minutes, stroking her purring cat, before realizing there was no delaying getting on with the day. She showered and dressed in blue jeans and a colorful, short-sleeved Western blouse. Before going downstairs to see how her employers were doing, she made the bed.

That was when she noticed the tiny microphone jammed between the mattress and wall.

"Well, good morning! And how is our wonderful new manager this bright and shiny morning?" Sidney Munson's cheery, musical voice welcomed Samantha as she came down the stairs. "I hear birds singing for their breakfast. Perhaps some morning after coffee you would like to go with me when I feed them."

Samantha waited until she could survey the dining room floor before answering. Not having a dead body to deal with made the day appear somewhat brighter.

Sidney noticed Sam's scrutiny. "Last night's business is gone without a trace to be found . . . ever. That is one of the niceties of the profession. A smidgen of work, then there's a lot of free time to enjoy life."

Esther sat at the dining room table, a fog of cigarette smoke hovering over her head like a cloud. "That's easy for you to say.

I'll have you know the cleanup's a lotta damn work."

"Yes, Mother," Sidney placed a delicate hand on Samantha's waist and guided her to a seat at the table some distance from Esther and her Marlboro haze. "Now be civil, Mother, our dearie is in a state of adjustment."

"Good morning," Michael came from the kitchen carrying a sliver carafe and empty china cup. Samantha noted how much more muscular he appeared today. The way the muscles rippled on his shoulders, he had to work out everyday. "We have a delectable Colombian coffee brewed using distilled water and seasoned with a slight essence of black walnut. Would the lady wish cream or sugar?"

"Black is fine."

"Ah yes," Michael poured a cup, giving a slight bow as he did so. "I prefer to drink mine in this manner also. An aged coffee bean, delicately spiced with only natural, organically grown herbs, always gives the best flavored brew."

She inhaled the wonderful aroma. "It smells delicious."

"And how is your kitty this fine morning?" Sidney's words sent a cold shiver trickling down Samantha's spine. "I do hope he is adjusting. I have heard some people actually get so attached to their cats they talk to them as if the sweet things understand every word."

"Shakespeare's quite happy here, just like me."

"You don't know how good that makes me feel," Sidney took a chair across the table from her. "All of us here at Sunset B&B have the greatest hopes that our fealty will be returned in kind."

Samantha blew on her coffee, sending up clouds of steam to meld with cigarette smoke.

Esther noted Sam's expression of bewilderment. "He means loyalty. Sidney always has been one to use a ten-dollar word when a nickel one will do just as good."

Samantha sipped on the excellent coffee while measuring her

reply. These folks had been rubbing people out for a long time. Any lie or deception on their part would be ferreted out before God got the news. There was no choice but to be truthful.

Well, there is another choice, Samantha thought. *It just isn't an attractive one.*

"I think I may need some . . . time to adjust to my new job description."

"Of course you will, sweetie." Sidney's dull gaze vanished. It was as if a deadly storm had blown away behind his blue eyes. "We fully expected that to be the case. No one ever goes into the profession with relish, or at least no one who lasts or is trusted."

"There are always hotheads or pure psychos who think being a hit-man is a macho thing to do." Michael came out carrying a baking tray of scrumptious-looking cinnamon rolls. "They are the ones you read about that are either dead or on death row. This is a business we are in, just like McDonald's or General Motors. The money is excellent. If a person keeps their wits about them, doesn't get greedy, and remembers to be loyal to their employers, they can retire as millionaires without difficulty."

"*Do* try one of Michael's famous rolls," Sidney said, extracting a small piece of black plastic from his shirt pocket. "I assure you they are the best you have ever tasted. Then, after breakfast, Mother will drive you into Tombstone and show you around. I do hope this does not offend, but I noticed that a nice permanent seems to be in order. Go to town, enjoy yourself."

Michael spread whipped butter on Samantha's cinnamon roll. "To ease the obvious temptations and trepidations you will experience during your training, Esther shall drive you wherever you go and attend to all your needs. Sidney and I took the liberty of removing a quite vital part of your Jeep. We will keep it safe. Later, after a few weeks of schooling, it will be replaced."

"Get with it," Esther grumbled. Samantha wondered if her deep scowl was chiseled into her pinched face. "I want to head to Tombstone before all the idiot tourists show up." She took a long puff on her Marlboro and blew a smoke ring. "And don't call the Sunset B&B the damn Bates Motel ever again. *That* place was creepy."

CHAPTER ELEVEN

A wide-eyed jackrabbit made a dash from a clump of catclaw bushes in an attempt to cross the road before being flattened by the speeding H2 Hummer. The dull *thump* from underneath Samantha's seat told her that the rabbit had failed spectacularly in its effort.

Esther Munson kept her gaze straight ahead; it was as if she wore blinders. A Marlboro cigarette with an inch of ash on the end dangled from her crimson lips. The numerous burned spots in the expensive leather seats gave evidence Esther wasn't very careful with her habit. At least she did have the courtesy to crack a window to let most of the smoke out.

Samantha often wondered how the prisoners she had seen being transported in the backs of police cars or buses with steel bars welded over the windows must have felt. Now she knew firsthand. Esther had made an obvious display of putting a nasty-looking pistol into her purse. While the overly painted old prune might have bad eyesight, the fifteen shots she said the gun could fire without being reloaded told Sam that the dead rabbit had had better odds.

"You'll like the beauty shop. They've done my hair for years," Esther said over the rushing wind and flying gravel.

The pile of purple hair on top of the old woman's head could have held an entire hive of bees. Samantha simply nodded, deciding to keep quiet and mouth a prayer for any living thing that happened to be on the road between them and town.

Tombstone. The very name of the town held a completely different connotation than it had yesterday. Violent deaths that had become bloody legends were the only reason the place had ever become famous. With the closing of the rich silver mines after they had flooded, the city of clapboard buildings and broken dreams should have faded into history, as had most boom towns of the West. Not so here. Hollywood, along with scores of writers, had built a tower of legends that people were willing to pay money to visit. Even the Boot Hill graveyard had become a tourist destination.

It seems, Samantha thought, *that another legend's still in the making. The Sunset Bed and Breakfast has been in operation for over seven years. They have likely done in more people than all of the bad men of the Old West combined. And now I'm expected to add to that number.*

A hard right turn brought a squealing of tires; they were now driving on blacktop. A skinny, gray-haired old man putting up a paper box alongside the road jumped aside, but surprised Samantha by giving a wave.

Esther flicked the ash from her cigarette out the window. "When you drive in Tombstone, be careful to keep it slow, especially around the school. We don't want the locals to think ill of us."

"Yes, ma'am." Samantha saw a blur as a cat barely streaked to safety before they roared past.

"There's a half-assed liquor store in town and a convenience store where I buy my cigarettes. Other'n that, we're forced to drive to Sierra Vista for most everything. Sidney won't let me go there anymore. I don't know why he blames me for those last few wrecks, but he does."

"Your son's just being caring," Samantha tensed and opened her mouth to yell, but the two kids on bicycles saw who was coming and decided riding into a cactus patch was safer than hoping Esther would miss them.

"Well, here's the school. That flatfoot sheriff, Bumps Turner, makes me slow down when I get to it." Esther rolled down the window and tossed out her still-lit cigarette butt. "I hate cops, but we gotta go along with the rules to keep on their good side."

"I'll do that."

"You'd better."

To Samantha's surprise, Esther slowed the huge vehicle to a safe speed. A local cop was sitting in his cruiser next to a flashing "school zone" sign, munching on a doughnut. Briefly, she thought of jumping out and running to the officer.

Esther said, "The cop's Joe Lomax, he works as a handyman out at the B&B on occasion." She gave him a slight wave as they drove past.

Scratch that idea.

"I guess a lot of people in Tombstone benefit from the Sunset B&B." Samantha asked, rolling down her window. The fresh air was cool, dry, and delightful.

"Dear," Esther said, lighting a new Marlboro, "ain't gonna be a soul in town who'll believe a bad word *anyone* says about us. Sidney and Michael donate a lot of money to the city every year. The new police station couldn't have been built without our help, same with the Senior Citizens' Center. And I haven't even mentioned the new fire truck everyone's so proud of."

All things to all men be.

"Smart thinking," Samantha's words brought a mirthless nod of satisfaction from Esther. *That old saw can cut both ways, you withered bat,* she thought as they pulled into a parking space in front of a dilapidated trailer house with a hand-painted sign on the door: *THE WILD HAIR BEAUTY SALON.* Across the street was an ancient adobe house announcing, *SPICE OF LIFE GOURMET VINEGAR WORKS.*

This just keeps getting better and better, Samantha thought as she climbed from the giant Hummer to follow the skinny old hit-man's mother inside the salon.

CHAPTER TWELVE

"And how's my favorite hairdresser doing this fine morning?" Esther Munson chirped happily. She stepped aside so Sam could enter the cramped confines of the old trailer. "This lovely lady is Samantha, our new manager for the B&B."

A willowy blonde was sweeping hair cuttings into a dustpan. She completed the task and stowed the broom in a closet before extending her hand. "Glad to meet you. I'm Minnet Page. I've been fixing Esther's hair for seven years now. If you have half of her sense of humor, I just know we'll be great friends."

Samantha could only force a numb expression of graciousness. The bubbly Minnet had wrecked her theory of the old bat's face cracking if she ever smiled. Esther hadn't stopped beaming since they had stepped inside.

Of course, Sam thought, *Esther is a chameleon, just like her son and Michael.* The old adage, "All things to all men be" echoed once again inside of her head. *If that quote hadn't come from the Bible, they surely would have coined it.*

"If you're ready," Esther said cheerfully, "Sam, as she prefers to be called, could use one of your wonderful perms."

"Samantha, what a pretty name, but Sam it is," the beautician said lightheartedly.

"Thanks, Minnet," Sam said, walking toward one of the two salon chairs that strangely enough appeared brand new.

"Hop in the chair and I'll get right to it. I always have time for folks from the Sunset B&B. Michael and Sidney both have me style and trim their hair too."

Samantha smiled as she regarded the bubbly hairdresser. Minnet was about her age, somewhat on the skinny side, with a cute face framed in a spray of freckles that set off her azure eyes delightfully. She wore no wedding ring, but some beauticians didn't wear them at work. The girl had an infectious smile along with an almost giddy attitude. After the way things had gone for her in Tombstone so far, Samantha couldn't imagine what anyone living here could find to be happy about. Under the circumstances, however, some diplomacy was called for.

"Tombstone is such a quaint place," Sam said, beginning to relax. "I'm surprised to find the climate is so refreshing."

"Aside from the wind blowing too much, it is nice." Minnet took a comb to Sam's auburn tresses. "Where'd you used to live?"

"Houston, I have lived there all of my life before coming to work for the Sunset B&B."

"You'll simply love working out there. Sidney and Michael are the sweetest, kindest people you can find in this world."

"They do seem nice." Sam sighed, then noticed Esther's head had drooped and she had begun snoring loudly.

"Poor Esther," Minnet said, "the dear lady is getting on in years. I've noticed every time she gets a chance to sit and rest, she nods off. I always leave her be."

My guess is a cat sleeps sounder than that old woman. Samantha took note of Esther's hand on her purse. "She works hard to help out her son's business."

"That is so true. Why, everyone in town loves those people. And Michael's such a fine chef. I have been there for dinner on occasion. No restaurant in the state can compare."

Remember to pass on the cherry pie. It was time to change the subject. "Are you married, Minnet?"

"No, I'm divorced, have been for three years. And you?"

"I'm divorced as well. My ex is a lawyer and still lives in Houston."

"Wow!" Minnet exclaimed, "A *lawyer!* I'll bet you get a pile of alimony every month."

"Oh right, that's why I'm having to work. My ex had all of our money invested in Enron stock. There wasn't much left to divide. We just went our separate ways."

"Isn't that the way things seem to go? My ex, Rodney, had a great job working for the city. Then he listened to Rush Limbaugh and so many of those radical talk shows on the radio so much he lost his mind. These days he's heading up the Tombstone Minutemen, the biggest bunch of nuts you'll find anywhere around outside of a Planters peanut factory."

"The Tombstone Minutemen?"

"Yeah, they claim there's a couple of hundred of them, but only about a dozen or so work at it full time. Three really keep folks riled up: Rodney, Wab Smith, and Carl Deevers. Locals call them the 'Unholy Trinity,' which pretty much sums it up."

"What do they do?" The hot sudsy water and Minnet's massaging of Samantha's scalp was relieving a lot of her stress.

"Mainly hold meetings where they drink lots of beer and complain about the government. Their big deal of late is defending the border from illegal aliens. The Minutemen claim those poor people coming into the country to find a job to keep from starving are really an advance force of al-Qaeda that's joined forces with a covert branch of the Mexican government to invade the United States."

"I always thought we kept an army around to take care of problems like that."

"Most sane people would agree with you. But listening to too much radical talk radio drives some people nuts. And Rodney's brain was skating on thin ice to begin with."

"I'm sorry to hear about your ex. Does it bother you that he lives so close? Being two states away from mine seemed like a grand idea."

"Oh, Rodney's no problem. He comes around on occasion trying to get me to join his bunch of kooks or let him put posters on the windows. Once he's out of sight I toss them in the wastebasket. Actually, he lives a few miles south of town on The Line, which keeps him a safe distance."

"What's The Line?"

"The Minutemen are building a line of bunkers across the desert using concrete septic tanks. They live out there in shacks and tents, waiting for the Mexican hordes to invade. In their newsletter, they described it as Arizona's maggot line. I think they meant to refer to the French Maginot Line, but with no more active brain cells than that group has to work with, I decided pointing out defects in grammar would be a waste of time."

Dante was wrong. There's a level of Hell he missed. It's called Tombstone and I'm stuck here.

"It seems there arc a few . . . oddballs in Tombstone," Sam said.

Minnet shrugged. "The town has been an idiot magnet for years. All of the movies, books, and magazine articles keep a few crazies showing up thinking this is still the Wild West. But they don't usually stick around long enough to cause a lot of trouble. Mostly there's nice people in Tombstone," Minnet smiled. "There's you and me along with Esther, Sidney, and Michael. Who could ask for better than that?"

Esther gave a startled snort and bolted awake in her chair. Even from her view with her head in the sink, Sam noticed Esther's hand shot into the purse before she realized where she was and pulled out her pack of Marlboros.

"Minnet," Sam said truthfully, "living in Tombstone is going to be the experience of a lifetime."

Chapter Thirteen

"You'll like this place," Esther said, tossing a smouldering cigarette out of the window as she pulled into a parking space in front of the terra cotta-colored bar a few blocks from town that Samantha had seen yesterday on her way to the Sunset Bed and Breakfast. "The food's always iffy at the tourist joints. All the locals come here."

Samantha noticed a rustic sign on the adobe building announcing it to be Johnny Ringo's Saloon. She decided whoever this Ringo character was, he almost certainly had been either an outlaw or lawman. Nearly every business in Tombstone appeared named after people who made their living with a gun.

After jumping from the Hummer, Sam held the door open for Minnet, who Esther had invited along for lunch. Being accompanied by someone who wasn't a professional killer had a salutary effect on her appetite. The aroma of meat grilling over a mesquite wood fire drifting on the clean desert breeze smelled delectable.

"It's been a while since I've had barbeque," Samantha said. "Texas has a lot of restaurants that serve it, but I've always preferred the little out-of-the-way places with a cooker in the back."

"Pete and Laura Fields own the joint," Esther said, firing up another Marlboro, making Samantha wonder why she'd tossed the lit one out of the window. "They don't serve barbeque here, and neither does Michael. All that damn red sauce gives people heartburn and gas."

Minnet stepped alongside Samantha, then they followed Esther's wake of cigarette smoke through the batwing doors.

"Hi Esther, Minnet," a smiling, somewhat overweight, silver-haired waitress met them with menus. "Pete's got cheeseburgers and fries on special today."

"You know what I'll have, then." Esther stepped aside, reached back with a bony arm and yanked Samantha close. "Meet our new manager for the B&B. Her name's Samantha, but we all call her Sam."

"Welcome to Tombstone, Sam," the waitress said, escorting them to a table in the rear. "There's lots of nice folks here, and you couldn't find better to start with than Esther and Minnet." She pulled out a chair for Sam. "My name's Laura, Pete's my husband. We're the owners, so anything you ever need, just ask one of us."

Samantha put on the plastic smile she was becoming used to. "I'm feeling at home already. A great cheeseburger with all the trimmings and a glass of iced tea sounds scrumptious."

Minnet nodded. "Then it's unanimous, Sam and I seem to have a lot in common." She chuckled. "Including ex-husbands."

Before spinning to leave, Laura said, "I can't help you in that department, I've been putting up with Pete for thirty years. Be too much work to break in a new one."

While Laura was getting their drinks, Samantha surveyed the crowd. She estimated maybe fifty people were inside of the obviously new building that had been decorated to look rustic. The long wooden bar held maybe twenty customers who were drinking their lunch while munching on peanuts or chips. The rest sat at round tables either dining or chatting loudly while awaiting their food. What was most interesting were the numbers of people dressed in period clothes—hats, vests, long coats, and revealing dance hall dresses—along with several wearing guns of every description. Without the televisions turned to CNN, the inside of Johnny Ringo's Saloon resembled a slice of life straight out of the 1880s. Sam found it oddly refreshing after spending so many years amongst the steel and plastic sameness of big-city Houston, Texas.

"Here you go," Laura said, shaking Samantha from her reverie. She placed a frosty glass of tea with a wedge of lemon in front of Sam and Minnet. Esther gave a look of satisfaction at her tall mug of white wine.

Both Minnet and the waitress didn't appear to think anything odd about Esther having a solid half-bottle of wine with lunch, so Samantha decided keeping quiet would be in her best interest.

Samantha ripped open a packet of sweetener and swirled the white powder into her tea while Esther guzzled most of her wine without stopping for a breather, then signaled for a refill. Sam worried anew for the safety of any living thing that happened to be on the road when Esther climbed behind the wheel of a vehicle bigger than a small truck.

The waitress set a cheeseburger in front of Samantha that nearly filled the platter; the French fries were served in plastic baskets lined with paper. Esther received only a sizzling piece of grilled hamburger to go with her wine refill.

"I follow that Atkins diet," Esther commented, eyeing her lunch. "The food keeps me thin and the wine keeps me happy, an unbeatable combination to my way of thinking."

Minnet squirted circles of yellow mustard on her toasted bun. "I've never had to worry about losing weight. I can eat anything I want, including ice cream, and never seem to gain a pound. I must say that Atkins diet really works for you, Esther, almost too well. You really could do with a few pounds to round out your figure."

"My figure's good enough for an old woman who ain't tryin'

to attract some damn man." She sliced open her hamburger patty and smiled at the blood-red center. "I can look like I want and eat and drink what I want when I darn well feel like it. You young gals still have men to worry with. Getting old ain't all that bad, I'm here to tell ya."

Samantha took a bite of what she believed to be the best cheeseburger she had ever tasted. Since she had been fighting a running battle with fat for years, Sam decided to leave half uneaten to spare her waistline. The nearly raw meat and glasses of wine apparently called for in the Atkins diet wasn't a pleasant alternative to simply not eating too much.

Minnet dabbed a napkin at the corner of her mouth. "Sam, I'm so glad you are in Tombstone. Perhaps we can get together some evening for drinks and girl talk."

"It'll be a while," Esther said over her now empty wineglass. "We really need her at the B&B. The place's gotten to be too much for the boys and me. We'll be teachin' Sam the ropes for a spell before she can get away."

"I understand," Minnet said, beaming her ever-present smile. "Work always comes first, but when you get time, we'll get together."

"I'm looking forward to it," Samantha said truthfully, watching Esther stuff a bloody piece of hamburger into her mouth. "I really, really am."

On the drive back to the Sunset Bed and Breakfast, Sam was surprised to find the copious quantities of white wine Esther had downed actually slowed her speed to where anything not crippled stood a chance of escape. The old woman had the first ghost of a smile she had seen cross her face as she tossed a smoking Marlboro out the window and lit another.

Samantha decided to venture being cordial. "That Atkins diet you're on, didn't I read Dr. Atkins died from a fall?"

Esther snorted. "We had nothing to do with that hit. Keep your trap shut about it. The Idaho potato farmers paid to have him done in."

Not another word was exchanged between them the rest of the short trip.

Through the scratched lenses of a well-worn pair of military field glasses, rheumy, hostile, dark eyes keenly observed the Hummer's progress across the desert. The watcher was making no attempt to hide; he was sitting Indian-style atop a picnic table in Landin Park, at the very south end of Tombstone. Daylight was for stalking. Every predator knew nights were for killing. The man kept his eyes to the binoculars while stuffing his lower lip with a fresh supply of Copenhagen, patiently awaiting the coming dark.

CHAPTER FOURTEEN

A dust devil appeared from out of nowhere to chase Samantha and Esther from the Hummer to the house. The duo barely made it inside before debris and small rocks began rapping at the ornate oak door like a demented woodpecker.

"Wonderful weather we have here in the desert," Esther snorted as she tapped a fresh Marlboro from its crush-proof pack. "Absolutely friggin' *wonderful.*"

"Mother, I am simply stunned by how nice our lovely Samantha's hair turned out," Sidney Munson said as he came to meet them. "Minnet is *so* talented. I really don't know how we could possibly manage without her services."

"I like Minnet," Samantha said. "We had lunch together at Johnny Ringo's Saloon. They have really good food."

"I am glad you enjoyed it," Sidney said. "Dining in Tombstone can often be a most trying experience. Pete and Laura work long and hard hours to keep their reputation as a quality establishment."

"At least the food there doesn't give me gas," Esther said, heading for the stairs. "I'm goin' to my room and lie down for a spell. Call me if you need anything."

"Get your rest, Mother. Michael is busy in the kitchen and I have the parlor set up to begin Sam's lessons." Sidney touched an open palm to his face. "I simply must tell what a darling cat Shakespeare is. That lovely pet caught and killed a mouse while it was darting toward our kitchen. Both Michael and I are *so* happy to have him. We gave the good boy a nice big saucer of milk to show our gratitude. The sweet kitty now has a bed in the kitchen, which is where he is now, so he can watch Michael while he works and keep a sharp eye peeled for anymore of those detestable mice."

Samantha smiled at the thought of her cat. She'd grown very attached to the feline. "Shakespeare will go after anything that will run from him. Back in Houston he once caught a beautiful songbird and killed it. Although I didn't like him to kill birds, I realized it was a natural thing for a cat to do."

"There is, hidden beneath a thin veneer of civilization, a killer instinct in humans too." Sidney again touched an open palm to his cheek. "Let us retire to the parlor and begin polishing your talents . . . hummm?"

Samantha took the single straight-back chair that sat in the middle of the room, in front of which a blackboard had been set up beside the bar. The scenario made her feel as if she were back in grade school, being tutored after hours for being unable to grasp the meaning of a lesson.

"Now you just relax, Sam," Sidney said in his usually syrupy sweet voice. "From the manner in which you handled the situation last evening, we know you are admirably blessed with self-control. This asset, as I am *certain* you are aware, is what separates the survivors from the statistics. In your new profession of helping with the, ah, *disposal* of troublesome individuals, it will be necessary to hone these skills to a razor's edge. You are most fortunate to have Michael and me as your instructors. I would, in all modesty, say that we are among the most successful in the profession. Of course, the simple fact we are here is, ah, *living* proof of that statement." He chuckled gleefully.

Sam adjusted herself in the uncomfortable chair, her mind awash with ideas on how to get out of this predicament.

Unfortunately, everything she came up with only assured her that she'd join the numbers of people who had visited the Sunset Bed and Breakfast only to become what Sidney had accurately termed "a statistic." There seemed to be no alternative to acting as if she really was interested in becoming a hit-lady.

Yet, Samantha realized she needed at least a show of honesty. The manner in which Sidney looked at her, as if those piercing blue eyes of his could see into her mind, was discomforting. "I hope you know that I didn't set out to make a career of killing people."

Sidney looked crestfallen. "Of course you didn't, my dear. I must say, neither did Michael, or myself, for that matter. A person who picked and delighted in such a career would not be trustworthy, or long-lived. This profession is *really* one where many are called, but few are chosen. Also, my dear, please refrain from using the word *killing*. We find it to be rather crude. After all, the people we dispose of are no different from a rabid animal that must be put down."

Sam took the opening, "Then how are the clients selected? All I know about Crossman Speaks is that he had grabby hands and was a lawyer."

Sidney clucked his tongue and adjusted his gold-rimmed glasses. "All in good time, my dear. Trust me when I tell you the clients are sent here only as a last resort . . . hmmm. No pun intended. None of these people are considered redeemable in the least. The world is a better, safer place after their removal."

"But what if—"

"—We have gone mostly over old ground here, Samantha. The Company has us on a most grueling schedule, which forces me to conclude the pleasantries. Today's lesson will be on the use of poisons." Sidney took a piece of chalk and wrote a column of numbers on the blackboard from one through six. "These indicate toxicity. One has the mildest effects. Six, such as the oleander plant we employed last evening, is among the fastest-acting and most lethal known to man."

Samantha could not help but be intrigued. "You use only plant poisons?"

"Why no, not at all." Sidney seemed pleased. "There are also chemicals such as cyanide and, of course, the old standby, arsenic, among others. Drug overdoses, especially of a prescription drug prescribed by a medical doctor that a mark—which is how we refer to clients away from their presence—is taking works quite well. The problem with chemical compounds is their disturbing tendency to remain in the body, which can often allow snoopy forensic scientists to obtain evidence. This is something that needs to be avoided at all costs."

Samantha noticed a folder on her desk. She opened it to find pages listing various poisonous substances along with their effects. "I thought hit-men always shot their marks."

"Excellent," Sidney clapped his delicate hands. "You are grasping the terminology already. I am *so* pleased. But to answer your question, the movies do not portray what *we* do at all accurately. The best disposals are those where the mark simply disappears, such as Jimmy Hoffa. Or they appear to have passed away from natural causes, such as a fall or heart attack."

"We arrange accidents, too?"

"Not here at the Sunset Bed and Breakfast. This is what is termed a permanent disposal site that will be used for many years. You should be aware there are also untraceable methods of causing disease."

Sidney cocked his head, as if thinking back through the years. "Michael and I once disposed of a most detestable drug dealer in a quite unique fashion. This mark was always heavily guarded; he knew full well he was high on our hit parade. He employed food tasters, wore bulletproof vests—all in all he seemed untouchable."

"What did you do?" Samantha was genuinely interested.

"It was Michael's idea. We performed two unauthorized entries. The first was into a veterinary hospital, the second into a hotel room where the mark was scheduled to stay. I dressed as a representative of the cable company and switched the sealed toothbrush in the bathroom with one I had brought along."

Samantha frowned in puzzlement.

"It was genius, really. From the veterinarian's records we found a skunk that had tested positive for rabies. We simply swabbed the dead animal's mouth out with a toothbrush, resealed it, and left it for the mark to use." Sidney sighed. "It took six weeks to know if we would be successful. We were. That man won't be importing any more drugs into our country."

In spite of the building heat of an Arizona afternoon, Samantha Sterling felt a chill trickle slowly down her spine. The sensation of being wrapped in the arms of a nightmare just kept getting worse and worse.

CHAPTER FIFTEEN

Luke Sutton sat in the back of the decrepit 1972 Dodge van that had been his home for two years, sipping the cheapest mescal he could buy across the border in Mexico while he waited in the stifling heat for the coming Apache moon. And killing time.

He admired the Apache, especially Geronimo. The wily chief had beaten back everything the government could throw at him for over twenty-five years. Now *there* was a lesson for all of those lily-livered, left-wing, pinko wimps who were turning the good ol' United States of America, Land of the Free, into a communist stronghold.

Just like Geronimo, Luke had suffered the slings and arrows of an oppressive government. Throughout most of his thirty-nine years he had been harassed and his opportunities laid low by a pinko government that gave people of dark skin preference over the decent white folks whom God had chosen above all others.

Two prison stints for simply attempting to even the score chaffed at him the worst. From here on he had to be careful to leave no pesky witnesses to testify against him in the future. That new commie-inspired three-strikes law would put him away for life if he wasn't diligent in taking care of business.

Luke had come here over a month ago and joined the Tombstone Minutemen, an organization that appeared to be made up of true Aryan brothers.

But coming to Tombstone had been a mistake. Rodney Page

was a softhearted fool, not a leader of true men who were strug-
gling to rescue the Land of the Free from a government
controlled by Jews.

No, Luke thought, *they kicked me out. Told me to leave or else.*

The experience with the Minutemen had only served to steel
his resolve. He needed money to find and attract *real* men to
help him in his cause.

And after he'd been so helpful to the Tombstone Minutemen.
The group claimed they wanted to "Clean up the border with
Mexico, scour the alien horde from our Land."

This was what Luke took to doing with a zealous fervor. Wetbacks weren't even on the level of good livestock. Their skin
color ranged from brown to black, an obvious indication of
Simian heritage.

That was why it was hard for Luke to understand him being
kicked out of the Minutemen for simply using a couple of young
wetback girls for his pleasure. They were here in the United
States of America illegally. He simply could see nothing wrong
with being allowed to use those dark-skinned girls for the only
good purpose a true Aryan had for Mexicans.

Rodney Page had ranted about the fact neither of the girls
were even twelve years old. As if that mattered. And the whip-
pings were meant as a lesson for them to stay out of God's
chosen land. It was an accident, plain and simple, that the last
one had died. The girls' weakness was proof, more proof, of
inherited genetic inferiority, nothing to blame him for.

Luke wasn't certain what genetics were, but he liked the
word and used it often. It showed him to be an educated man.

With the beginnings of a wonderful Apache moon rising
above the ragged hills, he would be able to soon move on to his
destiny with money to spare.

The only decent thing to come out of Tombstone had been a
good description of the pair of wealthy queers and one old

drunken woman who ran the exclusive Sunset Bed and Breakfast. They had to have loads of cash stuffed away in the remote home of theirs. Money Luke needed to save this country.

And faggots were even worse than Mexicans. They might be white-skinned, but their genetics were flawed. His visit tonight would simply be another much-needed cleansing of the rot that clogged the pipeline to true Freedom.

Luke Sutton cradled his prize possession, an Ingram MAC-10 machine pistol, modified to fire fully automatic, that he'd stolen from the Minutemen. He would employ this wonderful firearm to assure no witnesses would be left alive to cause him problems later. It was very helpful that the old mansion was so distant from town, without any snoopy neighbors to report gunfire.

He sipped more mescal and watched the moon rise. Then he remembered the Apache were actually scared of the dark. While they were vicious warriors, they would only fight during the daylight. Only a full moon gave enough light for the souls of the fallen to find their way to the land of *Usen*.

Just like frightened children.

On second thought, the Indians were genetically inferior, too. Geronimo had simply been lucky.

No matter. The cleansing would begin soon. Over the silver-laden hills of Tombstone, Arizona, the full moon was beginning its arc across the night sky, giving ample yellow light for a man to thread his way through the spiny cactus on a mission that required him to kill.

Luke Sutton would soon be on his way to rob the Sunset Bed and Breakfast.

Fern Birdsong stood on the porch of their home in the fading light, her clenched hands held hard to her hips.

"Tex," Fern squawked in a voice that reminded her husband of fingernails being drawn down a blackboard, "I want you to see Bumps Turner tomorrow about that dirty hippie living in that beat-up old van in the park. No one's supposed to stay there even overnight. He's been there for a solid month now."

"Yes dear," Tex came out, sipping a beer. He knew his wife disapproved of his drinking alcohol, especially since Fern had become brainwashed by the pastor of the local Baptist church she had joined for some unfathomable reason. Only it took a few beers to steady his frayed nerves to where he could stand being in the same house with her. "I'm sure the marshal knows all about it, but I'll drop by and see him. I have to go to the store for some more beer anyway."

"You drink too much, Tex."

"Yes dear."

"I fear for your eternal soul, Tex."

"Yes dear."

"I'll pray for you and for Esther Munson to drive slower."

"You do that, dear."

Tex Birdsong stared happily at the newspaper box he had erected across the road. Had he not been so preoccupied, the old fellow could have seen the distant figure of a long-haired, tattooed man stealthily moving amongst the building shadows as he made his way across Emerald Gulch heading in the direction of the big yellow mansion on the hillside a mile south.

After long moments of silence, the elderly couple went inside their house, where neither would say a single word to each other until the next morning.

CHAPTER SIXTEEN

"I'm beginning to believe Arizona sunsets are among the loveliest sights nature has to offer," Samantha said as she turned to leave the fading red embers on the Western horizon to die alone, reluctantly pulling herself from the window to take her seat at the dining room table.

"You'll get over it," Esther snorted after gulping a healthy swallow of white wine.

"Now Mother." Sidney came from the parlor to take his usual seat at the head of the long table. "Don't be a picklepuss. The desert has many delightful features if only one takes the time to enjoy them."

"People say the same thing about Italian opera. I can't stand that either. All that blasted screamin' gives me a headache."

Sidney filled his wineglass from one of the three bottles on the table that had been properly chilled, then uncorked to allow the wine to breathe. "Mother doesn't keep her opinions reined in. I find that to be refreshing, considering the masks many people wear, often for their own gain."

Samantha was spared a reply by Michael coming from the kitchen carrying a large, covered silver serving platter. "We will be dining this evening on mesquite-roasted quail nestled in a bed of wild rice that has been sautéed with herb butter." He set the huge dish on the table and removed the lid with a flourish. "The medley of organic vegetables were steamed using distilled mountain spring water and they have been delicately seasoned with the very best extra virgin olive oil along with a hint of fresh basil."

"My, my," Sidney beamed with pride, "such a delightful repast. Michael, you have outdone yourself once again. Please take your seat so we might enjoy a relaxing glass of wine together before dining."

Michael bent to check that the low flames from the alcohol burners were properly adjusted to keep his cuisine at a perfect temperature before taking the chair to Sidney's right.

"I do hope the other bottles will be an improvement over this vintage." Sidney filled Michael's glass. "The French wines, I feel, are riding on past reputation that has been surpassed by many of the California vineyards."

Picking up his glass, Michael tilted it from side to side to enable him to observe the film. "The texture is a tad weak. I am forced to agree about the superiority of our domestic wineries. The smaller ones, such as those in New Mexico, also turn out a very delightful product."

Samantha held out her glass for Sidney to fill from the bottle he beckoned with. "I must say, Michael, I'm very impressed with your culinary skills. If I'm not careful, I'll gain too much weight."

Esther said, "Don't eat any of the rice or bread, then you'll be fine. That stuff's what's bad for you. Too blasted many carbohydrates."

"Moderation," Sidney advised, "along with exercise is all that is required to maintain a healthy weight." He took a delicate sip of wine. "To change the subject, I must say that our Samantha is a *most* promising understudy. She appears to be an absolute natural to join us in our profession."

"I agree," Esther said. Her unexpected niceness came as a shock to Samantha, who had decided the old woman preferred her as dead as Crossman Speaks. "From what I've observed,

Sam has spunk, which is what it takes to survive nowadays."

"This is *so* wonderful to hear," Michael said, holding his wineglass high. "Keeping up with the kitchen and cooking is stressful enough. Add in whacking the occasional mark and it is quite taxing on my energies. Having our lovely Samantha to help will be *so* wonderful. I would like to propose a toast to her future with us."

"Hear, hear," Sidney tapped a fork to his glass, sending off a musical note before toasting. "Here is to Samantha Sterling, our new partner, who is, sorry to say, presently deceased."

Samantha nearly choked on a swallow of wine. "I'm *dead?*"

"Why, no," Sidney said, "you are a member of what we like to think of as *family.* What we mean is that your *previous* life has ended. There will be no more using of your surname, so I suggest that you give the matter some thought and come up with a new one. We have no problem allowing you to retain use of your first name, which will ease the transition considerably."

"You do understand why this is necessary," Esther said. "The Company demands that all of its employees be untraceable."

"And being dead is a real asset, should anyone start snooping where they could cause us problems," Michael added.

Samantha sat in silence, dumbstruck by the turn of events.

Sidney smiled at her. "It all came together so admirably just the past night. A Jeep similar to yours was involved in a terribly fatal head-on collision in New Mexico. The resulting fire obliterated all normal means of recognition of the bodies."

Michael said, "While you and Esther were in town getting your hair done so beautifully, Sam, Sidney and I utilized the Internet and employed our connections to place your name on the dental records of the unfortunate girl at the scene along with changing many other records, including the serial and license plate numbers that were registered to your vehicle in Texas. Once we make certain, ah . . . further alterations, you will be free to drive that lovely Jeep of yours once again. But you must realize that to everyone who ever knew you, you are dead from this day forth."

Samantha sputtered, "I was killed in a car wreck last night. Now, I need a new last name."

"See," Esther beamed, "I *told* you she's a natural."

"It beats being *really* dead," Sidney said with that cold smile of his, ". . . ummm."

"How about Sullivan?" Sam ventured after downing the much-needed glass of wine. "It's not far removed from my real name, which will make it easy for me to remember. Also it's Irish, which will explain the red tint to my hair."

"You are quite astute, Mother." Sidney refilled everyone's glass. "Our little lady appears to be a natural at surviving. With proper training and a little time, she will almost certainly be an admirable asset to our organization."

Michael held up his glass. "And here is to the late Samantha Sterling."

"May she rest in peace," Esther said.

Sam numbly joined in the toast, wondering if she might not have been better off if she had been killed in that car wreck last night.

Shafts of tangerine moonlight shooting through the parlor windows and undulating eerily on the floor with every fresh gust of wind that rustled the oleanders outside. In the distance, a coyote wailed a mournful tune to the star-studded desert night.

Samantha knew how sad the coyote must be, to wail so pitifully that a listener could feel its sorrow. She sipped on her third glass of wine and sat by herself. Even Shakespeare had joined her captors in the kitchen, leaving her to her thoughts.

By now her parents in Beaumont had undoubtedly been

informed of her death. They would be devastated. Kathy, her older sister, married for twenty years to a real estate agent in Cleveland, would be making airplane reservations to come to her funeral.

They'll bury a terribly burned body there in the family plot in Beaumont, believing with all of their heart it's me. It'll be a real shock when I show up and tell everyone what actually happened.

Samantha choked back a sob and took another sip of wine as the distant coyote grew silent.

Except that I'll be killed if I try to run. And no one ever looks for a person who is dead and buried. Damn, these people have thought of everything. It will take a miracle to get out of this mess alive.

A loud crash as a heavy army boot kicked open the front door shook Samantha from her reverie. There was the ominous clicking of a gun bolt, which she recognized from hunting trips with her father and ex-husband. The metallic sound was as frightening as the warning buzz of a diamondback rattlesnake.

Someone's come to kill the killers!

CHAPTER SEVENTEEN

Samantha stiffened with fright. A soulless voice filled with the venom of pure hate barked, "All right, you perverts, put your hands up where I can see them and don't even think of trying anything smart. This gun of mine will turn you into a pile of bloody meat if you do."

From the kitchen Sidney's musical voice sounded oddly calm, "That is an Ingram Mac-10, isn't it? They are quite splendid weapons. I do assume you have modified it to fire on fully automatic . . . ummm?"

"Make the wrong move, ya fag bastard, and you'll have your answer," the intruder blared.

Michael's voice: "There is really no need for the use of epithets or fulminates in this house, sir. I assume you are here to rob us. May I suggest we get on with the business at hand without the matter becoming, ah, *personal.*"

Esther shouted, "There's just the three of us! There's no danger to yerself. Would ya mind not waving that gun around, it might go off accidentally and hurt someone."

"Shut up, you old hag, or I'll kill you now instead of later."

That man doesn't know I'm here, Samantha thought. *And Esther is letting me know.*

Samantha's emerald eyes scanned the parlor for something, anything, to use as a weapon. The telephone was worthless. As far from town as they were, the robber would most likely be in Mexico before the law arrived.

In the mirror behind the bar, Samantha could clearly see a burly man with long black hair and a matted beard holding a boxy, strange-looking gun. He'd ripped the sleeves from his filthy "G. Gordon Liddy For President" t-shirt that showed off a myriad of colorful tattoos covering his arms and shoulders. All told, he looked the part of the boogeyman in every nightmare she could remember. The man was a stone killer, and it was up to her to stop him before it was too late.

If I can see him, he can see me.

Quickly, Samantha melted back into the shadows. She noticed her shoes had made a slight scuffing sound on the hardwood floor. Carefully she removed them and placed them on the sofa beside Esther's purse, where she had left it after they had returned from town.

In the kitchen, the robber's voice: "Listen up, perverts, I'm going to kill one of you right now just to motivate the other two if I don't start seeing money—a lot of damn money."

Sidney replied calmly, "There really is no reason for you to hold such hostility toward us, my good man. The fact of the matter is that we keep nearly all of our money in the bank or with our broker. I honestly must believe that you have never seen the movie *In Cold Blood.* I daresay we have even a thousand dollars cash among us."

"But we *can* write you a check," Esther added with urgency in her voice. "I believe that tact will give you the kind of money you're obviously expecting."

"The bank opens at nine tomorrow morning," Michael's voice said. "To calm any fears you may have, one of us can accompany you while the others can remain safely tied up. I believe you will find that not killing us will pay far better than what you were planning."

"How . . ." The robber seemed to be having trouble coming to a decision. "How much can you get?"

Sidney again: "We have nearly a half million dollars cash in certificates of deposit, along with our operating capital that will add up to well over five hundred thousand."

Michael said, "Compared to a few hundred dollars, that should be a no-brainer."

They're stalling. Samantha noticed goose bumps on her arms. She simply did not know what to do. Then she brightened.

The gun in Esther's purse!

Silent as a shadow, Samantha bent and clicked open the bronze clasp beneath a sheltering hand to deaden any noise. The cold, blue steel of the automatic felt reassuring in her now rock-solid grip. Both her father and Arnold had insisted on her having a working knowledge of firearms. When Texas passed the concealed handgun law, her ex-husband had insisted that Sam take the required course and she had received a license to carry.

Sidney and Michael knew that before they hired me.

Esther's pistol was a 9mm Beretta. Thankfully, it was a weapon Sam was familiar with and had fired before. It would have been prudent to pull back the slide to make sure a cartridge was in the firing chamber, but the noise would be a giveaway of her presence.

A DEAD *giveaway.*

Samantha forced herself to breathe deeply and evenly, as every firearm instructor always taught a person to do to steady their aim. Stealth as a cat, she moved from the safety of the shadows to quickly assume a shooter's stance facing the open kitchen, steadying the Beretta with both hands.

"Hey asshole!" she shouted.

The robber spun toward her, only to be rewarded by a slug of hot lead that stuck him square in the chest. The roar of the shot echoed loudly in the confines of the room.

Samantha watched with relief as the intruder's ominous gun crashed harmlessly to the floor, yet oddly enough the thug still stood alongside Michael, staring at her with wide, uncomprehending eyes.

Then Michael removed a hand from the back of the man's neck. A silver ice pick, its thin shaft red with blood, glistened in the florescent lights.

As the would-be killer slumped to the floor, Samantha noticed the black bone-handle of a bread knife stuck in the man's back all the way to its hilt.

Esther smiled at her, holding a very small revolver in a bony hand.

So much for my idea to keep shooting. With ALL *of them dead, I would be free.*

Samantha placed the Beretta on a coffee table and walked toward the body. Strangely enough she felt calm, oddly detached from the events that had just transpired.

"Never approach a mark unarmed," Sidney told Samantha in the tone of a schoolteacher. "Not even one who has quite obviously been dealt many fatal wounds. A human body can keep functioning for a while longer while than many would believe."

"I think this guy's plenty dead," Michael said. "An ice pick angled up into the brain acts to paralyze the mark."

"I killed him." *Why did I say that?* Samantha felt as if someone else was speaking. She looked down at the body and marveled there was so little blood.

"Very good," Sidney beamed. "You performed excellently, and beyond our wildest expectations."

"Shot him square in the heart," Esther added firmly. "I like that."

Michael smiled at her as he wiped the ice pick clean with a soapy dishcloth. "A simple 'yoo-hoo, Mister robber' would have given us the edge we needed."

Samantha shook her head sadly at the corpse. "That man was going to kill all of us."

Sidney stepped to Samantha's side and placed a comforting hand on her shoulder. "There are a lot of people out there, just like him. Some kill with a gun, others by selling drugs or attempting to destroy our country from within. We have taken on the task of eliminating them before they can do more harm."

Esther snorted, "While everyone's here jawin', they can help with the cleanup. That's always the most work, and I'm getting too damn old to keep doing it all by myself."

"Certainly, Mother," Sidney said. "I really do feel badly about Samantha having to do a *pro bono* hit so early in her career."

"She'll get over it," Esther said. "Now go fetch a tarp to wrap him in. I don't want any blood dripping on our new carpet."

Samantha kept staring at the still body, wondering how she had managed to shoot a man's heart out, yet feel nothing from doing so.

When Sidney went outside for the tarp, a pack of coyotes could be heard yipping in the distance, singing a mournful tune to an Apache moon.

Chapter Eighteen

"Now remember," Michael Herod said to Samantha as he grasped the handle of the knife stuck in the robber's back. "It is a lot less messy if you let a body set for a while before retrieving a blade. A beating heart is necessary to pump blood. In this case—" He jerked out the knife and smiled. "—see, no muss, no mess. A trip through the dishwasher and this wonderfully sharp bread knife can be returned to service. It's not part of my most expensive set, you know."

"That idiot caused me to need my hair redone," Esther complained, brushing over the hole left in her beehive hairdo from where she'd extracted the small silver pistol.

"You keep a gun in your do?" Samantha said, awestruck.

Esther snapped, "Of course. I plugged the bastard with it, too. Both of our shots went off at nearly the same time, dearie."

"Mother believes in always being prepared." Sidney unrolled a blue plastic tarpaulin alongside the corpse.

"Let me help you move him," Michael said, placing the knife into the sink. "He *is* quite a large fellow. I would not like to see you pop your back out again."

"Then I have to scrub up dried blood," Esther fumed. "There's nothing harder to get off without leaving a stain."

"At least we had the Saltillo tiles sealed very well, Mother," Sidney said, grasping the corpse's arms while Michael clutched onto the pair of worn boots. "If he had thrashed around and leaked blood onto one of our Victorian rugs, the cleanup would have been much more extensive and costly."

"Yeah, I suppose," Esther grumbled, watching the men lift the body onto the tarpaulin.

"I'll help you, Esther," Sam said with a nod.

"You go with the boys. Now that you're a member of our family, it's time you know how the disposal system works." Esther lit a Marlboro. "I've been scrubbin' up blood since before you were born. Anyone can do it, just takes a lot of elbow grease to fool luminol."

Samantha's brow furrowed in puzzlement. "Luminol?"

"Cops spray it to find traces of blood." Sidney stood and watched Michael fold the tarpaulin around the corpse. "The worst part of shooting someone is the blood splatter." He motioned to where Samantha's bullet had gone into the wall after passing through the robber's body and sighed. "We will be forced to replace the wall board along with the base boards. While we have no reason to believe any policemen will ever investigate us, it is always wise not to leave any evidence lying around that could cause embarrassment later."

"That's why we much prefer to use oleander," Michael added, standing and stretching. "The marks sometimes wiggle around on the floor and foam at the mouth, but that's a much easier and cheaper cleanup than replacing walls."

"I'm sure it is," Samantha said numbly.

"Don't let 'em go namby-pamby on you," Esther said. "Us girls did the right thing shootin' that bastard. The wall won't take 'em but a few hours to fix up good as new."

"Come along, Samantha," Michael bent to grab up one end of the tarpaulin. "Once we drag this fellow outside, we'll show you just how easy it is to make a body disappear."

The orange tractor's rattling diesel engine sounded loud and out of place in the still of a Sonoran desert night. A bright moon hanging low in a jeweled canopy of sable sky gave ample illumination for the proceedings without the necessity of using the tractor's headlights.

Samantha walked alongside Sidney, following in the tractor's wake. She'd taken his warning about rattlesnakes hunting at night as good reason to stay in the tire's tracks. Huge oleander bushes that lined their pathway on both sides cast undulating shadows with each gust of wind.

"We'll be there in only a few more feet," Sidney announced, speaking loudly so he could be heard over the engine's noise. "Just take care to stay close to me and behind the tractor."

Michael slowed the front-end loader to a crawl, then brought it to a dead stop. "Sidney, take a look to see where my front wheels are. I have an increasing difficulty driving at night these days."

"Of course, my friend," Sidney walked carefully alongside the tractor, eyeing the ground meticulously as he proceeded. "Move ahead about two feet."

Michael nodded. The machine crawled toward what appeared to Samantha to be a large hole in the ground.

"That's perfect," Sidney said, holding out a hand, palm open. He waited until Michael had set the brakes and turned off the engine to rejoin Samantha. The returning quiet of night felt oddly heavy and chilling to her.

"This is the main shaft of the historic Silver Cross Mine," Sidney said. "The old-timers were a persistent lot. They dug this hole down for over five hundred feet following a vein of silver that was too low grade to pay."

"They were vigorous, rough and tumble men in those days," Michael said wistfully from his seat on the tractor.

"Yes," Sidney agreed. "Those wonderful hardworking fellows never made a single dollar from their labors, but they did leave us with a hole deeper than a fifty-story building is high."

Michael said, "We occasionally dump in a sack of quicklime to avoid any unpleasant odors and aid with decomposition."

"Neat and tidy." Samantha stared at the tarpaulin-wrapped body in the loader bucket that was now well extended over the open maw of the mineshaft.

"It is nice that you approve," Sidney motioned with a hand to Michael. "Not only is it economical and handy, the capacity of the shaft is nearly limitless when one considers the efficiency of quicklime."

Michael moved a small lever with his right hand. There was a low, hissing sound as the loader bucket turned down to send the corpse plunging into the opening.

Samantha stiffened when she heard what sounded like a dull popping sound as the body began ricocheting off the sides of the rocky shaft.

Sidney had noticed her reaction. "Tut, tut my dear. I assure you he felt no pain from his rapid descent, and that the world is better off with him being tucked away down there."

"Yeah," Samantha took a deep breath. "I'm sure you're right about that. Shooting someone in the heart and then helping dispose of their body takes some getting used to, is all."

"We all must go through periods of adjustment in our lives, my dear." Michael shrugged. "Granted, the one you are going through is somewhat tougher than most, but from what I have seen, you will come through with flying colors. Not attempting to continue firing Esther's pistol was a most wise decision on your part and confirmed your loyalty to us."

Samantha gave Sidney a puzzled look.

"You honestly can't believe we left you with access to Mother's Beretta out of carelessness. In this profession, my dear, one can ill-afford to be too trusting. There was but a single bullet in that gun, and Michael and I are both wearing bulletproof vests under our shirts."

"That's one reason we were not overly upset when that idiot we just dumped down the mine shaft made his appearance," Michael said. "And since you passed our test and did the right thing, you won't be joining him."

"Now, for the final lesson of the evening," Sidney held out a hand to Michael who gave him the robber's MAC-10 wrapped in a towel. "We must always remember to wipe all fingerprints from any weapon used in a disposal, then either leave the gun at the scene or make certain it will never be found."

Sidney Munson vigorously scrubbed the boxy weapon with the cloth, then tossed both into the depths of the shaft.

"I do believe that after the way this evening has gone," Michael said, reaching for the tractor's starter switch, "a pitcher full of Tombstone Blues is in order."

"Why that sounds simply scrumptious," Sidney agreed before the engine began rattling once again.

Samantha followed the tractor back to the bed and breakfast with a numbness to her gait. She *had* thought of killing these people. Then, her trepidation fled. For some strange reason she felt a new emotion creep into her being.

Satisfaction.

CHAPTER NINETEEN

Tex Birdsong stood on the rear deck of his home, sipping coffee in the comfort of a warming sun that had first appeared over the eastern mountains nearly four hours ago. Occasionally he would set down his cup, put a pair of field glasses to his eyes, and carefully survey the distant, yellow mansion that was the Sunset Bed and Breakfast.

He'd retired after putting in forty years as a union longshoreman in the bustling port of Los Angeles. Tex was not a man noted for his patience, yet there really wasn't a lot of choice; he had to wait for Esther Munson.

It galled him just how slow *any* female could move and still accomplish anything. Back in his days of being a dock foreman, he kept his crew hopping or he fired their lazy butts. That was the way things were done, before the Republicans went and ruined this country.

Fern could be heard clattering about in the kitchen. At least he had been successful in keeping his wife from becoming a sluggard. It was just too bad that she had turned into a shrew.

With a little luck, that problem will be over real soon, Tex thought as he noticed a building cloud of dust heading down the distant mountain that was preceded by a speeding Hummer.

He studied the situation for a brief moment, placed the binoculars on the picnic table, then turned and hollered loudly through the open sliding door entering the kitchen.

"Dear, will you please go fetch the newspaper? My knee's acting up."

Fern yelled back, "It didn't stop you from walking to Johnny Ringo's Saloon last evening."

"The weather was a lot warmer then. You know I suffer with arthritis from all of those years I slaved away working to make us a living. The cold stoves me up these days."

"OK, I'll go get your blasted newspaper. For the life of me, I don't know why you wanted to subscribe to that Sierra Vista paper for in the first place. It's an added expense we could do without."

Tex heard the front door slam. He no longer needed the binoculars to see the Hummer. Far to his right the huge speeding platinum vehicle was already approaching the road running in front of their house.

This was going to work.

Then, the slamming of the front screen door caused his spirits to sink. He sighed and strode inside to find his wife changing shoes.

"How silly of me," Fern said as she balanced with one hand on the sofa to steady herself while she slid off a house slipper. "I might have gotten a sticker in my foot, those thin shoes don't offer much protection from mesquite thorns."

Tex Birdsong grimaced when Esther sped past heading for town. His wife did not even appear to have noticed the Hummer.

Well, there's always tomorrow.

"Your knee isn't bothering you too much to talk on the phone," Fern growled, finally getting the first slipper off. "I want you to call Bumps Turner about that hippie. I see his old van is still down there in the park. The marshal needs to check him out. I'm betting he's a druggie."

Tex shrugged. Considering how rotten his day had gone so

far, calling the police on some poor schmuck who was simply down on his luck and trying to scrimp by with free parking didn't seem like a bad idea at all.

"I'll get right on it, dear." Tex sauntered the distance to the wall phone in the kitchen before he remembered that he hadn't limped. Thankfully, the old bat was likely so engrossed with the simple task of changing shoes that she hadn't noticed.

Bumps Turner had took all of the particulars on the van and promised to drop by and see what he could find out before Tex once again heard the screen door slam. He glanced at a clock. Esther had sped by over ten minutes ago. He would need to take his wife's natural slowness into consideration the next time.

A thin smile crossed the old man's face. He hadn't thought about the fact that a really big rattlesnake might be coiled next to the paper box. After getting its hide peppered from flying gravel, a diamondback would really be pissed off. He refilled his cup with coffee and stepped close to the open door, where he would not miss hearing any delightful screams of pain.

CHAPTER TWENTY

When Samantha saw the battered, rusted-out, old Chevrolet truck towing a long trailer holding a concrete septic tank that was parked in front of the Wild Hair Beauty Salon, she surmised Minnet's ex-husband had stopped to visit.

"That bastard's blockin' my parkin' space," Esther grumbled, puffing furiously on a Marlboro. "People just don't have any courtesy these days, now back in my time—"

"There's a space just down the block," Samantha interrupted to spare the history lesson. "A little walk will do us good."

Esther snorted, gunned the Hummer around the truck, and skidded to a dusty stop beneath a mesquite tree.

Samantha decided not to say anything about the fact the huge Hummer was parked halfway onto the sidewalk. All that would accomplish would be to hear another lecture about how much better things were in the good old days. And another lecture of any type wasn't something she wanted to endure.

After an early breakfast and coffee served in the now less-than-uplifting confines of the kitchen, both Sidney and Michael had proceeded to give her a long and detailed lesson on the forensics of blood splatter and DNA.

Sidney had taken a gold Cross pen from his shirt pocket to use as a pointer. "Now observe the pattern of blood spray we have here on the wall. Your bullet passed directly through the mark's heart, which brought about such a dreadful mess as this one, but it *did* at least put a quick end to our problem. What I want you to observe is just how wide a spray of blood there actually was."

"And what most people don't realize," Michael added, "is that blood—well, fresh, warm blood anyway—flows as easily as cooking oil. It gets into nooks and crannies one would never suspect, such as behind baseboards. It trickles underneath walls and is generally a real challenge to clean up well enough to fool the police."

"Damn cops," Esther said, lighting a cigarette. "Nothin' but a royal pain in the ass."

"While we here at the Sunset house seldom need resort to bloodshed," Sidney said. "It will broaden your understanding of your new profession to pay attention. What Michael and I must do is remove this entire wall right down to the tile floor, then discard it in the depths of our wonderfully handy and efficient mineshaft."

"Did you find the slug yet?" Esther questioned, blowing a puff of smoke to the ceiling. "Bad idea leaving one around, even if it flew off into the desert."

"Yes Mother," Sidney chimed in his thin, musical voice. "You are quite correct in that many disposal artists are remiss in this area." His piercing blue gaze focused on Samantha. "I am certain you have seen enough of those insipid police shows to know that a bullet going through the rifling of any barrel is imparted with an individual identity from the lands and grooves that are easily matched by even the dullest of law enforcement personnel."

"Except for shotguns," Esther said, snuffing out her cigarette. "You can whack away with the same one of those again and again."

"True, Mother," Sidney continued, "but those things are *so* noisy and give such a nasty recoil it can bruise a delicate shoulder. I am quite certain that our lovely Sam will never need employ such a brutish weapon."

Michael said, "I would certainly hope not. To my way of thinking, *any* disposal method that draws blood is the sign of an incompetent or lazy practitioner. My little ice pick is quite a tidy instrument, I'll have you know. But to answer the question of the slug, Sidney and I pried it from out of a wall joist. A 9mm bullet is not noted for having great penetration."

"A person of my acquaintance," Sidney said, returning the gold pen to his pocket, "once shot a mark square in the forehead with a 9mm. He saw the slug come out the back of the mark's head, assumed the hit was complete, and went on his merry way, only to later be arrested for attempted murder. It seems that the bullet had not been powerful enough to penetrate the skull, and had followed around the bone to pop out on the back of the mark's head."

"Always plug 'em more than once, dearie," Esther had said. "Bullets're cheaper than lawyers, and a damn sight more efficient."

"Amen to that, Mother," Sidney had agreed, then he and Michael had kept on talking for two more solid hours, giving more detailed information as to how blood and DNA evidence could be avoided.

It's as if they actually think I'm going to make a career out of killing people, Samantha thought as she followed Esther to the beauty salon. *I shot that man last night in self-defense. The other man who ate that poisoned cherry pie wasn't my fault.*

"Blasted hippies," Esther complained, eyeing the septic tank. "Those idiots think a line of bunkers'll stop an invasion from Mexico. They should read how well that idea worked out for the French."

"I doubt they read much of anything," Samantha said, "or are able to."

Esther's reply was put on hold when the front door of the

Wild Hair swung open and three unkempt men stepped out into the bright desert sunlight.

"And Rodney—" Minnet's voice from inside the salon, "—stay gone longer this time."

"Ah babe, you know you still have the hots for me," the tallest of the trio said over his shoulder. Rodney Page was muscular; the sleeves of what was likely his cleanest dirty shirt had been ripped off at the shoulders, displaying a host of colorful tattoos that covered both arms. He sported long black hair drawn back into a ponytail that dangled down the center of his back. When he turned and focused deep blue eyes on Samantha while wearing a naughty boy smirk, she understood how Minnet had fallen for him; with some cleaning, Rodney would be considered handsome.

"Well, look at this, will ya?" a hugely fat man dressed in greasy overalls said, giving Samantha a lecherous stare, his sunken, dark eyes fixing on her breasts. "Tombstone's had a sexy, new chick come to town."

"She's too much for you to handle, Wab," the slickly thin man with a pockmarked face and slicked-back hair said as he headed for Samantha. "Let ol' Carl Deevers here show her what a good time is."

Samantha stepped back, but the lanky member of the Tombstone Minutemen never slowed until he stood close enough for her to smell his foul breath.

"Nice tits," Deevers said, reaching out with both hands open. "Let's see if them hooters feel as good as they look."

Carl Deevers froze in mid-grope, as if his mainspring had broken. His pale gray eyes widened in pain. "Uhhh . . ." seemed to be the only sound he could manage. Then Samantha glanced down to see Esther's boney hand fastened to the man's crotch so tightly that her knuckles were white.

"Dearie," Esther said in a syrupy-sweet voice, "if you don't apologize to my friend Sam here and start displaying some manners, I'm gonna start twisting. If I do, I promise you, it'll be a long, *long* time before you'll wanna even *think* about a woman."

"Uhhh . . . I'm sorry, ma'am," Deevers sputtered. "I was just teasin' the lady."

"Carl comes across a tad rough," Rodney Page said, stepping close, "but he's harmless, and I assure you he'll behave himself."

"I don't need your assurances," Esther said, keeping her grip. "This guy acts up again, he's a eunuch."

"Uhhh . . . lady, I'll promise you anything you want," Deevers whined. "Jus' don't twist my goodies an' please don't hurt me. I really mean it about that 'please' part, too."

Esther stared at him like a hawk eyeing a mouse. "See, being nice wasn't so hard." She released her grip. "Now be a good boy and run back to your village before they realize their idiot is missing."

Carl Deevers bolted away from Esther, his face molded into a mask of seething rage. He started to say something when Rodney placed a firm hand on his shoulder.

"Settle down and go sit in the truck," Rodney said, then turned to Samantha. "I'm sorry about this, ma'am. Carl's not a bad sort, just a tad short when it comes to manners. He won't bother you in the future."

Samantha noticed Esther now had a hand stuck inside of her purse. "I'm sure there won't be any more trouble."

Rodney smiled broadly, his blue eyes flashing merrily in the bright sunlight. "No, miss, there won't be, and once again let me apologize for Carl." He took a business card from his shirt pocket and handed it to Samantha. "My name's Rodney. Please don't hesitate to call on me if I can ever be of service. Being friends of the Tombstone Minutemen is a good idea, there's bad times headed our way."

"Dearie," Esther said in an oddly cheerful tone, "you really wouldn't recognize a bad time if it walked up and kissed you on the cheek. Now, why don't you morons take that turd coffin you're so damn proud of and go somewhere with it. Us girls need the fresh air."

Rodney nodded and, keeping his smile fixed, said, "Later, ladies." Then he climbed into the truck. After a few moments attempting to start the old pickup, the trio were on their way, leaving behind clouds of dust and oil smoke.

"I'm sorry you had to suffer being subjected to those guys," Minnet said, holding the door open. "Rodney had some decent manners and was a fairly nice guy until he burned out his mind listening to Rush Limbaugh and other talk radio shows. Carl and Wab were both born dumb and have been losing ground ever since."

"They're just men," Esther tossed her cigarette butt over her shoulder and traipsed inside the shop. "Being insensitive, smelly idiots pretty much covers the species. One agreeable thing about being old is getting over needing the only thing they're good for. Now let's get to fixin' my hair, it's a mess."

Chapter Twenty-One

Carl Deevers sat humped up in a red rage as he rode with Rodney Page and Wab Smith when they drove the old truck pulling a trailer carrying the septic tank to the camp of the Tombstone Minutemen and their budding Maginot line. The fact that his companions kept needling him about what Esther Munson had done only added to the pain in his crotch. The old bat had had a grip like an alligator.

"I hope you're still able to pee," Wab said, turning to check on the septic tank. "My brother Rob got kicked in the nuts once by some gal who knew karate or some such shit. His pecker swole up and turned black and I had to take him to the hospital. You know those docs put a big plastic tube all the way up his dick? Poor Rob wasn't able to enjoy nookie for over a month."

Rodney Page snorted, "Esther didn't kick Carl in his goodies, just gave him a reason to behave." He glared at his waspish companion. "Carl, if you wanna squeeze a girl's titties, at least buy 'em a drink first, make small talk. We're soldiers out to save America, so try and act like you have some manners."

"She shouldn'ta hurt me like that," Deevers grumbled, keeping his focus on the floorboard of the rattling truck. "I was just funnin'."

Wab Smith turned from eyeing the septic tank to give Carl a wry grin. "Rob was just playing around, too. If he hadn't gone to the doc, they said he'd have got an infection and they'd had to cut his dick off to save his life. I'm bettin' you won't be able to pee, either."

"That's a crock," Rodney Page said as he turned the smoking truck off highway 80 just south of the airport and headed east on a narrow, washboard road. "Carl will be fine, and I want y'all to forget this nonsense even happened."

Carl Deevers snarled, "When did God die and leave you in charge? That old battle-axe hurt me, made me look like a fool. I ain't one to let bygones be bygones, especially when my tool's involved."

Rodney Page swallowed and took a moment to answer. Sometimes the quality of soldiers he had to recruit to save America left a lot to be desired, yet each and every one of them were needed for the cause. Even Carl Deevers had value; the man owned and could run a backhoe to dig the holes for the bunkers. If Carl got angry enough to leave the Minutemen, they'd be forced to hire a backhoe. And that would cost a lot of money.

"Now Carl," Rodney Page said soothingly. "Esther Munson is just a crotchety old woman. You did come on a tad strong with that Samantha girl and Esther took it wrong. The incident was only a misunderstanding. Look, here we're almost to the line. Remember that the Mexicans could attack us anytime—they're not gonna phone ahead with their plans, you know—let's get this bunker in place so we can be ready for them."

Wab Smith nodded. "If you can still pee, Carl, I reckon we can get on with saving the country." He added after spitting a wad of snuff out the window to splatter on the door. "Even if we are forced to protect purple-haired nut crushers along with the good, innocent folks."

"That's the attitude," Rodney Page said as he geared down the truck to climb a small grade. "We have to focus on the border. That's why I'm a general in the Tombstone Minutemen. I keep my eye on the task at hand."

Carl Deevers started to say something when Rodney hit the air brakes, giving off a loud hissing sound signaling they'd arrived at the big hole he'd previously dug to hold the concrete bunker on the trailer. He waited until his companions had exited before he slowly climbed down. His crotch felt like it was on fire, but he was a soldier, damn it. No true Aryan ever let a little pain stop them from a mission.

"Gettin' hot," Wab Smith said, mainly to change the subject.

"This is Arizona, moron," Carl Deevers said with a snort as he walked over to check out the wooden ladder that gave access to a wide, shallow hole. " 'Course it's hot out."

Wab simply shook his head and said nothing; Carl needed to let off some steam. The pudgy man said nothing. After Rodney unsnapped the thick canvas straps that securing the concrete septic tank to the flatbed trailer, he walked over to a rusty old winch truck that had no doors, jumped in, and coaxed the engine to life. After the cloud of blue oil smoke had cleared enough for him to see, Wab shouted to Rodney Page, "Hook it up good. Those things cost more than a thousand bucks."

"Our commie-run government can send out billions of dollars in foreign aid," Carl Deevers said, gingerly climbing down the ladder to help guide the heavy concrete tank into position. "They give money to niggers and all kinds of worthless trash, but us God-fearing white men have to make do the best we can to protect their lily-white asses. This plain ain't right."

"Yeah, and it won't be for much longer." Wab Smith poked a fresh batch of Copenhagen behind his lower lip while he watched Rodney position the lifting cables into the hook on the end of the cable dangling from his winch truck.

"We'll be ready for the sons of bitches," Carl Deevers shouted from down in the hole. "Get that bunker over here, I'll make sure it's out of the ground far enough we can have gun ports. Those bastards won't be expecting us to be well dug in, protected. Hell, we'll mow 'em down like the weeds they are."

"You're right there, Carl." Wab Smith engaged the PTO and winched the concrete tank skyward. "We're smarter than they think and we'll be ready for them."

A few minutes later the groaning, decrepit winch truck had positioned the dangling tank directly over the center of the excavation. Wab set the parking brake for some reason he wasn't sure of—the thing had been broken for years. But the ground was level, so the truck would stay put. He climbed out and grabbed onto both of the levers necessary to safely lower the heavy load into the hole. Before he could move either one, a loud popping sound, much like a rifle shot from above his head, grabbed Wab Smith's full attention. He looked up just in time to jump back from the whipping end of the broken cable and watch in horror as the septic tank dropped into the hole with a dull thud.

"Jaysus H. Christ on a crutch," Wab shouted to Rodney, who stood on the rim of the excavation staring down with wide eyes. "Carl was in that hole."

"For some reason, he was standing square under the bunker. I can't see nothin' but a foot stickin' out. Poor Carl's flatter than a friggin' pancake!"

"Oh my God," Wab kept repeating as he ran over to stand beside Rodney. "Oh my God, it was an accident, the cable just broke, it wasn't my fault. Oh my God."

"Now calm down," Rodney said, trying to keep his composure. "This is a war we're fighting. Carl's a casualty of battle, an honored soldier who fell in the line of duty."

"I squashed him with a septic tank," Wab said, staring down at the protruding foot. Then he noticed a dark red wetness oozing from beneath the concrete tank and turned away. "It was an accident, I don't know what else to say."

Rodney Page put a comforting hand on Wab's quivering

shoulder. "We're soldiers in a war to save our country. What we need . . . no, *have* to do is use Carl's demise to further our cause. He wouldn't want to be remembered as being lost to a falling septic tank."

"No," Wab's voice was choked with emotion. "He sure wouldn't. What else can we do?"

Rodney gave a deep sigh and hesitated a few moments before answering, as did all successful leaders of men. It was important to show that you have given the matter serious thought, explored all avenues.

"Carl Deevers will become a martyr to the cause," Rodney Page said. "What we'll do is go ahead and finish the bunker, fill in around the tank like nothing ever happened. Then, after a couple of days we'll make an announcement that Carl was on routine patrol when he must have intercepted a group of drug dealers or terrorists. He is missing and must be presumed lost, a victim of our war that the government refuses to fight until it is too late. Shit, we should maybe make up a plaque and put it on the wall of our headquarters to inspire others."

"Yeah," Wab said, blinking his eyes dry. "That'll work, and I like it a lot better than the truth."

"I thought you would," Rodney motioned to the backhoe. "Do you know how to run that tractor?"

"Yeah."

"Then get on it and give old Carl a burial, then we'll cut in the gun ports."

Smiling now, Wab Smith began the task of fortifying the Tombstone Maginot line. After a few buckets full of dirt had been added to the hole, he'd forgotten all about Carl Deevers's unfortunate demise. Saving America was a lot more important than worrying over a whiner.

CHAPTER TWENTY-TWO

Minnet Page said nothing more about the incident with her ex or the Minutemen. And thankfully, from Samantha's viewpoint, the hairdresser didn't ask any questions about the bird's-nest-sized hole in Esther's tower of purple hair. Having to explain keeping a pistol in her hairdo might tax even Esther's abilities to worm around a subject.

A Tombstone police officer, whose nametag showed him to be Joe Lomax, came inside the Wild Hair Beauty Salon just as Samantha was getting a comb-out prior to their going to lunch. The officer's heavy footsteps on the wood floor caused Esther to snort harshly when she awakened from her nap.

"I didn't mean to startle you, Mrs. Munson," Officer Lomax said sincerely. "But I noticed your Hummer parked just down the street and thought you might be here, save me a drive out to the B&B."

"That damn thing stands out like a flashing billboard," Esther said. "I keep asking my Sidney to buy me something smaller, like a Porsche or maybe a Volvo, but he insists I need the safety of a big car." She glared at Joe. "What's so important you had to chase me down?"

Joe painted a strained smile across his face. "Oh, it's likely nothing, ma'am. Chief Turner asked me to check out an old van that's been parked in Landon Park for several days. Since you folks drive by there often, we thought you might have seen someone around it. The vehicle's serial number traces back to a junkyard in Lordsburg. Seems the van's been fixed up good enough to run, but we don't have a clue who owns the thing or has been living in it from all appearances."

He's not living anywhere *these days,* Samantha thought.

Esther Munson shrugged. "Can't say we know a thing about it," she turned to Samantha. "How about you, dearie, seen anything that might help the nice officer?"

Samantha waited until Minnet had removed the comb to shake her head. "No sir, I can truthfully say that I've never even noticed the van you're talking about."

Joe clucked his tongue. "I just had to ask was all. Most likely it belongs to some druggie who's caught a ride to another town. I'll have the old thing towed to the impound yard. That van's so decrepit it will give a junkyard an eyesore."

Minnet Page put a final swirl to Sam's hair. "There's something about this town that attracts a lot of idiots, Joe. Whoever drove that old van up there and abandoned it has likely moved on. They have a tendency to do that after they find out Tombstone's just another town, not the Wild West."

"I'm sure you're right, Minnet." Joe gave her a broad smile; he'd been attracted to the hairdresser for a long while. "You ladies have a good day now, y'hear?"

Esther Munson waited until the officer had gone outside and closed the door behind him. "Nosy cops, anyway. Why in hell would he think we'd know anything about some beatnik living in the park, for Pete's sake?"

"I think the term 'beatnik' went out in the sixties," Minnet said. "These days we just call them bums or druggies."

"Fits better than a leather glove in a Los Angles courtroom," Esther said, standing with a grunt. "Let's grab some lunch. I'm hungry enough to eat a horse."

Minnet gave a chuckle and stowed the comb beneath an ultra-violet light. "How'd you know what Pete has on special today?"

"Esther's good about things like that," Samantha said. "Nothing much gets past her."

"Hey," Esther said, heading for the door, "a few glasses of white wine makes *any* red meat taste good." She turned to the two girls. "If I'm paying, get a move on, I'm too old to afford to wait."

Minnet and Samantha exchanged grins as they accompanied Esther outside.

The women almost collided with a neatly dressed man with brown hair and a lean build who was walking past. He jumped back toward the street, gave a smile, and looked into the front window of the Wild Hair Beauty Salon.

"I don't see the fire," the man said, squinting into the glass. "Maybe if I ran and got a extinguisher we might be able to put it out and save the building."

"Nothing's on fire, Lucas," Esther growled. "I'm on a damn diet, it's lunchtime, and you were in my way."

"Then I won't slow you ladies down anymore," the man kept his smile and stepped closer to Samantha. "I would, however, like to make the acquaintance of your friend here. I don't believe I've had the pleasure."

Samantha instantly took a liking to Lucas. He was possibly in his early forties; there was a hint of silver lining his temples. But what she noticed most of all was his infectious smile and sparkling blue eyes that actually seemed to glisten in the midday sun.

"Samantha . . . Sullivan," she said extending her hand. "I'm glad to meet you."

"Sam manages our bed and breakfast," Esther barked. "She's livin' with us these days, which gives you two all the time in the world to make pleasantries later. Now we're going to make tracks before the special's sold out."

Minnet spoke up, "Lucas Levy owns the Spice of Life

Gourmet Vinegar Works just two buildings down. When Samantha finds time, I'll take her over for a visit."

"I'd like that," Lucas Levy said. "I not only distill my own
line, but I also import stock vinegars from all over world. I
would love to show them to Samantha."

"I've never seen a vinegar store," Sam said. "Actually, I've
never even heard of one, not even in Houston."

"Tombstone holds many wonders," Lucas Levy said as he
watched Esther scoop up both girls, one with each arm, and
pointed them to the distant Hummer. "I'll see you when you
have a bit of free time and Esther's not starving."

"See ya, Lucas," Esther grumbled over her shoulder as she
herded the girls away. "Come out to the Sunset House some
evening. The boys would love to have you visit, give you a chance
to get to know Sam better, too."

"I'll do that," Lucas said, turning to head for his shop. "I'll
give you a call in a day or two." Then he realized he was talking
to empty space. For an old woman, Esther Munson could really
get a move on when the spirit moved her. It gratified him to
know age hadn't slowed her.

CHAPTER TWENTY-THREE

Sidney Munson stood alongside Michael on the front porch of the Sunset House. They were taking turns with a pair of binoculars while watching a tow truck hook up to a junky, old van that had sat in Landon Park for days.

Michael Herod clucked his tongue and passed the powerful and expensive set of field glasses to his companion. "I'm of the opinion that the lovely chap who tried to rob and kill us last evening very well might have called that terribly weather-beaten vehicle his home."

"I do believe it is a very distinct possibility, my friend. His personal hygiene was simply dreadful. I doubt the fellow had had a bath or shower for days."

"Undoubtedly correct, Sidney," Michael said. "He had not even cleaned his teeth for a very long while, which accounted for his awful breath. And the dirt beneath his fingernails was loathsome to behold."

"At least he has gone to an appropriate place . . . ummm."

"I will double the usual amount of quicklime we add to the disposal site to make certain his foulness doesn't attract buzzards or coyotes. A few dollars of prevention is worth a pound of cure, or so the old saying goes."

Sidney Munson lowered the field glasses from his piercing blue eyes and returned them to their leather case. "I *was* most impressed with that darling Samantha. The little dear had a gun in her hand and did not attempt to shoot any one of us. I believe her conditioning is going as well or better than we hoped."

Michael Herod gave a low chuckle. "As our instructor at The Company was so fond of saying, 'Many are called, but few live long enough to be chosen.' "

"True, true, my friend. Let us keep an optimistic outlook and hope for the best. We both desperately need a relaxing respite from our grueling labors. A nice, reliable, and responsible hit-lady working for The Company will enable us to enjoy that Alaskan cruise we have been looking forward to."

"Yes, Sidney, I do believe we may very well have a potential manager of sterling dependability to rely on."

Sidney chuckled. "Why, my friend, that was an unexpected pun, I do believe."

"Why it was at that. Too bad the little lady can never use her real surname ever again." Michael slipped his silver ice pick from its hidden sheath. He held it up to the sun, delighting in the way the thin sharp point glistened in the bright light. "Should she ever . . . ah, forget or become disloyal, we can cure that malady so easily."

"Ummm . . ." Sidney gave a gentle sigh. "Yes, my friend, we can always start over, as we have done before too many times. Considering my arthritis and your poor knees, we both surely need Samantha to work out."

"Esther is keeping a close eye on her. She believes there is better than a fifty percent chance of success."

"Mother is most perceptive in these matters. She has trained, I believe, at least a dozen people in the art of interment."

"Too bad they are all dead. An experienced interment specialist would be most welcome indeed."

"Our profession is not for the dull or unwary, but it does offer excellent pay, along with a general lack of boredom."

Sidney Munson stepped to the edge of the porch railing and pointed down to where some thick bushes were covered with shadows from the high yellow mansion. "Look Michael, there is a pesky diamondback rattlesnake crawling toward our oleander farm."

Michael Herod did not hesitate a second. He came forward, drew back with the hand holding the ice pick, and threw it downward, impaling the hapless snake through its triangular head.

"I honestly detest those creepy things," Sidney said. "But your aim is true as ever, my friend. From appearances, your wonderful ice pick has not only dispatched the hideous reptile but has also been driven hard enough to hold the snake firm to the earth."

"When it quits wiggling I will retrieve my ice pick. Perhaps I many be lucky enough not to have dulled the point too badly or even worse, bent the shaft out of true alignment. There is one tool that must be perfect in every detail to be thrown true."

"And you are *so* skilled in its use. Remember that time in Toronto when you were forced to throw your ice pick well over fifty feet in a crowded train station? You deftly struck the mark in the base of his neck and he collapsed as if he had had a heart attack. I daresay we were a mile away preparing to enjoy a hot cup of tea before the truth became known to the authorities."

"Yes, that was sometime ago, wasn't it, my friend? I still recall my sadness at not being able to recover that ice pick. Finding them well balanced along with holding a keen point can be a trying task."

Sidney Munson kept his focus on the writhing snake. "Operating the Sunset B&B does have its advantages. We have far more control over choosing the time and method of interment than those who work in the field."

Michael Herod grinned down at the impaled rattler. "I am hopeful Samantha will make a success of the business. There is a certain bearing about the little lady that tells me she is a survivor, along with being levelheaded and intuitive."

"We shall find out soon enough. While you were spraying insecticide along the base of the house I had a phone call from The Company. We can expect two customers tomorrow, a Mr. and Mrs. Steve Lowman. His wife's name is Judy, by the way. I know how much we both intensely dislike getting stuck having to do a twofer, but it is the price we must sometimes pay to keep receiving good contracts."

"In every occupation a little rain must fall. Are they driving in or must we pick them up at the Tucson airport?"

"Neither, Michael, they will be dropped off by charter helicopter directly here at our place of business. The couple think they are coming here to meet a potential business associate who has a desire to purchase a stock of VX nerve gas they have managed to smuggle into our country."

Sidney Munson beamed. "Such delightful customers, a twofer for those two won't be too bad. In fact, we should consider it our patriotic duty."

"My friend, this will also give us another splendid training opportunity."

"I have already decided the same thing. Samantha needs the experience of performing a double internment all by her sweet little self."

"Of course, we will take care that nothing goes awry."

"Vigilance is always our watchword here at the Sunset House."

Sidney Munson decided the snake had ceased its writhing sufficiently for Michael to retrieve his beloved ice pick. He placed a hand on his friend's shoulder and accompanied him down the steps, both enjoying the warm desert air.

CHAPTER TWENTY-FOUR

Samantha was in an oddly serene, almost giddy mood when Esther pulled the big Hummer to a dusty stop beneath the carport at the Sunset House. She briefly pondered if this was a common feeling after shooting someone, then Esther jerked her from her reverie when she climbed out and lit another Marlboro cigarette from the butt of the one she had smoked on the short drive from town.

"You got gall, dearie," Esther said through a cloud of smoke. "I think you might not have to be put down and might become an asset to us. But heed the word, *might*. Now come inside where it's not so damn hot and help me comb a pistol into my new hairdo. A person never knows when they'll have use for a gun. The people who have to spend time looking for one are usually referred to as statistics."

Samantha felt her glow vanish as if a dark cloud had passed beneath the rosy sun. She was still a prisoner, held against her will by people who killed for money. She simply nodded when she joined Esther Munson and silently followed her inside the imposing, yellow mansion that gave her a chill upon entering the foyer.

"Well hello, Mother," Sidney met them with a smile. "And our lovely Samantha." He grabbed up Sam's right hand and pecked a small kiss on its backside. "I trust you two had an enjoyable visit to town."

Esther adjusted her pink cat's-eye-shaped glasses. "Pete and

Laura had sausage and potato salad for lunch. Damn sausage always gives me gas."

"Come into the kitchen, Mother," Sidney chimed. "I shall ask Michael to fix you a glass of bicarbonate of soda with a twist of lemon. We have some news to share with you two."

"I'll just have another glass of white wine. Bicarbonate gives me even more gas than sausage." Esther lit another Marlboro and turned to Samantha. "Well, come along dearie, I want to get this over with so I can take my afternoon nap."

"I must say you two are cheerier than a rainbow," Michael Herod said when they came into the kitchen and took a seat at the table. "I could not help but overhear about that dreadful sausage." Michael placed a cold, sweating glass of white wine in front of Esther. "This will make your poor tummy feel much better."

"Makes more than just my stomach feel better, that's why I drink the stuff," Esther snorted. "What's up? I need my power nap."

"Just a brief and wonderful announcement," Sidney said, taking a bottle of Perrier water from the stainless steel refrigerator. "You would never guess who phoned."

Esther took a healthy swallow of wine, lowering the contents of her glass by half. "I told you, son, we play games after dinner. Now get to the point."

"Lucas Levy called," Michael said happily. "He said that he had a brief meeting with our lovely Samantha. He mentioned just how much he would enjoy coming to dinner and getting better acquainted."

"Of course we said, why wait? This evening is open, we have no guests." Sidney opened the green bottle with a flourish. "We already have some nice, thick, juicy New York Strip steaks marinating in red wine and some secret spices. Michael is planning a vegetable medley, along with potatoes au gratin, to accompany our repast. It will be an excellent dinner for us all, especially considering the wonderful cherry pie that is baking in the oven."

Samantha cocked a worried eyebrow. "We're not going to kill the man?"

Sidney gave a musical chuckle. "Oh, you poor dear. Of course you would be concerned over another cherry pie, considering your last experience with one here. We should have been more thoughtful. Lucas is an honored guest, not a client."

"We haven't been paid to whack him," Esther chugged the last of her wine. "That's the gist of that. Dinner sounds good. I'm off to take my nap. Wake me by six if I'm not up." She stood and stomped off.

"Gas always makes Mother testy," Sidney said. "I believe you'll enjoy getting to know Lucas better, Sam. He seems to be a solid member of the community and a prosperous gentleman."

Michael turned to Samantha. "And speaking of gentlemen, that wonderful Shakespeare has caught yet another pesky mouse. We are all getting so attached to your sweet kitty, I simply don't know how we made do before his arrival."

Samantha watched as Shakespeare rubbed against the hitman's legs, purring loudly. Her cat was obviously happy with their new life. *Loyalty, thy name is not cat.*

Michael reached down and stroked Shakespeare's head, eliciting a fresh round of loud purrs. "He is such a delightful pet, along with being the ultimate predator. Cats make no apologies for what they are. Every time Shakespeare makes a kill, he brings it over to proudly show me what he has accomplished. I always reward him with a little bowl of sweet cream along with a few bits of that honey-cured ham that he adores so much."

Sidney gave Samantha a pensive look. He swirled the Perrier water around in his glass then said to her, "You *do* see the analogy, don't you, my dear? Shakespeare is no different than us. Those filthy mice carry disease, foul food supplies, and destroy clothing. No sane person can argue the logic of removing them from existence . . . ummm."

Samantha gave a meek nod, which seemed like the safest response. "I believe I'll go to my room and rest as well. I'll wake Esther if she's not up when it's time for dinner." She hesitated. "Thank you for asking Lucas over, he does seem nice."

Michael gave a dismissive wave before turning his attention to chopping celery with a large knife. "Why we always love to entertain, my dear. We are simply glad you like the gentleman."

Samantha nodded, then turned and went upstairs. She was undressing to take a long, hot shower when she realized Shakespeare had remained in the kitchen.

Probably hoping for another mouse to kill.

Chapter Twenty-Five

Tex Birdsong rode his bicycle somewhat unsteadily as he made his way from Johnny Ringo's Saloon back to his house, where he'd undoubtedly suffer through a tirade of bitching from Fern.

That woman simply had to go; she had turned his life into pure agony. Tex thought back on five years of wedded bliss. Unfortunately, that had been over forty years ago. His wife's transmogrification into a witch had been insidiously slow.

When he'd been a longshoreman working the docks as a union boss things had been different—a lot different. If someone got out of line, mouthed off at him, they received a knuckle sandwich for their insolence. And by damn, he'd taught many men that Tex Birdsong was not to be trifled with. Not by a long chalk.

Now, he was forced to kowtow to a shrew every day. To add to his sad situation was the fact that his pension fund had been raided, stolen actually. The suited bastards had invested his retirement in something called derivatives, along with mutual funds that were loaded with stocks like WorldCom and Enron, and lost nearly all of his hard-earned savings as a result. These days, he relied mainly on his and Fern's Social Security just to get by.

The damn bicycle he was riding saved buying expensive gasoline. On the good side, his wife couldn't come along to harp at him when he went to town to buy stamps, a quart of milk, or such. Today he'd gone in before noon on the pretense of buying a pair of shoelaces he didn't need. He had gone straight to Johnny Ringo's and bought the first good lunch he'd eaten for weeks. Fern couldn't boil water without making a botch of it, never had been worth a damn at cooking anything.

Sure, he'd spent over twenty dollars, but he had been the one who busted his ass all those years to make a paycheck. All his wife had done was work at the phone company doing some kind of soft indoor deskwork and raised their three ungrateful kids who never called, never wrote, never sent their parents any money to help them out in their so-called golden years.

Tex Birdsong was working himself into a red rage fueled by alcohol. He decided if Fern started yelling at him, he'd slap her around some, teach the bitch a lesson. He had done it before, shaped her up too. At least for a while, anyway.

He pulled over, almost hitting an ocotillo cactus to let some asshole driving a damn rattling diesel pickup by. A quick glance at the truck showed it to be Lucas Levy, the bastard who owned the vinegar works. What a thing for a man to have to do to make a living. Back in his day men did men's work. They sure didn't lower themselves to sissy stuff like making gourmet vinegar. People didn't need mamby-pamby things like that. Meat and potatoes, bread and beer had made this country strong. Now the hippies, queers, and milksops were running the United States, tearing it down by breaking its backbone. If only he weren't so old he'd join the Minutemen, show them what a *real* man could do.

But he *was* old; his joints hurt all the time these days. And his eyeglasses needed replacing, they'd gotten so bad he knew he was better off riding a bicycle than attempting to drive their ten-year-old car.

Tex pedaled on, coming to a stop by the newspaper box he had put up in hopes that Esther Munson would run his wife over. He studied the situation for several minutes. A couple of bushes could be planted close to the post, give better cover for rattlesnakes. He made a note to do that soon. In the distance Tex watched a cloud of white dust rolling across the desert floor. Lucas Levy was headed out to the Sunset Bed and Breakfast for some reason. He checked his watch and was surprised to find it was almost six in the evening. Maybe he'd spent more than twenty dollars. What the hell, he'd earned that money; he could spend it if he wanted to.

The retired longshoreman gave a dismissive shrug as he rode the bicycle to alongside his house, got off, and securely locked it to a steel fencepost. There were lowlifes out there who would steal an old man's bicycle. When Tex Birdsong walked to the front door he folded his hands into fists again and again. Then he went inside.

"Hi honey," Fern said cheerfully. "I hope you enjoyed your afternoon out. I've been thinking on the matter and I believe you need to go to town once in a while, be good for you."

Tex Birdsong blinked a couple of times to assure himself that he wasn't asleep or had passed on. He was fine. "Are you all right, dear?"

"Never better. And Eunice brought by a rack of pork ribs along with nice big bowls of mashed potatoes and gravy. I'll heat them up for you when you're ready."

Tex Birdsong was so taken aback by his wife's unexplained niceness he couldn't answer for some time. Here he had come in full of mettle and spoiling for a fight, only to have his wife actually be nice to him. As Riley used to say on television, "what a revolting development this turned out to be." After studying the matter he decided to take advantage of being in the eye of the storm. Tomorrow, however, he would definitely plant a couple of bushes next to the newspaper box, plan ahead for the tempest that would surely hit once again.

"Thank you dear," Tex said. "I'll go outside and smoke my

pipe, give you plenty of time to set the table. Call me when you're ready." When he went out the door he realized with a start that niceness could be catching. Damn it.

CHAPTER TWENTY-SIX

The final throes of day had been extinguished in a red blaze of glory behind the rounded Tombstone hills to the west when Samantha and Lucas Levy took a stroll in the oleander-hedged courtyard of the Sunset Bed & Breakfast. Night was shrouding the desert, soft as black velvet. The twinkling evening star became the centerpiece of a jewel-encrusted heaven. Not a breath of wind moved so much as a leaf. The only sound was that of crickets singing their rhythmic mating call in a ritual timeless as night itself.

Samantha realized that since arriving in Tombstone, this was the first time she had been away from the prying eyes of professional killers. The idea of confiding in Lucas crossed her mind briefly, then a familiar smell of cigarette smoke wafting on the still air announced Esther's unseen presence as clearly as if she was standing in the open shining a flashlight and whistling.

Scratch that idea girl, a few wrong words will not only do you in, but also an innocent man who seems really nice.

"So, Lucas, you're a retired postal worker," Samantha said loudly enough that Esther wouldn't misunderstand a single word and possibly do something rash, like start shooting. "What motivated you to come to Tombstone?"

"It seemed like a good idea at the time," Lucas said in his smooth, even voice. "My home for most of my adult life was in Detroit, Michigan, where the winters were cold enough that when someone yells, their words froze, so you'd have to go inside and thaw them out to know why they're upset."

Sam chuckled, "That *is* cold." She liked the man's humor. Lucas had a handsome face, bronzed by sun and wind. His coal black hair glistened in the starry night. "Did you throw darts at a map to find a warmer climate or what?"

"Wherever I was aiming for, I missed somewhat badly." His expression turned serious. "My parents and my wife were driving home one snowy night on the interstate. The car slid on ice into the path of a semi-truck. They were all killed instantly."

Samantha reached out and grasped Lucas's hand. "I'm so sorry. You must have been devastated."

"That's one of the words that pretty much describes those times. After the funerals were over, I retired. I was an only child, so with my parents' inheritance and my wife's life insurance I realized I could go live just about anywhere I saw fit. For some reason, I've always have had a desire to own a vineyard and make fine wines. California was too crowded for my tastes, however. Then, while searching real estate listings on the Internet, I found a few acres already planted with grapes for sale in St. David, just down the road from here, that attracted me so I bought it sight unseen. There was no house on the property, so I purchased the shop here in Tombstone that has some small living quarters in the rear. There's just me, so I don't need much room."

Samantha realized she was still holding Lucas's hand; it was a good feeling. "I didn't know you were a vintner."

Lucas's usual smile returned. "I'm not, it turned out. The first two years I had to dump my entire production. Then it occurred to me that making vinegar was awfully easy. As a matter of fact, it came downright natural to me. And since I owned a shop to sell it from . . . and the rest is history."

"I suppose vinegar is nothing but bad wine. I never have given the matter any thought."

"The worse the batch, the stronger it smells, so more people believe me when I tell them that it's gourmet vinegar. Add a few oddball ingredients like peppers or berries, bottle it up in pretty jars with a fancy label, and the idiots can't buy it fast enough, God love 'em."

"I like your attitude. Most people would have given up and gone on to some other line of work."

Lucas shrugged. "For some reason, the longer I live in Tombstone the easier strange ideas are to come up with. Where else could a person still make a living running a stagecoach, putting on gunfights, or turning out wine so bad it needs to be diluted with distilled water to make decent vinegar."

You would not believe some of the other *ways people make money in Tombstone,* Samantha thought. "The town *is* different than any I've ever visited, let alone wind up living in."

"Ah, but the climate is good, the people are nice—for the most part anyway. I believe Esther and you had a slight altercation with some of our more unsavory citizens earlier today. A few of the Minutemen are decent, well-meaning folks trying to help the government tighten the border. Then there's Rodney Page and his group, who don't have enough active brain cells between them to change a lightbulb without either breaking it or falling off the ladder."

"Or electrocuting themselves. You left that one out."

Lucas Levy chuckled. "I see you do know them."

"The weasely one, Carl I think his name is, tried to get a little too familiar with me. Esther set him straight."

"Isn't Esther just a hoot to be around? Everyone in Tombstone either loves her to death or takes pains to stay out of her way. I really admire her spunk."

Sam noticed the red glow of a burning cigarette behind a row of tall oleander bushes and decided the subject definitely needed changing. "So, how long have you known Sidney and Michael?"

"I made their acquaintance soon after I bought the shop. They're members of the city counsel and both of them have been very kind and helpful to me. Those two go out of their way to welcome people, make them feel at home. Their sweet attitude is the reason they have such a successful business as this bed and breakfast."

Samantha slapped at a bug crawling on her cheek to mask a cough she was unable to suppress. "The Sunset house does have an exclusive client list."

Lucas Levy looked at her with caring blue eyes that sparked in the night. "We should return to the dining room. Michael has baked one of his scrumptious cherry pies. It would be a shame to pass on such a treat, and I do believe the gnats are becoming a nuisance, as often happens this time of year."

"Michael does make a memorable cherry pie." Samantha gave Lucas's hand one final squeeze then turned and followed him back inside the sprawling yellow mansion. She was totally taken aback to find Esther sitting at the kitchen table in front of a half-eaten slice of pie. Michael and Sidney were both there as well. *Who was smoking in the courtyard?*

Esther glowered at the couple. "I got tired of waitin'. I'm old and need my sleep. We have guests coming tomorrow, be a busy day."

"Now don't be curt, Mother," Sidney said in his cheerful, musical voice as he carried two plates each holding a piece of cherry pie to the table. "Lucas and Samantha were simply spending some time together getting acquainted."

Lucas slid a chair out for Samantha, his display of manners greatly impressing her. "After I have a delicious piece of Michael's pie, Esther, I must be going myself. The grapes need watering quite early in the morning while the weather's still cool to be effective."

Sidney set out the slices of pie in front of Lucas and Samantha. "I do hope you enjoyed the visit as much as we enjoyed having you, Lucas. Perhaps we can do this again soon."

"Just ask, the company of a lovely lady and great food. How much more could a person want?"

Sidney beamed and went back behind the island counter to help Michael clean up.

Samantha smiled at Lucas, then turned her eyes to the thick slice of cherry pie. After a moment of trepidation and concern about what tomorrow's guests would bring, along with continuing to worry over who was shadowing them in the courtyard, she grabbed the fork and helped herself to a big bite of Michael Herod's memorable cherry pie.

CHAPTER TWENTY-SEVEN

Samantha awoke the next morning, a bit startled that she'd awakened at all, considering the reputation of Michael's cherry pie. But she felt fine, invigorated for some reason. A loud purring from the pillow next to her told Sam that Shakespeare hadn't totally abandoned her to live in the kitchen with Michael.

"Good morning, kitty," Sam said, reaching over to scratch Shakespeare's ears, which the cat loved dearly. "Mommy ate some of Michael's cherry pie and lived to tell about it."

Then she remembered the microphone and pulled back the covers to check it out. The microphone was no longer there. Even the holes where the wires come out of all had been patched. It still was a good plan to believe everything she said was being overheard. "That was really tasty pie without the oleander juice, little guy."

She gave Shakespeare a good rubdown, sending him into sounding like a happy buzz saw, then she wiped the sleep from her eyes and went to take a long, hot shower. There were guests coming. The question of the day was would she have to help whack them or not. Time would tell; first the shower then after a couple of cups of Sidney's strong but excellent imported coffee, she'd try to find out.

"Good morning dearie." Esther met Samantha at the bottom of the stairs holding out a comb. "Take this and brush over where my little gun is, will you please?"

The word *please* coming from Esther shocked her so badly Sam smiled, took the comb and began fixing her hair without hesitation. "There you go. No one will suspect a thing."

"Thanks dearie, now let's get to the kitchen. Michael's serving eggs benedict, which I love. Plays hell with my Atkins diet, but that doc's dead as Abraham Lincoln, so he won't get upset."

"Good morning, Samantha." Sidney poured a cup of coffee into a china cup and handed it to her when she drew near. "This is another of my special blends. In this one I use an admix of cocoa, nutmeg, walnut, and cinnamon in the scantiest amounts to deliver a delightful, nutty taste that accents the hand-picked Colombian coffee we have flown in especially for us directly from the growers."

Michael Herod added from behind the island counter, "We occasionally do business with people from Colombia. The contacts give us the ability to obtain the freshest and finest coffee beans available."

Why doesn't that surprise me? Samantha gave a demure smile and took a testing sip. "Sidney, you have outdone yourself. This is quite simply the finest coffee I have ever tasted." And she honestly meant it.

Sidney beamed; he loved compliments.

"Take your coffee to the table, dearie," Esther said. "We can drink it there so as to enjoy Michael's eggs benedict the very second they are done. Time spent beneath warming lights is one reason restaurant food tastes so insipid."

"Right you are, Esther," Michael said while stirring a bowl. "I cannot understand such general lack of respect for good food as restaurants display these days." He nodded to the kitchen table. "You will also find some fresh-squeezed orange juice in chilled glasses already set out for your enjoyment."

These people are being too nice, Samantha thought with a chill.

There is a really big storm headed my way, I just know it, I can feel it in my bones.

Sidney refilled Sam's coffee cup while Michael brought her a steaming hot plate of eggs benedict along with a slice of buttered toast. Samantha had to admit that Michael's breakfast was better than any she could remember and told him so.

"Enjoy, my dear," Michael said with a thin grin. "Later, after Sidney and I have tidied up the place, there is a short movie we want you to watch."

"A *movie?*" Samantha was taken aback.

"For now," Michael said, turning his attention to the overhead oven. "Just enjoy the cuisine. You can trust me on this."

Samantha felt her appetite flee, but she continued to poke listlessly at the eggs benedict. Whatever the family of killers had to show her, they would do so whether or not she ate breakfast.

Steeling herself, Samantha found her appetite had returned, and once again she ate with relish.

Chapter Twenty-Eight

The worst were the bodies of small children. Like the adults their eyes were open, staring blankly in death. Whatever had killed the many hundreds of people in the videotape, it had done so quickly and violently. The bodies of seemingly hundreds of people lay in contorted positions; some had obviously been trying to run away from whatever had stricken them. They had not gotten far. Intermingled with the humans were the still forms of birds, dogs, cats, goats, and cattle. Whatever had struck here was obviously a quick destroyer of all life.

To add to the horrors on the big-screen television, Samantha saw the group of men, all wearing what appeared to be white spacesuits, walking among the bodies in total apathy, some even kicking the dead aside like trash.

"Why don't they try to help them?" Samantha's voice was tight with rage as she fought back tears. "There might be someone still alive."

"*Help* them, my dear," Sidney said, speaking almost in a whisper. "They *caused* this to happen. They're enjoying the victory."

"The scenes you are watching," Michael said, "were filmed in a Kurdish village in Iraq a few years ago to document the event for Saddam Hussein's personal pleasure. What we are seeing is the effects of an attack by the use of VX nerve gas, one of the deadliest substances ever created by man."

Sidney Munson turned to Samantha. "All real monsters wear

human faces, never forget this. These people may look normal, act normal, come across as benevolent and caring, but their souls, if they even possess one, are black as sin itself."

Esther sipped some coffee. "Most estimates are that Saddam Hussein gassed over seventy thousand of his own countrymen to death. What we're lookin' at is only one lone incident in one small village."

Samantha was stunned. "I thought when we invaded Iraq there were no weapons of mass destruction found. Now you're telling me there was nerve gas at Saddam Hussein's disposal. If this is true, why didn't he use it against us?"

Michael said, "Because we were prepared. Nerve gas isn't effective against an army who has defenses. Also the use of a weapon like VX would have given us good reason and incentive to use tactical nuclear and chemical weapons ourselves. Even a monster like Saddam Hussein was not stupid enough to take a risk as big as that."

Samantha jerked her face away from the television to look at Sidney, who sat beside her on the sofa. "Where did Saddam get nerve gas, and if he had a stockpile, what happened to it?"

"My dear, you have arrived at the precise reason we have chosen to show you this terribly gruesome videotape." He grabbed up the remote control and shut off the television. "I believe we can spare ourselves the pain of watching more of this."

Esther said to Samantha, "The world is a damn sight more dangerous place than most people believe . . . or want to know. There are stockpiles of worse substances than nerve gas out there, and a lot of it is for sale to the highest bidder."

"You must understand, my dear," Sidney said, "people and governments who deal in drugs and WMDs do so in the shadows. Their actions are protected by various laws and treaties meant to protect. But these vile monsters use those myriad laws to hide behind."

Samantha felt a shiver of black fright course through her body. "I thought our government had the CIA and branches of the Army to take care of these things."

Michael Herod clucked his tongue. "Have you noticed news crews often arrive at accidents and crime scenes before the authorities do? Remember the people who sell death for gain go to great lengths to appear innocent, kind, and gentle. They have the protection of the law and lawyers. And you must remember that under our system of government everyone is innocent until proven guilty in a court of law."

"That means nothin' can be done to 'em 'til after the bomb goes off, sweetie," Esther said. "And the bodies of the innocent have been buried."

Sidney got up and refilled both his and Samantha's cup with coffee. "Now you know there are some events that cannot be allowed to occur. As we mentioned, the bad guys operate in shadows, then so must some certain operatives of the government operate in total secrecy."

"Meet 'em on their own level," Esther said. "And whack the bastards before they pull a job, so to speak."

"Somewhat crudely worded, Mother," Sidney said, "but quite an accurate description." He again turned to look at Samantha. "Many years ago, the leaders of our government realized their legal limitations, along with the cold, hard facts of what steps had to be taken to remove threats to our country."

Michael said, "When a doctor recognizes a cancer in a patient, he cuts it out before it can spread. This is the same pragmatic approach the government decided upon; kill the disease before it can kill others."

"The branch of government entrusted to protect us against clandestine threats realized that civilian contractors were a necessity, contractors who could never, for any reason, be connected with any form of recognized law."

Intense astonishment shone in Samantha's face. "You're telling me the United States government employs hit-men?"

Esther spoke up, "Not just the United States, dearie. A lot of our funding comes from Great Britain and other at-risk countries. There's a lotta bad guys out there who desperately need whackin'."

"*Our* funding?" Samantha felt her heart skip a beat. "We here in Tombstone are killing people and being paid to do it by the *government?*"

"Just refer to our employers as 'The Company,' please, my dear," Sidney said with a sly grin. "And do remember, as the narrator always used to say to Mr. Phelps on the television show *Mission Impossible,* 'If any of you are caught or killed, the secretary will disavow any knowledge of your activities.'"

Esther gave an ominous chuckle. "Have you ever *really* wondered about those thousand-dollar toilet seats and such the government pays for? That money wasn't lost, it went to a damn good cause, and we're one of them."

Samantha felt weak, confused. "The first one, the lawyer Speaks from California who ate the oleander pie. He was hit at the request of the government?"

"Tsk, tsk," Michael waved a finger at Samantha. "The *Company* paid us to do him in. Please take care to always use that term."

"Wha—what did he do?" Samantha stuttered. "Speaks had roaming hands and an abrasive personality, but that's nothing to kill a man over."

Sidney said, "Mr. Speaks was not only a lawyer, he was a very good lawyer. The lovely gentleman was preparing a quite possibly effective brief to present to the Supreme Court. If Speaks had been successful in his efforts, a kingpin of finance to the drug trade would have gone free."

"The risk was too big to chance," Esther said. "Drug dealers kill the same as bombs, only quieter. The big money they make also goes to a lot of wrong hands."

"But . . . but," Samantha said, her mind awash with contradictory thoughts. "Speaks had to have family, people who knew where he was going. They'd look for him and trace the man straight to Tombstone and the Sunset House."

Michael gave a shallow chuckle. "One of the benefits of working for The Company is the effectiveness of their janitorial services."

Samantha's lowered brows told Michael she did not understand, so he elaborated. "There are untold thousands of people every year who simply disappear, seemingly from off the face of the earth. The Company has the abilities, helped along these days by the Internet, to cause records to become erased. This is a very nice function for those in our business."

"Michael," Esther scolded, "you'd use a page full of big words to tell someone to duck." She turned to Samantha. "What he means is, we have powerful protection at the highest levels where it counts. There's not a shred of proof that Speaks ever set foot in Tombstone, let alone here."

Sidney smiled and continued, "Actually, making a person disappear is much easier these days than it was back when we started with The Company. Nearly all records are stored in computers. A few delete buttons get pushed in Quantico . . . poof, the man done gone."

"I always loved that line," Esther said, lighting a Marlboro with the stub of another. "But we can't let Sam think we're sexist. Hell, we'll whack any woman who's in need of it, so long as we get paid for the job."

"True, Mother," Sidney said with a slight sigh. "It is a shame, really, how many lovely ladies have to be disposed of these days. I suppose it is a sign of the times, along with being a testament to the success of the Women's Liberation Movement."

"We don't need to keep jawin'," Esther said from a cloud of cigarette smoke. "This meeting was set up for Sam's benefit. The lesson either took or it didn't. I hope it did because we need the help. The damn Company's drivin' us plain crazy with business, and I ain't gettin' any younger."

Samantha took a moment to consider Esther's words before turning to Sidney. "That videotape about what nerve gas can do was shown to me for a reason."

"Yes, my dear, it surely was. There is, as we speak, a truly loathsome couple by the name of Steve and Judy Lowman preparing to come to the Sunset Bed and Breakfast later this afternoon by private helicopter. They believe they are to meet the buyers for nearly a hundred cylinders of that nasty VX nerve gas they have stashed in the hold of their yacht, which is anchored off the coast of San Diego, California."

"A hundred cylinders," Samantha exclaimed. "That sounds like an awful lot. Where did they get it . . . why sell it, and who would buy the stuff . . . ?" She realized she'd already answered her own question. There were *always* buyers for weapons. The more casualties they could cause, the more money they would fetch on the market.

"Imagine," Sidney said, "a single cylinder being released in the air-conditioning ducts of a Las Vegas casino. The estimates are over a thousand dead. A few more cylinders released at the Superbowl, the bodies would fill warehouses."

Michael said, "The economy would shut down as the country ground to a halt from fear. 9/11 was only a wake-up call for what could happen if we fail to stop the events beforehand."

"A hundred cylinders," Samantha stammered. "And the couple who smuggled these terrible weapons into our country are coming here."

Sidney gave a grim smile. "The buyers are also coming in.

Their airplane should suffer a malfunction over the remote mountains of Montana due to a missile." He looked at his gold Rolex. "Why, I do believe they will be deceased in about five hours and twenty minutes, should the Johnson brothers have no difficulties with their mobile launcher. If they fail, however, all is not lost. We have *lots* of room in our deep mine shaft."

"The Johnson boys," Esther snorted. "They love bombs and blowing things up. Being around 'em always gives me a headache."

"As we speak," Michael said, "the Coast Guard has attached the Lowmans' yacht for failure to pay certain taxes and fees. They will tow it to a nice safe naval yard where the contents in the hold will be most safely and effectively dealt with."

The image of bodies of dead children with open pleading eyes filled Samantha with rightful rage. "I'll help squeeze the oleander for Michael's delicious cherry pie."

"How thoughtful you are my dear," Sidney said. "My poor hands hurt terribly from that process." His eyes sparked like flint when he added. "And welcome to the family."

Esther coughed. "All right, the lollygaggin's over. Sam's either gonna make a trustworthy hit-lady or else. Now let's get to work. There's people coming that need to be whacked and time's a-wastin'."

CHAPTER TWENTY-NINE

Tex Birdsong was not about to allow himself to be taken in by his wife's newfound, phony niceness. He was no fool. Not anymore. Years ago he'd done too much thinking from below the belt line, now he was, as some of his cronies at Johnny Ringo's were fond of saying, "Getting screwed back for all of the screwing he'd gotten." Most men his age could well agree with that statement.

This morning Fern had actually been singing in the kitchen while she'd fried up his favorite breakfast of thick peppered bacon, country potatoes, and three eggs, over easy, with four buttermilk biscuits covered with sausage gravy. A man's breakfast.

Then, to top off his frustration, she had given him a neck rub after filling his cup with the last of the pot of coffee. No, this type of behavior would never last, it was simply a lull in the storm in which he was destined to live out his years. Unless . . .

Tex rode his bicycle into town and for once didn't stop by the saloon. He had decided on a goal. He had a plan to execute. Esther Munson flattening Fern with that speeding Hummer of hers was a glorious scenario, but the math had to be perfect. Too damn perfect. Ten seconds one way or the other, all that might be accomplished would either be a hospital bill or having to listen to his wife complain for hours about getting peppered with flying gravel. No, this was not nearly certain enough.

After lunch, he worked about the house doing minor repairs

until the late spring sun had warmed the desert to where his arthritic bones would not hurt too badly when he dug a few holes for bushes around the newspaper box across the street.

The holes he dug that afternoon were placed just so to give a nice deadly rattlesnake a grand hiding place from where it could strike Fern's bare leg. There were lots of rattlesnakes in the country around Tombstone. Big, fat diamondbacks with a disposition worse than Fern's mother had had, and that woman had had a glare mean enough to stop a clock. Tex realized his mother-in-law had been a warning he had missed.

Once the holes had been dug, Tex's shoulders and back ached. He blinked against the bright desert sun and surveyed a nearby shady draw that was lined with green leafy bushes that were called greasewood or something like that. He really didn't care what the species was so long as they were big enough to shelter a deadly rattlesnake. And best of all, these bushes were free for the taking. No expensive nursery in Sierra Vista for Tex Birdsong; he was too smart to get taken in by advertising. Sure, the state of Arizona had laws against transplanting vegetation and cactus without obtaining a permit. But there was no one about, not even a sign of anyone who might notice his movements. Shovel in hand, he worked his way into the shadow-filled, shallow chasm.

Tex Birdsong hadn't descended five feet into the opening when it happened. First had come a loud hiss, like a tire going flat, then a hard whack to the calf of his leg, followed by an intense, building pain. Only then did the huge diamondback rattlesnake that had been snoozing beneath a sheltering rock have decency to rattle a warning.

It took a moment for the realization he had been bitten by a snake to sink in. Tex wanted to use his shovel, kill the damn buzzing snake that had bitten him without so much as even a token rattle to cause him to step back. But he knew time was of the essence. He needed to get home to Fern. She'd call an ambulance; she'd know what to do. God, the pain was worse than having a red-hot poker jammed against his leg.

Tex tossed the shovel aside and stumbled to his house. Just as he knew she would, Fern made him sit down in a chair on the porch while she ran to call 911, tears streaming down her cheeks.

A few moments later the town ambulance came roaring to a stop. The two paramedics assured Tex Birdsong that rattlesnake bites were rarely fatal and that he would be fine once they got him to the hospital and injected something they called antivenin. Hell, he didn't even know there was a cure for rattlesnake bites. In every movie he'd ever seen, they killed anyone they struck.

As Tex Birdsong was being strapped onto a gurney, he noticed a sleek red helicopter landing at the Sunset Bed and Breakfast. That was a new pisser to deal with. Not only were rattlesnakes not likely to get rid of his wife, now Esther Munson might be relying on helicopters instead of a speeding Hummer for transportation. *Life really sucks,* he thought before they shoved him into the ambulance and roared off, sirens blaring in the still desert air.

CHAPTER THIRTY

In the deserts of the Southwest, it is not unusual for both the birth and death of the day to be bathed in the crimson color of fresh blood. Unlike the high mountain country, where the events are sudden as the drop of a guillotine, in the desert the colors ooze over the desert horizon, building slowly, like the crescendo of a grand opera, only to fade slowly into sunlight or the mute black of night.

It was one of those shafts of red sunlight streaming through the window of her bedroom on the second floor of the Sunset Bed and Breakfast that awoke Samantha from her slumber. She reached above her head to where a heavy weight was attempting to drive her skull into her neck. A few rubs on a soft, hairy body caused Shakespeare to fill the room with his soothing purring. Having the cat in her bed was reassuring that he hadn't totally abandoned her to live in the kitchen.

Samantha was somewhat shocked to realize she not only had enjoyed a restful night's sleep, but also pleasant dreams. She remembered on her drive from Houston to Tombstone how she had tossed memories of her ex-husband at each milepost on the interstate. Last night in her dreams it had been Arnold Wilkins himself that had splattered onto the signs to explode in a spray of gore. Apparently killing people who desperately needed it agreed with her.

After sliding the ponderous tomcat to a more comfortable position alongside her, Samantha continued petting Shakespeare while going over in her mind the events of the past evening with clarity of retrospect.

The shiny red helicopter carrying the Lowmans had set down on a plateau next to the Sunset house and idled while the couple ran through a shower of flying dust to shelter. Then the Belljet had immediately sped up and taken off before Samantha had even gotten a glimpse of the pilot or pilots sitting behind the bubble-nosed front of the aircraft. Obviously they were in a rush to be somewhere else. After spending only a few scant moments in the company of the Lowmans, she could well understand all too well why the pilot had wanted to be rid of them.

Esther Munson, who'd been standing next to her, stomped a half-smoked Marlboro into the dirt and snorted. "It looks just like a big bird stopping to take a quick shit before heading to happier places. I'm bettin' these two schmucks are gonna be a real test, at least for a while anyway."

"Smile, Mother," Sidney said with a forced air of cheerfulness. "Think of the fifty grand stacked up in nice untraceable hundred-dollar bills that these fine folks are going to provide us."

The Lowman couple was nothing at all like Samantha had expected them to look. Steve Lowman appeared to be in his early fifties, slim and trim, with a hint of silver on the temples of an expensive haircut. His wife Judy was model-thin with short brown hair, wearing a pantsuit to complement her husband's casual blue jeans and sport shirt. All in all, they seemed to be a normal, happy couple.

Then Steve Lowman had stepped close and opened his mouth. "What a hellhole of a place Tombstone turned out to be. I've never set foot in such piss-poor country in my life."

Judy Lowman chimed in while patting her hair back into place from the buffeting of the helicopter downdraft. "That prick of a pilot is going to get a letter in his file, a damn scathing one, too. My husband and I do not allow ourselves to be treated in such a disrespectful, uncaring manner. I do believe I may have turned my ankle attempting to run away from the terrible shower of dirt that man subjected us to."

"We'll certainly sue that helicopter charter company for damages, my dear," Steve Lowman said. He fixed his gaze onto Samantha and shoved a small suitcase toward her. "Take this to our room and hang up our clothes before they become even more wrinkled."

Samantha remembered reaching out and taking the obvious expensive-looking hand-tooled leather grip without hesitation. Lowman had that powerful of a personality. Both he and his wife came across as if they were God's chosen people, to be kowtowed to by all others. The realization that this was only a temporary condition caused Samantha to nod and answer, "Yes sir, right away sir."

As Sam turned to carry the suitcase back to the Sunset Bed and Breakfast, Esther and Sidney both began profusely apologizing for the pilot's lack of courtesy and promising the Lowmans a most memorable stay in historic Tombstone, Arizona.

Monumental is a more accurate description of your visit here, Samantha thought as she reached the welcome shade of the veranda that was lined with colorful oleander bushes. *Just wait until you try the cherry pie, now that'll change your attitude, make a better person out of you.*

At least an hour had passed before Samantha came into the Lowmans' presence again. The couple had insisted on the privacy of their second-story room to make what they curtly described as personal business calls on their cell phone.

When the Lowmans came down the stairs, they still wore the same clothes and were plainly in an even more acute dour mood then they'd arrived in.

Esther Munson seemed to genuinely enjoy giving them a buoyant greeting. "How 'bout I run you fine folks into Tombstone for a nice visit? There's lots of shops and things to see. The most famous gunfight in the Old West happened there, maybe you'd like to see the site or possibly visit Boot Hill Cemetery. One of the headstone's is a real hoot, 'Here lies Les Moore, six shots from a forty-four, no Les, no more.' "

Judy Lowman snapped, "We collect only Zuni and Navajo artifacts and ceremonial figures of the highest quality. We have no desire whatsoever to purchase the type of trashy items the average tourist does. And I cannot imagine why either of us would wish to visit a cemetery, of all places."

"The people who were supposed to meet us here must have been delayed for some reason," Steve Lowman said. "I can only get a 'no service' message when I tried to phone their cell."

Sidney stepped forward, beaming. "Why, there is no problem at all, I'm most certain. Here in the rugged mountains of the Southwest, I'm afraid that cellular service is spotty at best. I do believe our other guests are not scheduled to arrive for another couple of hours or so. If there have been any difficulties, I am sure a message would have been received on our always reliable landline. A modicum of patience is required from those of us who live in remote areas . . . ummm."

"Shitkicking damn hick spot on the frickin' map," Steven Lowman growled. "These are valuable customers we're expecting. The deal's worth enough we could buy this place, burn it down, and not miss the money."

Judy Lowman added, "I can't understand why they asked to meet us here, dear, but they did. Let's have a drink and settle down. Remember, winners like us do not allow themselves to become unduly worked up."

Steve Lowman gave a sigh. "You are quite right, my dear." He turned to Sidney. "My wife and I prefer Glenlivet single-malt scotch whiskey, neat. I assume such a drink is available?"

Sidney Munson retained his smile. "Why of course. Here at the Sunset House we strive to maintain a fully stocked bar, along with the cuisine of a five-star restaurant."

"Allow me," Esther had said, already behind the bar rattling glasses.

"Make mine a double," Steve Lowman said as he hoisted himself onto a barstool. "Excellent whiskey helps pass time better than wandering through the detritus of a town that should have been torn down years ago."

"I'll join you, dear," Judy Lowman said. "History has always bored me to death."

When the Lowmans decided to "settle down," they did so with rare gusto. The couple kept complaining until they'd emptied two bottles of scotch and their speech was becoming slurred. Then the phone rang. Esther Munson answered, listened for a brief moment before the drunken Steve Lowman could make his way across the room, then hung up.

"That was Mister . . ." Esther thumbed through some paperwork, "Rathburn. He was one of our other scheduled guests."

"Well what'd he say, damnit?" Steve Lowman shouted.

"He apologized and said for us to go ahead and have dinner without them. A series of severe thunderstorms has unfortunately grounded their airplane. He said that it will likely be morning before they make it to Tombstone."

"I needed to talk to him," Steve Lowman said to Esther.

"The connection was being patched in from his cell to his office. He mentioned the thunderstorms were interfering with the communication quite badly."

"See dear," Judy Lowman said with newfound sweetness, "all is well. Come back to the bar and let's have another drink, then enjoy our dinner. Things are coming our way. I can feel it."

Samantha couldn't resist saying, "Michael Herod had been a chef in some of the very finest hotels. I assure you fine folks that you'll never have a better meal than the one you'll enjoy this evening."

"*We*'ll be the judge of that," Steve Lowman said. "Pour me another damn drink."

Esther Munson whispered in Samantha's ear as she walked past, "That was the Johnson boys. They said it was a shame the Fourth of July wasn't this afternoon, I guess they made quite a show over the Montana mountains when that plane blew up."

"I'll begin setting the dining table," Samantha stated.

Two generous slices of Michael Herod's cherry pie had done their job once again. Samantha wondered if the copious amounts of whiskey the Lowmans had consumed kept them from twitching as much as Speaks had. Both of the would-be nerve gas merchants had fallen off their chairs and only kicked around on the floor for a few brief minutes before growing eternally still.

"Great way to make a hit." Esther lit her first cigarette since the guests had arrived. "Not a lotta work to clean up after."

Sidney smiled and added, "The best part of using the bed and breakfast method is they never see it coming. Well, not normally, anyway."

Esther stared down at the still forms of the Lowmans. "At least they weren't on some damn diet or such. Michael had to resort to using his ice pick on that one skinny asshole of a drug dealer we whacked last year," she snorted. "At least that method's cleaner than bullets or knives."

"I have a surprise for you," Sidney said to Samantha. "We are going to teach you to drive the tractor. That makes light work of moving bodies."

"First we gotta drag 'em outside," Esther grumbled from a

cloud of smoke. "I'm gettin' too old for that task."

"Oh Sam dear," Michael Herod said, coming from the kitchen. "Sidney and I worked very hard to place a wooden wheel stop for the tractor to keep a misjudgment on your part from causing a tragedy. This will safely keep the tractor from falling into our deep mine shaft."

"That tractor's got an automatic transmission," Esther lit another Marlboro from the butt of her first. "Take the village idiot to not know forward from backward with one damn lever. And Samantha's no dummy."

Esther Munson's compliment not only came as a surprise, but it felt genuine. "Thanks," she said, then turned to Michael, "I appreciate Sidney's and your thoughtfulness and hard work."

"Well, let's drag them outside and help Sam with the tractor," Sidney said. "Then, I do believe we all deserve a nice cold Tombstone Blues."

"Damn straight we do," Esther said, following the bodies outside.

After the Lowmans had been disposed of, not another word had been said about them. Their luggage had followed them down the shaft. It was as if Steve and Judy Lowman had ceased to exist.

Samantha had remembered thinking before coming to bed that such an attitude as the hit-men showed was totally necessary to maintain a professional outlook on their chosen line of work, much like doctors or morticians must learn to do. Strangely, Sam could honestly say that she felt no remorse or guilt. Not in the least.

In the fresh light of a new day, nothing along those lines had changed.

CHAPTER THIRTY-ONE

Samantha luxuriated in a long, hot shower. After drying off, she decided to take special care with her makeup. This was a day when it felt great to simply be alive. Samantha chose to dress in faded blue jeans, cowboy boots, and a tight western shirt, leaving the top three buttons undone. Adding a turquoise squash blossom necklace, along with a couple of Navajo-crafted silver rings, and she was ready to head down the stairs for a cup of Sidney's scrumptious coffee, the aroma of which wafted tantalizingly in the dry desert air like a promise.

Shakespeare ran past Samantha halfway down the stairs, his purr machine on high. The big black tomcat darted into the kitchen to rub fawningly against Michael Herod's legs while he was busying himself kneading loves of organic wheat bread. The chef repeatedly admonished that buying any factory-made breadstuffs was a gauche act.

"Well, good morning, sweet kitty," Michael said without looking down. "I will give you your little bowls of cream and a bit of imported cheddar cheese in just a moment. For now you must be patient with me, I am at quite a delicate stage with the yeast."

Esther, who was sitting at the island counter smoking a cigarette, snorted, "Asking a cat to have patience is like believing an investment banker or a used car salesman has your best interests at heart."

The big tomcat put a period to Esther's words with a long, loud, pathetic meow that was akin to a shriek.

Sidney Munson came from a side room. "I'll feed that poor kitty." He frowned at Samantha. "The little guy is simply starving to death."

"Shakespeare is neither little nor starving, Sidney," Samantha said. "He's gotten Michael and you wrapped around his paw and is making the most of it."

"Well, we just love the tabby, and I am simply not going to allow him to suffer in want."

After Sidney had fixed and set out the cat's matching china bowls and Shakespeare was purring while eating, a feat difficult to understand, Sidney focused his attention on Samantha. "How did you come to give this darling pet his name? Michael and I have been wondering about that."

Samantha said, "It came from one of Shakespeare's works, *Henry the Sixth,* to be precise. I adopted the cat from the pound after divorcing my lawyer husband. The name Shakespeare came perfectly natural at the time, considering the Bard wrote, 'The first thing we do, we kill all of the lawyers.' "

Esther Munson choked on a combination of cigarette smoke and coffee. When she was able to speak she chortled, "I love that line, but if people had the good sense to follow those instructions we'd be out of business. Most of our special clients are lawyers."

Michael Herod clucked his tongue. "A sad but true commentary on our society, in politics one is forced to look long and hard to find someone who *isn't* an attorney."

"Ol' Bill Shakespeare knew his elbow from a hole in the ground," Esther ground out her Marlboro and frowned when she found her pack was empty. "A tolerable good writer, once you get past that style of his that went out of date before gunpowder was invented."

"No, Mother," Sidney said then cocked his head in thought.

"I honestly believe they had gunpowder back in Shakespeare's day."

Michael washed and dried his hands before pouring a cup of coffee and setting it on the counter in front of Samantha. "When those two get started, it's like their minds got stuck to the tracks with super glue. Here, my dear, enjoy your coffee, I have some very delectable pecan rolls in the oven that will be ready shortly." He beamed at her. "Your performance last evening was commendable, most commendable, my dear. We all are *so* proud of you."

Esther grunted and stood. "I gotta go get some more cigarettes. Those things are so damned expensive us old people have to keep working our fingers to the bone to be able to afford them. And yes, Samantha did good. Be nice to have some dependable help around this place. Work, work, work, that's all I've had to look forward to, and here I am a feeble seventy-five years of age. It's about time I could take a break, read a book, or just enjoy the day, spend maybe an entire month without having to whack someone and suffer the cleanup."

Samantha had to bite her lip to keep from making a comment that might possibly be taken out of context. There was no way the crotchety old hit-lady could be described as feeble. A lot of other words came to mind, but the day was starting off much too well to take any chances. Actually, there was an opportunity here.

"Esther," Samantha said, "I understand your being tired, but I really do need you to teach me more. This business is rather new to me."

Sidney spoke up, "Why what a sweet thing to say, Sam dear." He smiled his thin smile at his mother. "I am so proud to have her as part of the family."

"Yeah," Esther said. "But she'd better be a quick learner, I ain't gettin' any younger, ya know. I'm going upstairs and get more cigarettes." She turned and stomped off.

Michael Herod said, "Esther was taken aback by the compliment. Unfortunately, we in this profession receive *so* few of them."

I can believe that, Samantha thought, but said, "She has been a survivor in a tough business. And there's a lot I need to learn."

"And so you shall, my dear," Sidney stepped over and laid the familiar keys to her Jeep alongside her coffee cup. "As a token of our trust, Michael and I have restored your vehicle to operating condition. Feel free to visit Tombstone whenever you feel the urge."

"You know, Sidney," Michael said, peering into the oven. "I really do need a couple of bottles of Lucas's vinegar, the kind only he makes with garlic and lots of habanero peppers."

"Why, what an excellent opportunity to drive your Jeep," Sidney said to Samantha. "The battery likely needs a charging and the outing will do you good."

"I think I would like that. It will give me a chance to see Lucas again. I enjoy his company."

Michael slid a tray of delicious-smelling sweet rolls from the oven, sat them on the counter, then fished in a drawer to come up with a few twenty-dollar bills, which he laid in front of Samantha. "Here is money to pay for my vinegar with some left for shopping. Please buy me two bottles, large ones. I believe Lucas calls it 'Desert Fire,' which is actually quite an accurate description. Habanero peppers are the hottest grown, I do believe."

"Damn things'll burn the lint out of your belly button," Esther said, coming into the kitchen trailing smoke. "I tasted one twice, the first time and the last time."

"Habaneros have an excellent flavor," Michael said to Esther. "When used as a spice in moderate amounts, the taste is unique to Southwest cuisine."

"All I know is they're hotter than hell and give me gas."

"Samantha is going into town after enjoying a pecan roll," Sidney said to his mother. "Is there anything you wish her to bring back?"

"A carton of Marlboros. No, make that two cartons, I hate running out."

Michael Herod returned to the drawer to fish out more money to add to Samantha's supply of twenty-dollar bills. She sipped more coffee while pondering the possibility of at last being able to escape the clutches of living in a houseful of professional killers.

CHAPTER THIRTY-TWO

Sidney Munson, Michael, and Esther all stood on the front porch of the Sunset Bed and Breakfast watching a diminishing trail of gray dust that marked Samantha's departure for Tombstone in her shiny red Jeep.

Michael said, "She's driving too fast, that's not a good sign."

"Mother drives even faster, Michael," Sidney said. "We mustn't be quick to rush to judgment here. I honestly believe the little dear has joined the company in both words *and* spirit."

Michael Herod focused on a GPS screen. "Using that little tracking device we placed under the hood of her Jeep, we can follow her movements to within a few feet, even if she goes to Canada."

Esther snorted, "Hope you put plenty of C4 under the seat in case she's faking. We're too darn busy to put up with any crap from the law."

"Now, Mother, please don't fret," Sidney said. "We have all been in the business too long to allow for any error. Hope for the best while preparing for the worst is the motto that all successful hit people live by. To answer your question, a simple flick of a switch and that Jeep will blow a crater in the road so big the highway department will have to work overtime to fill it."

"I really hope she makes it, for more reasons than one," Michael said, keeping his eyes on the GPS. "The vinegar is needed quite badly."

Sidney eyed the rose bushes that surrounded the porch. "Are

those pesky aphids back again?"

"I am sorry to say you are correct. A couple of bottles of Lucas's disastrously potent vinegar added to a gallon of water then sprayed on the roses is the quickest way to kill aphids that I know of. They drop like flies the second that stuff touches them."

Esther snorted, "And I need my damn cigarettes." She flipped a smoking butt over the porch rail then glared at Michael. "Well, keep an eye on her. If she's stupid enough to make a run for it, wait until she's on the interstate before blowing her up. The farther away from Tombstone she is when it happens, the better."

"Life is a crapshoot," Michael said. "You two go about your business. I'll keep an eye on things here and let you know how Samantha's dice roll turns out."

"Won't take long, that's for sure," Esther lit a fresh cigarette and followed her son back inside the stately old mansion.

CHAPTER THIRTY-THREE

Tex Birdsong raised a shaky hand of greeting to the pretty girl with long auburn hair driving a red Jeep as she sped by in front of his house. Having two speeding vehicles to take potshots at his wife when she crossed the street would be a plus, doubling the odds of flattening her. He'd decided Esther would surely still be driving the big Hummer. That old bat was mean enough to outlast God's dog.

He was sitting on the porch in a cheap canvas chair, enjoying the desert morning while reflecting back on yesterday's disaster with a rattlesnake that didn't have the decency to rattle. The doctor in Sierra Vista had made him stay overnight for what he called "observation." The damn sawbones wanted more money was all. Where the snake had bitten him was swollen to the size of a golf ball and sore as hell. But that was the sum of the matter. His plan of having Fern done in by a so-called deadly rattlesnake was a bust.

The money grabber in the hospital had gone to great lengths to describe how snakebites are handled, told him more than he ever wanted to know. It turns out that rattlesnakes have control over how much venom they inject. They do not wish to waste it as a large amount injected in its usual prey, say a mouse, acts to help digest the rodent even before the snake swallows it. Many times when a rattler strikes a human they merely inflict a "dry bite," which is a warning where only a tiny amount of venom is injected. The snake is simply telling you to stay away and that it has no desire to attack. Fortunately, that was what the snake that bit him had done. The doctor gave him only a small amount of antivenin along with a tetanus shot, then watched for swelling to determine if an additional dose was required. It wasn't. Hell, he'd been hurt worse hitting his thumb with a hammer. The real pisser was yet to come. The bill for the ambulance, the damn doctors, and all the tests and shit would add up to thousands. He was covered by Medicare, but hadn't bought into any damn expensive "supplement" policy. The government knew how to waste money like it was water, but they were too greedy to take care of the hard-working people who built this country.

"Would you like some more coffee, dear?" Fern asked sweetly from inside the screen door.

"No, I'm okay," he answered gruffly. He couldn't expect his wife's sweetness to last. Not by any stretch of the imagination. No, he would soon be subjected to more bitching and meanness that any human should have to endure. Then he brightened. There was a ten-thousand-dollar life insurance policy on Fern. A windfall like that would soothe a world of hurt. He smiled upon the rapidly departing red Jeep, then the newspaper box across the road. *If at first you don't succeed, try, try, again.*

Samantha slammed on the brakes when she realized just how fast she was driving. The flashing school zone sign had come as a glowing reminder. Driving now at a safe speed, Samantha pondered her newfound freedom and the trust being shown her by three professional killers. It seemed out of character for those experienced hit-people to be so trusting so quickly. Sure, the job last night had gone well, and she'd done her part to rid the world of a threat, but still a nagging thought kept nipping at her like a pet dog trying to get attention. *I'm missing something here.* Then a light flashed on in her mind.

Landin Park was only a couple of blocks back. She spun the Jeep around and headed there, waving at the silver-haired old man on the porch who always seemed to be so friendly, then pulled to a stop at the very far corner of the park to be allowed complete privacy.

Samantha had not studied automobile technology in school without good reason. Actually, she was sort of a car buff. In short order she found what was obviously a GPS tracking device that was not very well hidden low on a fender well under the hood. The bricks of plastic explosives taped to the frame beneath the driver's seat also came as no real surprise, a relief actually. The hit-people of Sunset Bed & Breakfast were doing exactly what Samantha had expected. Trust was a luxury that could not be wasted on them.

Very carefully, while remembering Sidney's lesson on disarming bombs, Samantha removed the aluminum detonator cap from the explosive charge. Then using a pair of wire cutters she kept in a toolbox, she cut the wires from the radio transmitter that would fire the charge. A few minutes later the C4 along with the deactivated detonator were stashed in a grocery bag on the rear floorboards. The GPS she decided to leave alone. A brief thought of how much fun it would be to toss the device on the back of a truck headed from Mexico quickly passed.

Smiling with satisfaction, Samantha started the Jeep and drove toward Tombstone. She had two cartons of Malboros to buy, then stop by Lucas Levy's gourmet vinegar shop. With good timing and a little luck he might allow her to buy him lunch at Johnny Ringo's Saloon. There was no hurry, being late would have the enjoyable effect of helping repay for having had enough high explosive placed beneath the seat of her Jeep to blow up a train.

CHAPTER THIRTY-FOUR

"Oh wow, two bottles of Desert Fire," Lucas Levy's blue eyes sparkled at Samantha with the happy enthusiasm of a little boy up to mischief. He turned to scan the shelves of his small, quaint store. "Now that's not one of my better sellers. Actually I believe Michael Herod is the only one to ever buy a second bottle. I may have made that vinegar a tad too hot for a lot of people's taste."

"Michael used to cook at a five-star hotel," Samantha said. "I'm sure he knows exactly how to use it without offending anyone's palate."

"Michael is quite a wizard in the kitchen, isn't he? Ah, here we are, my last two bottles. I'll make up a new batch once I can locate or possibly grow some more Red Savina habaneros. They are very difficult to come by. With a Scoville count of 577,000, the *Guinness Book of World Records* claims it's the hottest pepper on Earth."

Samantha smiled at Lucas as he set the tall, colorful bottles on the glass countertop. "I believe I've heard of the Scoville scale of rating peppers, but I can't say I know what it means."

Lucas Levy punched numbers into the keys of an antique brass cash register. "Since you asked, Wilbur Scoville, the man who made the list, did so many years ago when he worked for a large eastern pharmaceutical company. Most people believe the testing he did was quite scientific and complicated, when actually it was simply auditory."

"I don't understand," Samantha said honestly.

"They used a decibel recording of how loud ol' Wilbur screamed when he bit into a pepper. Not long after he chomped down on a Red Savina habanero his family had to put him in a home, poor fellow."

Samantha chuckled and tossed two twenty-dollar bills onto the counter. "At least he's remembered." She asked Lucas. "I have some time off, how about letting me buy you lunch?"

Lucas counted out the change. "As long as no habaneros are involved, there's an offer I can't refuse. I'm even out of rubber gloves to handle those peppers that are hot enough to cause a hazmat team to worry."

"If they're that hot, why do you ever use them?"

"Because, my dear," Lucas turned and closed the cash register drawer. "Of the immense satisfaction it brings me to offer a unique product to the culinary world. The very fact that a five-star chef purchases my product is solid proof there's a market for all types of vinegar, including some rather extreme varieties."

Samantha smiled. "For lunch, I was thinking of seeing what Pete has on special at Johnny Ringo's."

Lucas lowered his eyebrows in a thoughtful frown. "Today is liver and onions, I'm fairly sure." He sighed. "In the past, gunfights erupted over less."

"Cheeseburgers and fries it is."

"Without hot peppers."

"Maybe a few jalapenos, for flavor."

"You're buying?"

"Only if we can get there while I'm still young."

"Madam, shall we walk or take the chariot?"

Samantha gave a genuine smile, it was refreshing to be away from professional killers and be able to engage in some fun banter. "It's only a few blocks, but my Jeep's outside sitting in the sun. There's a nice shade tree close to Ringo's that, if we hurry, I might be able to park under before someone less deserving beats me to it."

Lucas moved with the speed and agility of a cat to open the door for her. "Lunch with a lovely lady who's buying and a chance to park beneath a big shade tree makes for a rare day in Tombstone."

The second Samantha hit the remote, Lucas opened her door for her then walked around and hopped in the other side. She felt a wave of apprehension when the first thing Lucas did was turn around to inspect the brown paper bag containing the bomb she had removed from beneath the Jeep.

"If there's any fresh milk or ice cream in here," he said without touching the bag, "it'll be extinct in a matter of minutes. I can run and put it in my refrigerator if need be."

"No," Samantha was careful to say nonchalantly. "It's only some hardware items I'm taking back to Sidney and Michael."

"Then let's not waste time, noon's not far off and there's only one tree," Lucas said as Samantha slid the Jeep into gear and began the short drive to Johnny Ringo's Saloon.

CHAPTER THIRTY-FIVE

Rodney Page climbed out of his battered old pickup truck, adjusted his sleeveless "wife-beater" T-shirt to show off as many of his numerous tattoos as possible, flicked a stub of cigarette onto the steps of a shop, and surveyed the street with a scowl. Not only was he as irritable as a pit bull with a toothache, he was nearly broke.

The Tombstone Minutemen were finally getting the media coverage they so richly deserved, after the damn Mexicans and foreigners of all sorts had nearly wrecked this country. But the new people coming in didn't want him even around, let alone be in charge of anything. That was a real pisser. And he was the person who had sounded the first alarms, organized the freedom fighters. Now he was an outcast from his own organization that had been infiltrated and taken over by wimps and gays for their own causes.

Briefly, he wondered if George Washington or Abraham Lincoln had suffered the same slings and arrows of outrageous misfortune that he was now enduring. He vaguely remembered hearing those lines, most likely in the tenth grade, his last year of school, and decided to use them in the future. The limp-wristed scum who had taken over the Minutemen loved big, fancy words. He'd use some on them, make the bastards reconsider ousting him.

Being removed from the Minutemen and nearly broke was not Rodney's biggest problem. Not by a long chalk. He smiled when he realized he had come up with another fancy line. No, Rodney Page's biggest concern was Wab Smith; the little weasel had become obsessed with Carl Deevers being beneath bunker number twelve, as the concrete septic tank that had crushed him flat was now numbered on the Maginot Line of defense that *he* had built.

Wab Smith was growing increasingly nervous over questions about what had become of Carl Deevers. It turned out there were not only a hundred or so Minutemen watching the border that day, but the Border Patrol was holding some kind of exercise using another couple of hundred men along with a dozen or so helicopters and various spy devices. Their story about Deevers being abducted by Mexicans was not working well. Not well at all.

It turned out a lot of people had seen Carl Deevers leave town with them and not return. Worse, one of the snoopier bastards had contacted the sheriff's department who had came out and asked him a lot of questions. Then they went so far as to even list Carl officially as a missing person. And Wab Smith was the only person outside of him who knew exactly where Deevers was and what had happened.

Hell, it was an accident pure and simple, not like he'd killed anyone. The cable had snapped at the exact moment Carl had been under that septic tank. Wasn't his fault in the least. But the law wouldn't look at it like that, never did. At the very least they'd throw him in jail for months, ruin his reputation, make certain he'd never again head up the Minutemen.

Rodney Page steeled his resolve not to let that happen, but to also come up with a plan to prevent Wab from ever revealing what actually happed that day at bunker twelve. But now he was hungry and nearly broke. Then he saw a shiny new red Jeep parked beneath a shade tree. And there was no one else in sight. Possibly his luck had improved.

151

He felt the extendable steel fighting wand tucked into the back of his jeans and hidden beneath the T-shirt then walked over to inspect the Jeep. Rodney's hopes fell when he saw only a single bag in the back seat along with what looked to be two tall bottles of something other than decent liquor.

"Damn cheap-assed tourists," Rodney swore, deciding not to use the wand to break the glass without good reason. "Why couldn't they have bought something valuable that I could sell?"

"You need something in there?" Lucas Levy's soft voice caused Rodney to spin to face the man he had not seen. To further frustrate him, that new girl, the pretty one who worked out at the bed and breakfast, was standing alongside of Levy. The fact that he had missed seeing either of them burned his soul like an attack of fire ants.

"Just lookin', asshole," Rodney snarled at Lucas. "What's it to you, anyway?"

Lucas Levy stepped away from Samantha and closer to Page. "Because, Rodney, I honestly believe you were thinking of using that fighting wand you have tucked in your butt crack that stuck up like a little flagpole when you bent over to break into Samantha's Jeep. *That's* what it is to me."

Rodney Page was in no mood to be insulted. Not on top of everything else going wrong. He grabbed onto the steel wand and started to pull it when the stars came out. After gaining some of his senses, he realized the vinegar salesman had somehow managed to kick the wind out of him. A second swift kick to his shin caused him to collapse onto the dirt street, writhing in pain.

Lucas Levy looked down at Page, turned to Samantha, and clucked his tongue. "Such a terrible display of manners from that fellow. A simple apology would have saved him a *lot* of pain."

Samantha was becoming far more hardened than when she

had first arrived in Tombstone. "I believe Minnet would agree that Rodney's attitude could use improvement."

Lucas said to Samantha, "If we walk around to the front of your Jeep, I believe we can drive away without running over Mr. Page." He bent over the writhing man who was holding his leg and extracted the wand. "I believe I'll take this, it might save you problems in the future. Someone not so nice as me might take it away from you and really hurt you with it."

"I'll get you for this, Lucas," Rodney Page growled through clenched teeth. "Believe it."

Lucas Levy clucked his tongue again and climbed into the Jeep. He turned to Samantha who was keying the ignition. "I can certainly understand why Minnet divorced that man. I honestly do believe if Rodney Page was marginally smarter, he could be considered dangerous."

Samantha grinned. "Minnet said Rodney was born dumb and has been losing ground ever since. Now, we know she was right." Then she put the Jeep into gear and drove away, leaving Rodney chocking in a cloud of gray powder dust.

Several minutes later, Rodney Page sat in the shade, recovering his composure. By the time he limped back to his truck, he was struck by what was surely an epiphany.

"Now I know just what to do," he said aloud to himself. "I gotta get rid of Wab anyway. I'll kill him, and make it look like Lucas Levy did it." He hesitated while considering this. "All I need to do is come up with a plan. A foolproof plan."

Then he drove back to the desert, to bunker twelve, which he called home, to heal and plan how to accomplish his goal.

Chapter Thirty-Six

When Samantha braked her Jeep Liberty to a dusty stop in front of Lucas's Spice of Life Gourmet Vinegar Works, she was amazed at how calm she remained after the incident with Rodney Page. Only scant weeks ago, such a harrowing experience would have sent her to the doctor for a Xanax prescription to calm frayed nerves.

But now, when Samantha lifted her hands from the steering wheel, she was pleased to note they were steady as a brain surgeon's. Obviously living with and helping out professional hit-people had a tendency to put minor incidents, such as the encounter with Rodney Page, into the entertainment category. Rodney was big, muscular, and acted mean as a junkyard dog, but she now knew a dozen ways to kill or disable any man in the blink of an eye. Esther had combed a long sharp hatpin into Samantha's auburn tresses just this morning after carefully describing exactly where to stab a person with it in such a manner as to instantly paralyze the attacker.

"*Always* be prepared, dearie," Esther had said. "Cemeteries are full of trusting people."

Yes, Esther had certainly been correct. Only now it dawned on Samantha that Lucas seemed to share her nonchalance. After kicking senseless a much younger and bigger man who had a weapon that struck her as odd, Sidney had demonstrated how vicious one of those steel fighting wands could be in combat. He had laid a ham bone on a bench outside where the resulting splatter would not create any mess for his mother to complain about. Then he had whipped out the wand that clicked open with a snap that reminded her of a .22 short being fired. Then faster than her eyes could follow, with one hard, quick blow, Sidney had crushed the ham bone into pieces.

"Don't ever let anyone who has one of these things get close enough to use it," Sidney wisely advised. "Shoot them if you can. If you have been disarmed for some reason, throw dirt in their eyes to blind them, then try to get behind them. If all else fails, run. After you get a gun, look them up and shoot them before they can tell many people what happened. A skilled hit-person builds a reputation from successful jobs. Don't concern yourself over strategic withdrawals. The final outcome is all that matters."

Samantha let the air conditioner run until it began to send out cold air. In the building heat of an early Arizona afternoon it felt like a blessing from Heaven. After a brief hesitation, she turned to Lucas. "Where did you learn to fight like that? Rodney is tough, mean, and had a weapon, yet you didn't work up a drop of sweat beating the crap out of him."

"Surely you've heard the term 'go postal'." Lucas's happy blue eyes showed he was enjoying himself. "I simply employed some of my training in handling unruly patrons. Actually Rodney was no problem, a little ol' lady with a cane, now there's a world of hurt coming your way."

Samantha didn't buy for a single second that the post office trained their personnel in the martial arts, and surely even if they did, not to the proficiency Lucas had demonstrated. "You paid attention in class. Minnet's ex will be sore for days, then he'll come around to even the score. His kind aren't ones to let bygones be bygones."

Lucas gave an indifferent shrug. "Whatever. I'll oblige him, but I can't see his point. Not only am I older, smarter, and more devious than he is, I'm a much nicer person, and only an idiot messes with nice people." He turned to Samantha, his eyes sparkling in the sunlight. "I do hope he behaves himself. The next time he might really get injured."

Samantha couldn't suppress a chuckle. "Minnet once said that Rodney's gene pool needed chlorine. She might be right."

"Hey," Lucas said as he grabbed onto the door latch. "Thanks for lunch, I enjoyed it along with being in your fine company once again." He then surprised her by turning, grabbing her right hand, and giving it a kiss. "Perhaps, madame, I might be honored to repay your kindness by asking you to come here for dinner in the near future. I'm afraid I don't have Michael Herod's culinary skills, but I can grill a hot dog and place it in a bun with the best of 'em."

"All you have to do is call." Samantha meant every word as Lucas opened the door, sending in a blast of heat. "Not many girls can resist tempting offers like that."

"See you soon." Lucas shut the Jeep door and disappeared into his shop with the grace of a ballet dancer.

Samantha took a moment to ponder just what Lucas Levy's story would be in the light of truth. While on the subject, she had to wonder just how many people in Tombstone were actually what they appeared to be. The way things had shaped up, if she was careful enough to watch her backside, she would be around long enough to learn the facts. Tombstone was certainly no place to let your guard down, that much was certain.

For some strange reason Samantha wished for a cigarette. This baffled her, as she'd never smoked one in her life. Then she remembered that she had forgotten to buy Esther's two cartons of Marlboros, along with the four bottles of white wine she'd ordered.

Living with professional hit-people could be reason to start smoking, Samantha thought as she drove into the hot desert day.

Then she grinned when she pictured Sidney's stunned expression when she returned to the B&B and handed his bomb back to him. There was a line from *Alice in Wonderland* that came to mind. Sam couldn't remember who spoke it but it sure as hell fit: "Tut, Tut child, everything's got a moral if only you can find it."

"Yep," Samantha said to herself. "That author undoubtedly spent time in Tombstone." Then the traffic near the convenience store caused her to focus on her driving. The day had gone much too well to mar it with a fender-bender now.

CHAPTER THIRTY-SEVEN

Tex Birdsong, who was in his front yard trimming the oleander hedge, glanced up and smiled at the pretty young lady driving a red Jeep Liberty as she sped by, kicking up gravel. He adjusted his wide-rimmed straw hat to keep the bright, hot afternoon sun at bay as much as possible in the desert.

He gauged the Jeep's speed to be adequate to flatten his wife. The mental image that thought conjured up was immanently agreeable. Fern's syrupy sweetness was becoming even harder to deal with than her bitching had been. She doted on him worse every day, it seemed. Especially after the rattlesnake had bitten him.

Tex took a moment to ponder just how hard it was to do in a wife. Having a handy rattler take care of the job was definitely a bust. That was painfully clear. To add to his hardship, he'd stopped by the library and read up on black widow spiders, scorpions, and those terribly vicious-looking desert centipedes, all of which were of epidemic proportions in Tombstone.

The information he'd gleaned was another pisser to deal with. Hell, the damn desert was supposed to be a dangerous place, full of all kinds of deadly reptiles and insects that were plentiful and anxious to bite human beings just to enjoy causing them to writhe in agony while awaiting a sure death.

That entire scenario turned out to be a crock. Honeybees, it turned out, were responsible for more fatalities than all of the so-called dangerous creatures in Tombstone combined. Not only were most scorpions only mildly poisonous, even the awesome black vinegaroons that were the size of crayfish and sported a long whip-like tale whose stinger looked like it virtually guaranteed a trip to the undertaker turned out not to be poisonous at all. Their only defense was a distasteful vinegar odor the bugs gave off when stepped on or run over by an automobile. Now that Tex thought on the matter, he couldn't see how giving off an odor after being killed could be considered much of a defense. He shook his head at the sad facts of life, and at just how difficult the task of removing his wife from the land of the living had become.

But Tex Birdsong was a man of focus and determination. He also wanted—hell, he *needed*—Fern's life insurance policy to pay the medical bills from his snakebite episode. The image of holding a check made out for the admirable sum of ten thousand dollars beckoned like the glint of gold at the end of a rainbow. And all he needed was a new plan to accomplish his goal.

Esther Munson speeding by with that big Hummer and running Fern over still seemed like a good idea, only now Tex realized he needed a backup plan. Only any idea that wouldn't put him in the slammer eluded him like a will-o-the-wisp.

Tex Birdsong gave a snort of disgust, then returned to the task of trimming the oleander hedge that grew like weeds. He'd come up with a way to get rid of his wife, all he had to do was study up on the matter a bit more. The method was out there, he just had to come up with a plan, and damn soon, before those medical bills started hitting the post office box. He wiped a trickle of rare sweat from his brow. The desert was so dry a person couldn't even work up a sweat. Then he concentrated on stuffing the oleander cuttings into bags so he could go to Johnny Ringo's Saloon and enjoy a few cold beers. He did his best thinking at a bar, always had.

Soon, very soon, Tex would once again be blessedly single.

CHAPTER THIRTY-EIGHT

Old timers who had lived many years in the desert would have said the temperature in Tombstone that afternoon was hot enough to not only fry an egg on the sidewalk, but the chicken, too. Every living thing, with the exception of the ever-present black vultures circling against a blue sky seeking out death, had retreated to shadowy places to await the coolness that followed a bloody sunset.

Samantha wondered briefly why that frail-looking, silver-haired old man had chosen this time of day to trim oleander bushes. The gentleman was certainly retired. Perhaps boredom had simply gotten the best of him. Anyone who'd ever suffered through an afternoon of network television, as Sam had done, could easily understand him choosing to bake his brains instead of withering them. She gave the old fellow a smile and wave, then continued on up the dusty road to the imposing yellow mansion of the Sunset Bed and Breakfast, where she parked in the blessed shade of the long wooden carport. Then Sam grabbed up the bags carrying the contents of Esther's wish list along with the bomb she had removed from beneath her Jeep and strode inside. This was going to be *fun*.

"It's about time you got back," Esther Munson growled as she pounced on the bag containing the cigarettes. She ripped open a carton, tapped out a pack, and had a lit cigarette in her mouth before Samantha had time to say a word. "I need my damn Marlboros, they're the biggest pleasure I get these days . . . well, at least *one* of 'em."

"Mother," Sidney said, coming into the kitchen to join them. "The doctor told you to quit smoking. Cigarettes are bad for your health."

Esther turned to her son. "Both docs who told me are deader than doornails. Natural causes too, I'll have you know."

Sidney wasn't going to drop the subject. He pointed a manicured fingernail at one of the colorful packs. "Take note, Mother, it says that they are dangerous on every pack."

Esther snorted, "Yet I'm still here. I tell ya, Son, there's no truth in advertising these days. Now when we promise to whack someone, they'd better pick out their casket and be damn quick about it."

Sidney shrugged, knowing he was fighting a losing battle. His mother had a way of ending any argument in her favor.

"I had a nice long lunch with Lucas at Johnny Ringo's," Samantha said cheerfully as she placed the remaining bags on the kitchen island. She extracted the four bottles of white wine. "I'll put these in the freezer to chill," Sam gave Esther a grin. "Happy hour will be here before they can freeze."

"You've got a good head on your shoulders, girl," Esther said. "And an understanding of old people's needs. I like that trait in a person."

Michael Herod, who had been occupied mixing dough for some of his delicious cinnamon raisin rolls, took a moment to survey the countertop. "Ah, good. I see Lucas did have the bottles of habanero pepper vinegar. I was quite concerned he might not have any, and Sidney and I have a pressing need for the product."

Samantha lowered her eyebrows. "I can't imagine any dish that would require peppers as hot as Lucas said those are. Certainly not two bottles of the stuff."

Sidney gave an evil grin. "It is a rather, ah . . . unusual recipe, my dear, one that we seldom get around to making."

Michael added, "A diligent chef keeps a pantry full of spices." He came to take the bottles of vinegar when he noticed the bomb in another bag. "Sidney, my friend, you simply *must* come here and see what our darling Samantha has brought us."

Sam gave a satisfied grin. "I disarmed it just like I was taught. I know there was no way you people would give me an opportunity to simply drive away." She chuckled. "I toyed with the idea of tossing the GPS on a passing truck to give you a thrill."

"I think it is quite fortunate for you that you did not do that, Samantha," Sidney said seriously. "People in our profession have, by necessity, a somewhat limited sense of humor."

Michael Herod grabbed the rectangle of plastic explosive. He sniffed it and said, "This is a nice brick of cooked sugar held together by a glue of my own design."

"The bomb you found was a dummy," Esther announced from a cloud of cigarette smoke. "Anyone in our business can't take chances with loyalties. We have to *know* who we can trust and who we can't. From the fact that you're standing here, we can trust you from here on out."

Samantha felt a building chill along her spine. "If the bomb was a dummy," she turned to face Sidney, "why did you tell me I was lucky to have left the GPS in my Jeep."

"Tut-tut, dearie, all's well that turns out well," Sidney said.

Esther grunted. "The *real* bomb was well hidden over your gas tank, girl."

Michael said, "You certainly don't think we would ever be so crude as to put a bomb anyplace it could be easily seen. Why, we are professionals, after all."

Sidney's grin returned. "Michael and I shall endeavor to remove the active device after dinner and our visitors have left. The weather will be much more agreeable by then. This has been a dreadfully hot day."

The chill along Samantha's spine had turned into a strcak of icicles. "*Two* bombs! You put two bombs in my Jeep."

"Now now, dearie. Only *one* was real, after all." Esther shrugged and tapped out another Marlboro. "Think of it as a lesson; nobody, especially people who're expecting something like that, ever thinks to look for a second bomb."

"Gets them every time," Michael said cheerfully, returning to his bread dough mixer.

Sidney said, "Well, now that this little episode is behind us, Samantha, my dear, you should be happy to know we are having some very distinguished guests coming to visit us this evening."

A bomb under the seat of your car is not a "little episode," Samantha thought as she began to realize the less said about the subject, the better she would sleep tonight. The facts were she had lived through the day. For a hit-person, that alone was cause to celebrate.

"Are we going to whack them?" Samantha asked, a tad embarrassed when her voice broke.

"Oh no, my dear," Sidney said. "These are our employers from Washington. The matter must be most serious because the director himself, along with a couple of four-star generals, will be joining us this evening. I must say, this is quite an unprecedented event."

Her mind already awash with conflicting thoughts, Samantha came straight out and asked, "Are the generals from *our* army and the director from the CIA?"

Sidney gave a sincere chuckle. "Yes, Samantha. We have been quite truthful with you on *that* matter. The 'Company,' as we much prefer to call the CIA, has been contracting with us and other professional hit-men for many years. Being able to go directly to the guts of the matter is such a time and money saver for the government."

"Normally they never come to the field," Michael said without looking away from his cooking. "We were told this is an emergency of extreme proportions. I can't say that I have ever heard such strong language from The Company before."

"Well, let's all pitch in and help Michael serve up a memorable dinner for these fine people," Sidney said. "I feel certain that in due time." He focused his piercing blue eyes on Samantha with a cold gaze. "We will *all* know what our new task shall be. Then, working together as a team, we shall carry out the contract, which will most certainly be quite lucrative."

Samantha came very close to asking Esther for a cigarette. The existence of a second, *real* bomb that could easily have blown her into pieces so small no undertaker could put back together again kept bothering her. If she had given into temptation and tossed the GPS onto the back of a passing truck . . . but she hadn't, fortunately.

"I'll start setting the table," Samantha said, forcing a cheery note into her voice.

"Good girl," Esther said with a hack. "I'll help you."

As Samantha began working to entertain the distinguished guests, she found herself placing the events of the day on a shelf in her mind, and concerned herself with wondering about tonight's event along with everyone else. What could possibly be so important as to bring the director of the CIA, along with high-ranking military personnel, to visit the remote town of Tombstone, Arizona? A quick glance to the wall clock told her she wouldn't have to wait long for the answers to her questions.

CHAPTER THIRTY-NINE

The growing sound of manmade thunder brought everyone outside the Sunset Bed and Breakfast to greet their distinguished guests. From out of a crimson sunset, a pair of jet-black helicopters roared in low over the craggy Tombstone hills. They circled, then sat down side-by-side on the flat section of mountainside that was large enough to serve as a heliport.

Esther Munson tossed her cigarette to the rocky ground and stomped on it. She knew that most people frowned on smoking these days, and did not want to look bad in front of the CIA director. He was a real stickler about image.

"Look at that," Esther said loudly over the roar of slowing rotors while elbowing Samantha, who stood by her side. "Both choppers have signs on them sayin' they belong to Evergreen Airlines, outta McKinnville, Oregon. Every bad guy in the whole damn world smart enough to shoot a gun and not hurt himself with it knows that outfit's a front for the CIA." She snorted, "Dumb-ass bureaucrats."

Samantha still had a hard time believing that high-ranking generals, let alone *the* director of the Central Intelligence Agency, was on board either of the now idling helicopters. The entire affair was most likely another ruse being orchestrated for her benefit, for some reason she had yet to understand.

She felt a sense of awe when four black-suited soldiers bolted from the closest helicopter. They held mean-looking submachine guns at the ready while surveying the area. One of the soldiers, probably the leader, barked something into the microphone of his headset. Then they stood aside when two men wearing more medals and stars on their spiffy uniforms than Samantha had ever seen outside of news media photos strode toward them, followed close by a trim, silver-haired man wearing gold-rimmed glasses and carrying a small briefcase. Not a single one of the arrivals showed even the slightest hint that they'd ever smiled in their lives.

Sidney and Michael stepped forward and received the trio with quick and friendly handshakes. It was obvious they had all met before.

"I believe you gentlemen have met my mother, Esther," Sidney said with a sweep of an arm toward the two women.

A subdued but definitely pained expression on the three visitors' faces confirmed Samantha's assumption that they had indeed made her acquaintance.

"It's been a while, Mr. Director," Esther said in a surprisingly pleasant tone. "And General," she added with a nod.

Sidney Munson ushered the three men closer to the two women. He beamed when he announced, "The lovely lady is Samantha. She had only recently joined our team. We have the greatest confidence that, with some additional field experience, she will become a valued asset to us all."

The silver-haired man wearing a suit extended a hand and gave Sam a limp greeting. He spoke with all the emotion of someone ordering off a menu, "James Burr, director of the Central Intelligence Agency." He then turned and headed for the mansion.

"I'm Air Force General Frank Hawk." The man gave Samantha a firm handshake. His eyes were deep green, piercing. "Please forgive the director's curtness. He is, as are all of us, under intense pressure."

"Glad to meet you, Samantha," the second general pumped

Sam's hand while giving her first smile of the visit. "My name's Gall. Howard Gall, of the Marine Corps." His coal-black eyes reflected the dying red sunset like embers in a campfire. "I look forward to working with you. Sorry that our first operation together has to be such a quandary as this one, but we really don't have time for pleasantries."

"I understand," was the only response Samantha could manage before the general yelled at the soldiers so sharply it caused her to jump. "Sweep the area for hostiles and listening devices. Then set up and maintain a security perimeter around the entire structure. Remember, this is a Pinnacle Empty Quiver situation."

A chorus of "Yes, sirs!" answered as the four soldiers Samantha had first seen were joined by at least a half-dozen more. All were armed to the teeth and dressed in dull black that extended to their faces. The men ran off carrying various metal boxes. Whatever the hell a Pinnacle Empty Quiver situation entailed, it was certainly serious. *Very* serious.

Samantha felt her heart race and her palms turn clammy as she followed the procession inside the Sunset Bed and Breakfast while shadows darted about the cactus-studded desert hills in the gathering darkness of the coming night.

"I can offer you gentlemen anything you wish from the bar or kitchen," Michael Herod said as their guests began seating themselves at the formal dining room table. "There are also some appetizers that I put together when we learned of your arrival. I believe you gentlemen will find them acceptable."

Director Burr gave a grunt as he slid his chair close and opened the briefcase in front of him. "I'll take a scotch and water is all. This state of affairs has taken my appetite, I'm afraid."

General Gall gave Samantha another smile and slid out a chair for her next to his. "Have a seat, little lady. I'm going to take Michael up on his offer of a drink. I think a nice cold martini with three olives is in order." He leaned his head close to Sam. "And I'm betting our newest hit-lady would enjoy a nice drink as well."

It was apparent to Samantha that no matter how grave the situation, it didn't stop a Marine General from coming on to a woman. "I'll have a glass of white wine. The same as Esther."

General Gall swallowed hard when he looked at a scowling Esther, then scooted Sam's chair close and took his own seat while Air Force General Hawk refused any refreshments, demanding they get down to business.

A few minutes, later, Sidney, Michael, and Esther joined Samantha and the three men at the table to learn what had brought them here in such an obvious state of tension. When they learned the answer, even the seasoned hit-peoples' blood ran cold.

CHAPTER FORTY

Rodney Page awoke from an afternoon nap in the coolness of bunker twelve with a splitting headache. He blinked at the empty bottle of cheap Mexican brandy and snorted. The quality of everything produced across the border was definitely inferior and declining steadily. Now, back in the good old days when white men ruled the whole damn world and the pepperbellies— along with niggers, chinks, and all of the other simian races— knew their place, things were better. A *lot* better.

"And they're gonna get better real soon, thanks to us true patriots," Rodney mumbled to himself. He stood as tall as he could in the confines of the low concrete tank and strapped on his pistol. A true soldier was always armed, but the bulky .45 revolver kept poking him in the leg. No matter, the weapon was always close at hand and there wasn't anyone around to witness his giving in to comfort.

Rodney, as did all of the Minutemen with a genuine calling, took a rest period in the heat of the afternoon to allow themselves to stay up late at night and listen to talk radio. This was when the airwaves sparkled with God's truth. Not only did Rush Limbaugh speak out against the dark forces, nowadays there were many more. The Savage Nation was wonderfully filled with insight and factual observations of the sad state this country had slipped into. The list went on and on. Anyone with a radio could drink a beer and learn what was *really* going on.

But most of the masses were too busy watching reality TV,

which was, in actuality, paid for clandestinely by big business to keep people from thinking or even—God forbid—reading newspapers while being subjected to subliminal physiological suggestions to buy this or that product. The same facts held for all of the cable news channels. No, the Minutemen were the last hope of the white race, of civilization itself.

Rodney stretched, using proven isometric techniques that had been hidden by the heathen Chinese for thousands of years, then placed a boot on the low rung of a stepladder and climbed out of the concrete septic tank to stand in the red glory of a drying desert day. He was a man on a mission. No one burdened by a true calling had time to idly enjoy nature's beauty. Being a soldier, he surveyed his surroundings for danger. The first thing he saw was that idiot, Wab Smith, the man he really needed to remove from the Earth, standing atop the adjoining bunker. It had been numbered fourteen to avoid the use of thirteen, which everyone knew carried the curse of bad luck. Always had.

Wab held a pair of field glasses and was apparently studying something to the south with great interest.

"Likely watching jackrabbits screwing," Rodney grumbled. His head throbbed like some pimple-faced little kid was learning how to play the drums between his ears. It would be too painful to climb back into the bunker to retrieve his own set of binoculars. He decided to walk over and use Wab's to survey whatever the hell the idiot was looking at, find out if it was important, which he sincerely doubted.

Rodney Page took a testing sniff of the air and wrinkled his nose. Carl Deevers was definitely getting ripe. That was an unexpected turn of events, as a body beneath a concrete septic tank that was surrounded with dirt shouldn't stink. How it was possible eluded him. Perhaps, Rodney mused, the stench was coming through the inferior Mexican concrete the tank was made of. The problem with that theory was the fact that he hadn't smelled anything inside the bunker.

"Cheap concrete," he spat. Rodney Page knew what to do. Tomorrow he'd drive to a discount lumber yard in Sierra Vista, buy a sack of quicklime, then spread and rake it around the bunker. That'd do the trick. If anybody other than Wab Smith— who would know damn good and well what the problem was— asked, Rodney decided to tell them he had been plagued by rattlesnakes and had heard that quicklime drove them away.

All that was *really* necessary to cure the problem of the odoriferous Carl Deevers would be to have Wab Smith join him in the netherworld. What Rodney needed to do was come up with some way to blame Wab's demise on Mexican drug dealers. No one would question that story. Everyone knew those guys were nothing but a bunch of bloodthirsty killers. By exercising a little patience, he would find his opportunity. In the meanwhile, he decided to go see what had Wab so fascinated that he kept the field glasses pressed to his eyes as if he was watching a strip show at the tittie bar.

Wab Smith jerked the binoculars from his face and bolted back while emitting a girly squeal of surprise that was worthy of a San Francisco fairy, not a soldier on America's only line of defense. If Rodney Page needed any other reason to see the man done in, he had it now.

"Jaysus H. Hillbilly Christ on a crutch!" Wab spurted. "You scared the shit outta me. How about saying something like 'Hi Wab,' or 'What's up, Wab?' or something like that instead of sneaking up and trying to give me a heart attack."

Now there's an idea, Rodney Page thought. "Soldiers are supposed to always be aware of their surroundings." He gave a head nodded to the south. "What's the activity out on the front?" Rodney always enjoyed referring to everything using military terms, gave him an air of authority.

"Looks like a shitload full of wetbacks," Wab pointed to a

gathering of vehicles on the barren desert. "They're a good mile off the Bisbee highway and there's no roads to where they are, just flat ground. Bet they're dodging the Border Patrol."

"Lemme see," Rodney grabbed the binoculars. A moment later he gave a low whistle. "I think you're right, Wab. There's a semi-truck loaded with watermelons. There's two old, beat-up vans and three cars to match an' every one of 'em has Mexican license plates. There ain't a green card among 'em, I bet. Looks like the Minutemen got a job to do, apprehending wetback pepperbellies."

"You'll want to call in help. I'll use the CB in my pickup, have a dozen boys here real soon."

"Nah," Rodney Page gave a dismissive shrug as he gave the field glasses back to Wab. "I'll get my shotgun, you've got a rifle. The two of us can scare a few wetbacks from across the border, or we don't deserve to be called Minutemen."

"You always said that having the odds on our side kept them from trying something stupid. And Rod, I counted almost a dozen men out there."

"See any weapons?"

"No."

"Well, surprise, surprise. The Mexican government don't allow *its* citizens the right to keep and bear arms."

"Makes our job safer, I reckon."

Rodney Page suppressed a groan. Dealing with idiots was becoming tiresome. "I think two armed soldiers can handle a dozen unarmed wetbacks. Once we get them captured and tied up, then we'll call in the Border Patrol, show them how efficient we are."

A glow of anticipation grew in Wab Smith's eyes. "Yeah, grab your gun an' let's go take some prisoners, make a name for ourselves."

"Be right with you. We'll need to take your truck. The battery's dead in mine."

A half-hour later, the two Minutemen approached their quarry in the shadows of twilight. It had taken longer than expected to get any vehicle started, and finally they'd had to take the battery from Wab's winch truck and put it in Rodney's pickup. Wab's truck, it turned out, had an empty gas tank.

"We oughta park a way's back and walk up to 'em," Wab suggested. "If they spook an' run off like rabbits, all we'll have to show for our efforts will be some junk vehicles and a load of watermelons that won't keep long in this heat."

"Yeah, I hate watermelons anyway." Rodney Page shut off the ignition and coasted his decrepit pickup to a shop alongside a copse of greasewood bushes. He grabbed the twelve-gauge riot gun he was so proud of, patted the revolver on his hip, then fought the balky handle to open the door. "Let's go show everyone what the Minutemen can do."

Wab beat him outside, and stood squinting into the dull black of night that had began to envelope the desert. Overhead, a jeweled canopy of sky was unfolding to welcome a rising moon. In the distance, a pack of coyotes sang a greeting to the dark hours they'd waited through the torrid day for.

Rodney Page slid back the pump on his shotgun to send a charge of double ought buckshot into the chamber. The ominous metallic sound echoed in the still desert air like the sound of a nail being driven into a coffin lid. "Let's go round up these trespassers on American soil."

The pair of intrepid Minutemen began working their way toward the semi-truck that stood stark in the moonlight. They had decided to stop darting about behind bushes for fear of stepping on a snake. There was plenty of open ground that was a lot safer to traverse. Most likely the wetbacks were busy cooking beans and tortillas, and wouldn't notice their approach anyway.

When Wab and Rodney were within a couple of hundred feet of the vehicles, they stopped in the open to study the situation. What they saw wasn't at all what they expected.

"They ain't cooking anything," Wab whispered. "I don't see even a little fire."

"I can't understand why they're all milling about. What bothers me is, I understand a lot of Mex talk, but what they're speaking don't sound like any Mexican I've ever heard."

"Might be from southern Mexico," Wab said.

A look of tension crossed Rodney Page's face. "I don't think so." He took a step back. "Wab, I think we should—"

Three dark-skinned men standing at the back of the watermelon truck saw them. Then they began yelling in words the Minutemen did not understand.

"You all are under citizens arrest by the Tombstone Minutemen," Wab Smith shouted, brandishing his rifle.

Rodney Page felt a chill. He hadn't said a word. Seconds before Wab starting acting like an idiot, Rodney had seen the dark ominous forms of automatic rifles leaning against a nearby van.

"Wab," Rodney shouted. "Take cover, the bastards are armed!"

Before either of the two Minutemen could move more than a few feet they were almost cut in half by a deadly spray of 9mm submachine-gun fire from a group of men who knew how to use them and also had no trouble making decisions.

No trouble at all.

CHAPTER FORTY-ONE

Sidney Munson's eyes narrowed, but no one spoke. Everyone had been stunned into silence at the director's words. The dining room was quiet as the inside of a thick stone tomb. The situation that had brought the head of the Central Intelligence Agency, along with two four-star generals to Tombstone was more dangerous than they had expected. *Far* more dangerous.

Esther was the first to break the silence. She tapped out a Marlboro and lit it in front of the director. The situation simply screamed for a cigarette, decorum be damned. "Well, the bastards finally got themselves a nuclear bomb. Surprised it hadn't happened sooner."

General Gall took Esther's lead and fished a cigar from his pocket. "A bunch of them have tried, God knows. Radicals, terrorists, and arms dealers who want to get rich. We managed to stop them all." He lit the cigar, rolling it slowly in the flame. "Until now."

Director Burr said, "We had intelligence of a Soviet missile warhead that went missing from the Ukraine. The informants traced its passage to Mexico where, unfortunately, the device disappeared into the rugged Sonoran desert. Satellite sweeps for radioactive materials turned up negative. The warhead had to be stored deep underground, possibly in a mineshaft, to avoid detection."

Air Force General Hawk wrinkled his nose at the building cloud of smoke. "Detectors picked up the radiation signature this morning, moving toward the border." He noticed the questioning expressions of his audience. "All nuclear weapons emit distinct patterns of radiation. Much like fingerprints, none are exactly the same. This device is a thirty-year-old Soviet tactical warhead with the rather impressive explosive value of thirty kilotons." He hesitated a moment. "That's thirty thousand tons of TNT. A bomb that big goes off in any large city, it will not only be utterly destroyed, but the residual radiation will turn the area into a wasteland for thousands of years."

Samantha felt butterflies in her stomach. Not so long ago she had been a girl living in Houston, Texas, who was so bored with life that playing with her cat had become the highlight of her day. Now, not only was she a hit-woman, somehow fate had dumped a nuclear bomb at her feet, and she just knew they were going to fit her into the plan of recovering the warhead. Since there was little choice, she asked no one in particular. "If you were tracking the bomb, how did it get across the border and wind up just outside of Tombstone?"

Director Burr gave a slight cough and shot a scathing glare at the two generals. "The goddamned ball got dropped is what happened. The plan—the one that didn't work—was to intercept it at the border, treat the incident as a routine drug bust. Keep the whole incident nice and quiet." He sighed, reached across the table to pick up Esther's pack of cigarettes. He tapped one out and lit it. "But that's not what happened, *is* it gentlemen?"

Marine General Gall snorted, "The Border Patrol is lax, they screwed it all up. Now if *my* men had been there—"

"The bomb is *here*, General," Director Burr said coldly from a cloud of cigarette smoke. "There will be plenty of time for finger-pointing later. *Lots* of finger-pointing and blame-laying. And there will be even more blame to go around if we don't focus on the issue at hand, which is recovery and damage control."

General Hawk said, "In all fairness to the Border Patrol, the scenario of border-crashing has been brought up before, only to be ignored for budget reasons."

Sidney Munson cleared his throat. "I believe we would like an explanation of this 'border-crashing' and more detail as to how a very nasty nuclear weapon of mass destruction came to be only a short distance from our lovely home."

"I'll be, by necessity, quite brief," James Burr said gruffly. "They brought the device across the border by using overpowering firepower. The perpetrators simply machine-gunned everyone who got in their way. Two helicopters called in to help were shot down by SAM'S . . . shoulder-fired surface-to-air missiles. From listening to their radio transmissions, the only reason the WMD didn't make it to a waiting rental truck was because the truck it was on, hidden under a load of watermelons, overheated and stalled out on them."

"We got lucky," General Gall said. "They're out there in the desert, cornered like rats. The rest of the bastards waiting in the rental truck are now in custody. The incident at the border is being handled as a battle between Mexican drug lords. The two helicopters were rushing to render assistance and unfortunately were both struck by a severe dust devil that caused them to begin spinning, collide with each other, and crash."

Director Burr said, "It is imperative we keep a total news blackout on what is *really* going on here. This administration is very much pro-business. The presence of an enemy nuclear bomb on American soil would be disastrous for the markets. If the device detonates, then we will do what we must. The reason we are here is to employ your admirable skills of removing people who need it from the face of the earth." He gave another glare to the generals. "And your ability to do the job nice and quiet with as little fanfare as possible. Keeping this entire incident treated as if it were a routine drug bust and out of the media as much as possible is why we are here having this discussion."

Michael Herod came from the kitchen, where he had been listening to the conversation, and placed a steaming hot plate of supreme nachos on the table. "We understand your point. If the facts were known there would be more newsmen here from CNN, Fox, and other networks than military and bad guys combined. Recovering a nasty nuclear bomb while whacking a number of people would be rather difficult to do in front of cameras *and especially* keep it all nice and tidy."

"My point exactly." Director Burr eyed the nachos. "And this brings me to the business part of our visit. If, and *only* if, you are successful in keeping this operation quiet enough that we can blame the entire incident on drug dealers, which will also have the salubrious effect of giving the administration reason to tighten the border, I am empowered to be most generous in payment for your services."

"Just *how* generous?" Esther inquired.

The director gave a thin smile. "I see you are still the pragmatic one, Esther. Satellite tracking has revealed that from our best estimates there are approximately ten subjects at the site. I am authorized to pay you double our usual rate, or one hundred thousand dollars for each one that is permanently neutralized."

Esther snorted, "That's only a measly million bucks. Hey, we're talking about a frickin' nuclear *bomb* here . . ."

Director Burr held up a hand. He'd dealt with Esther Munson before and had already anticipated her demands for more money. In this particular instance unlimited funds were available, but when dealing with professional hit-people, wrangling over the price seemed to be part of their enjoyment. "My dear Mrs. Munson, there are terrorists on our soil. Look upon the job as being one of doing your patriotic duty."

Esther blew smoke from her nose. "We're plenty patriotic every April fifteenth. This is July and I'm askin' for a damn bonus. 'Specially considering the risk involved."

The director realized the delicious-looking nachos were growing cold. It was time to end the business and become sociable. "Considering the circumstances, the president has personally authorized me to, upon successful completion of the contracts, place in your Swiss bank account the totally tax-free amount of twenty-five million dollars."

Samantha couldn't suppress a gasp. *All I have to do is go kill a bunch of well-armed and trained terrorists and recover a nuclear bomb, then I'm rich? Oh by the way, I need to live through it, too.*

"*Now* you're singin' our song," Esther nodded at Michael. "Well, don't just stand there like some damn wooden cigar store Indian. Bring some plates for those nachos before they cool off."

"I am so pleased," General Hawk said, "that we have reached an equitable agreement. While we are enjoying our snack, I'll take a few minutes to fill you in on this particular bomb and what we know about circumstances that might cause it to become armed and how to possibly disarm the device should it become necessary. If this terrible, but distinctly remote situation does occur, disarming it will be your *only* option. A nuclear bomb has a very large kill radius. No one at the site will have time to leave the blast area if it starts counting down."

Samantha had been looking forward to Michael's scrumptious nachos. Now the butterflies were back in her stomach. And there was every reason to believe they'd moved in to stay for some time.

CHAPTER FORTY-TWO

Samantha held a hand over her eyes to shelter them from flying dust and debris as the two black helicopters carrying their guests lifted from the desert and roared off to the west beneath a blanket of twinkling stars. The soldiers had wasted no time gathering their various boxes of spy devices and jumping on board. They knew full well, as Samantha now did, that a Pinnacle Empty Quiver meant a lost or stolen nuclear bomb. Putting a lot of distance between themselves and the device was a grand idea. The military personnel were certainly well trained in atomic weaponry, knew exactly what the hazzards were. And they were headed the opposite direction she would soon be going as quickly as they could.

Smart men, Sam thought. *I suppose trying to jump on a runner of one of the copters like people did when they evacuated the embassy in Saigon wouldn't have worked anyway. Falling a couple of hundred feet or being shot by a hit-man would kill me just as dead as being in a nuclear explosion. And I'd be better off trying to live through this situation. Actually, several million dollars better off. Esther's always telling me that eventually something gets you. It's what you do from now until then that counts. Might as well go for the gold.*

The roar of the departing helicopters faded, leaving only the thick stillness of the Sonoran desert at night in their wake. Not even the plaintive howl of a coyote or chirping of crickets broke the stone silence. It was as if all of nature was holding its breath. Or taking cover.

Sidney Munson clucked his tongue and gave a very thin smile. "I believe our best course of action is discretion, along with proper prior planning. First, let's go to the kitchen and enjoy some of Michael's delightful cuisine, which was rather rudely turned down, I must say. Then, once our palates have been sated, we can focus on the matter at hand and develop some tactics to whack those nasty terrorists while making ourselves a sweet addition to our retirements."

"I really like the part about retirement," Samantha said.

"No one here's alive 'cause a taking unnecessary risks, dearie." Esther stomped out the stub of her cigarette. "At a hundred grand a hit, those idiots with the bomb are the ones who oughta to be smart enough to worry." She spun and strode off, saying over her shoulder, "We can talk later—I'm hungry enough to eat a damn horse."

Sidney placed a comforting hand on Samantha's shoulder. "Mother always has been one to not let trying circumstances upset her appetite. I believe we can learn from her example . . . ummm."

Samantha's stomach was still a butterfly sanctuary, but he was right, a nice meal might help bolster her resolve to go kill a bunch of bloodthirsty, radical terrorists with a WMD. "Lead on, Kemo Sabe." She was taken aback with her flippancy in the face of death. Keeping company with Esther was certainly having an effect on her attitude.

Sidney beamed as he escorted Samantha to the door. "My, my, I must say we are all *so* proud of our little flower and the way she has blossomed so wonderfully."

I haven't had a lot of choice, Sam thought, but decided it best to keep the conversation upbeat. "You folks have been so nice to me, how else could I repay your kindnesses?"

Sidney's white teeth glinted in the starlit night. "Many are called, few live to be chosen. Now, let's enjoy our meal."

Chapter Forty-Three

Tex Birdsong sat on the back porch of his home, enjoying the cool night air along with a tall glass of Long Island Iced Tea made strong, just the way he liked it. He had surprised himself when he'd asked Fern to join him, but she'd refused, saying there was a reality show on television she wanted to watch. It was just as well, gave him time to reflect on some new methods to get rid of the old bat and not get caught.

Watching the two helicopters take off from the Sunset Bed and Breakfast put him to thinking of paths not taken. It occurred to him those words were from some poem, probably written by some skinny fairy who'd never busted his butt as a longshoreman. But they did give him cause to think.

The people who owned the bed and breakfast were obviously doing well. Hell, they had more money than they'd ever need. Controlled the whole damn town is what they did. And from the looks of things, business was booming. Only the super rich flew around in private jet helicopters.

Tex sipped his Long Island Iced Tea and frowned when he found it was getting warm. With a snort of disgust, he chugged most of the watered-down drink. He wondered when and why he'd ever developed a taste for the stuff. It wasn't a real *man's* drink. That much was for certain. Back in his union days, if he'd seen anyone on his crew ordering a Long Island Iced Tea, he'd have decked them just for the fun of it.

But those fun days were gone now. Tex was old and felt it. He knew his days of bar fights were over, goddamn it. The only enjoyment left to him these days were going to Johnny Ringo's Saloon, or if his knees didn't hurt too bad, walking to the VFW where beer was a quarter cheaper.

Tex Birdsong thought bitterly. *How'd I wind up old and broke, living in a dusty desert town where people's main pastime was arguing over history? Hell, nothing excitin's happened here since that damn gunfight back in 1881. Never will again either, most likely.*

Tex slugged some more of his drink and tossed the rest onto an oleander bush. That was what was wrong, he was bored shitless. Back in his salad years, he'd been a boss of men, a mover. He had been someone who mattered. Not like he was nowadays, an old fart with a nagging wife and basically no money except Social Security. The bastards who'd raided his union pension fund had done so legally, but they were robbers, the same as if they wore masks and stuck up banks. Yet they'd gotten away with it. The damned system was at fault, needed changing.

Bile rose in Tex's gut, as it always did when he thought of what had happened to his money and his beloved union. He'd heard that today's longshoremen weren't allowed to fight anymore, got fired if they did. Back in his day a few bruises along with swollen knuckles were a badge of honor. The goddamn wimps who run this country needed their asses kicked out of office while we still had a country.

Now he knew how he had been able to stay married to Fern all of those years, he'd had a mission, a goal. And he'd damn well been the toughest longshoreman in the business. A focus worthy of his abilities to get things done, kick some ass when it needed kicking. He stood slowly. Where the rattlesnake had bitten him was still sore.

But Tex Birdsong had made a decision. The Tombstone Minutemen were trying to save this country. He'd heard Rodney Page speak a few times, especially on nights when the beer was free. He might be old, but he could make a difference. There were battlelines that needed manned, observation posts to be filled. By God, he was able to shoot a gun when the time came, too. He had a .38 revolver and a box of hollow point shells. Those things would expand like mushrooms when they hit human flesh, blow a hole in a person big enough to read a newspaper through.

Tex Birdsong shook with enthusiasm. The dozen beers he'd drank earlier were still doing the trick. It was time for action. He strode back inside of his home with a purpose to his step. The Minutemen needed him as much as he did them. And time was wasting.

Chapter Forty-Four

Sidney Munson stabbed a small, ruby-colored piece of salmon tartare with a silver fork and studied it intently for a moment before delicately dipping it in some Bleak caviar sautéed with extra virgin olive oil then chewing it with obvious zest.

The very idea of anyone eating raw fish did nothing to calm the flutters in Samantha's stomach. Back home in Texas, most of her friends would have referred to the pale red chunks of salmon as bait. It also struck her as odd that everyone was sitting here at the dining room table, calmly eating a belated dinner, when they faced the task of whacking about ten terrorists before dawn. Then there was the matter of a Russian nuclear bomb to deal with.

Samantha couldn't help but reflect on how much she had looked forward to moving to Tombstone, make a new life for herself and Shakespeare. Oh yes, and add a little spice and adventure to what had become a stale, mundane existence.

Be careful what you wish for in the future girl, sometimes wishes come all too true, then Samantha's stomach found a new place to quiver. *There might not be a future, not if anything goes wrong—or that damn bomb blows up. If that happens I'll at least go out with a bang. No whimpers for me. There won't be time.*

"You really need to eat something," Esther Munson said to Samantha. "It's important to keep up your strength."

Michael Herod said, "It's often hard to judge how long a job will take. Take Esther's good advice." His voice grew soft. "I remember what it was like for me when I first entered the business. I can fix you a couple of slices of whole-grain toast with organic butter and add a couple of soft boiled eggs on the side if you would like."

Samantha gave Michael her first simile of the harrowing evening. "That would be sweet of you. I must admit my stomach's a little queasy."

Esther snorted, "You'll get over it. A few more hits and you'll look at a job with no more personal feelings than a doctor takin' out an inflamed appendix."

Sidney forked another piece of salmon with obvious glee. "Michael, my friend, you have once again outdone yourself. This tartare dish is simply scrumptious." He glanced at Samantha. "Mother is right, my dear. Ours is only one of many occupations where a professional, detached attitude is absolutely necessary. When you think of a mark, don't picture a human being in your mind. Focus only on how wonderful the check for your services will look in a nice safe Swiss bank account . . . ummm."

Samantha said, "I admire the way you folks can stay so calm, even when you've surely never recovered a nuclear bomb before. Just thinking about the devastation one of those can do is enough to scare any sane person."

Sidney said, "There, my dear, you have just identified one of the traits of the people we will soon be dealing with. Very, very insightful."

"They're crazy as hell," Esther said, scraping her plate clean with a slice of bread. "Religious zealots always are. If they get themselves whacked they have a direct pass to heaven, makes 'em unafraid and causes 'em to make easy targets of themselves. That can really be helpful."

"I read they also get seventy-two virgins in the next life," Samantha said.

Michael Herod gave a shrug. "I never have understood the benefits of that part of their misguided religion."

Sidney gave a thin undertaker's grin. "They wish to go to their god. I believe we should arrange the meeting as quickly as possible."

"They'll certainly be expecting us to go after them," Samantha said.

Sidney Munson kept his skeletal smile. "Those terrorists are driven to succeed in their mission. After the bloody incident at the border along with the roadblocks and ensuing capture of their companions and the seizure of the moving van for the bomb, they know full well an attack on their position is imminent."

Esther turned to Samantha. "We know from the intel given us they all have powerful personal radios for communication."

Michael Herod added, "You can bet your last bullet those marks are very confused by the radio silence from the military. All they'll be receiving will be local police and highway patrol chatter pertaining to roadblocks to catch drug dealers. Pretty routine transmissions considering the unnerving cargo they have hidden in that truckload of watermelons."

"Every good hit-person," Sidney said, looking straight at Samantha, "uses a diversion whenever possible. Throw the mark off balance, give them the surprise of their life, so to speak, when they finally figure out what's going on."

"And that, my dear," Esther said, "is why we are not charging across the desert carrying an armload of guns and ammo. The direct approach is for armies or idiots. We're in this for the money and all the loot in the world doesn't do you any good after you're dead. Samantha, we're a success in the whacking business because we plan ahead. And we *never* play fair. Winning is all that matters, because the losers get buried."

"Mother is correct, as always," Sidney chimed in, "our

instruction so far has been mainly of techniques, and we have been sadly remiss in instructing you in the fine arts of deception. Unfortunately, due to the unforseen pressures and time restraints being placed on us by these unspeakably nasty people, I'm sorry to say your training in this area of the field will be rather much of a crash course."

Samantha said, "In this situation, I'll be a fast learner."

From the kitchen, Michael said, "I have not a single doubt you will be, dearie. There is a room just off the pantry that you have yet to enter. This is where we keep all of the, ah . . . *special* items we used to employ on a regular basis. Running this bed and breakfast is such an efficient method of disposing of marks that we have not needed to resort to field methods for some time." He hesitated to place two eggs into a pot of boiling water. "But rest assured, we all know exactly what it will take to whack those ruthless men and live to put money in the bank for doing it."

"What about the bomb?" Samantha questioned.

Sidney Munson stabbed another piece of raw salmon. "I must say that is a whole new ball of wax for us to contend with. But life without new experiences would be terribly boring . . . ummm."

Michael brought in a china plate and set it in front of Samantha. "After you have finished, we shall all remove ourselves to the situation room. You'll feel much better dearie, once you have a little food in your poor, stressed tummy and we have a plan in place."

Esther lit a cigarette. "Nuclear bombs're tough things to cause to blow up. There's been some on airplanes that crashed and nothing happened. And we sure as hell aren't going to be *that* rough with the damn thing. Once the bad guys are home with their ancestors, the first thing we'll do is radio the military and let them take it from there. I'm too old to mess around with bombs of any kind. They *all* kill you dead, black powder or atomic, the results are all the same if you're on the receiving end."

Samantha forced herself to begin eating. The sooner she learned what the plan was these professional killers had laid out, the better. It would be pleasant to think she might stand a chance to live long enough to see the sunrise.

CHAPTER FORTY-FIVE

Tex Birdsong rode a wobbly bicycle along the dirt road by the bright yellow light of a newly risen full moon. It wasn't his fault the bicycle wobbled like it was made out of rubber. The damn Chinese who'd built it after putting a lot of fine American workers—fine *union* workers—out of their jobs had undoubtedly used cheap, inferior metal to make the axles. These days a person couldn't buy anything decent that was made in America. Everything was all cheap, foreign shit engineered to fall apart and need replacing the day after the warranty ran out, not like in the grand times when America was run by Americans who had a backbone instead of the limp-wristed, politically correct morons who controlled the country nowadays.

Then, as he approached the first streetlight, Tex saw that some idiot had dropped a piece of pipe in the road. A really big pipe by the looks of it. His heart jumped up to the bottom of his throat and started hammering when he noticed the so-called pipe had over a dozen rattles on the end, held high beneath the night sky.

Tex's recent painful encounter with a rattlesnake had taught him they were not to be trifled with anymore so than a longshoreman of olden days. He whipped the handlebars to one side and shot past the snake, nearly running into what had to be the largest cholla cactus plant in Arizona. Luck was riding with Tex Birdsong that night. He regained control of his bicycle once he was safely past the deadly reptile and came skidding to a dusty stop to catch his breath.

To his annoyance, the huge snake stayed nonchalantly stretched across the road, completely ignoring his passing. The thing didn't even have the courtesy to coil up and begin buzzing and striking at him like they were supposed to. He wanted to pull out his pistol, walk over, and teach that damn snake some respect, but he couldn't. Tex had been unable to find his .38 revolver, and it galled him too much to ask his wife where it was. No man, no real man, ever asked a woman for anything. Took it, by gawd, and let the chips fall where they may. He was no wimp—never was, never would be.

After taking a deep breath and letting it out slowly, Tex was able to focus on what was more important than shooting a rattlesnake, the Tombstone Minutemen. A few minutes later he parked his wobbly bicycle near the front door of Johnny Ringo's Saloon, safely locked it to keep the low-life scum that abounded these days from stealing his only cheap mode of transportation, then went inside the bar.

A scan of Johnny Ringo's disclosed no one he knew. Tex had hoped possibly Rodney Page or his deputy, Wab Smith, might be there. No, those men had important work to do and were undoubtedly out on the Maginot Line defending our country from rabble. Tex realized it was too late at night for him to go riding his bicycle all the way to The Line, especially considering the abundance of dangerous rattlesnakes. He decided his goal to join the Minutemen could wait for daylight, or maybe even until another of their meetings, which always included free beer.

Tex Birdsong climbed up onto his usual stool at the far end of the bar and signaled to Wendy, the night barmaid, who wasn't at all hard on the eyes, to bring him a beer, which he knew would take a while. The two bits a beer he tipped wasn't enough to speed up *any* bartender.

But then, nothing, it seemed, ever happened fast in the desert.

Tex realized that for him to get into a dither over joining the Minutemen was wasted effort. This was the land of tomorrow. He watched Wendy's ample bosom jiggle when she bent over to fill his mug and decided to enjoy the night. After all, like the Mexicans were so fond of saying, there was always tomorrow.

CHAPTER FORTY-SIX

Aswad and Zahid were the forward guard of the al-Qaeda detachment. Their job was to be the first to intercept the attack from the infidels they knew would be forthcoming. That death would find them soon was a cheering thought. They had come here to the land of the Great Satan to die for Allah, and the rewards that awaited them in heaven would be glorious beyond measure.

It was just too bad their mission to destroy a large American city had come to this sad state of affairs. And all due to their stupid leader, Husam al Din, insisting they buy an old, worn-out truck that had overheated and broken down on them. Now, the best they could do would be to try and detonate the atomic bomb where it sat. Blowing a huge hole in the barren desert, while only destroying a little town like Tombstone and killing a measly thousand or so infidels wasn't what they wished. Still, it would send a strong message and definitely hurt the Great Satan's booming economy.

The message would be plain to all the world that their god was great. That alone was incentive enough to die for with a smile. But so far the desert had remained quiet, only an occasional animal rustled the sparse vegetation. In the full moon's brightness they could see well enough to prepare for any attack and stall the infidels long enough for their companions to unload all those damn watermelons and prepare to bomb for detonation. For the time being there was nothing to do but keep a sharp eye peeled, and talk about the afterlife they would soon be enjoying.

"I am looking forward to bedding my thirty-six virgins," Zahid said.

"My brother, there are seventy-two virgins awaiting us. The Mullah in Afghanistan was quite plain on the number."

"Seventy-two is a very good number. After all we have endured, it is more fitting than the paltry number thirty-six I was told."

"Because we are al-Qaeda, my brother, we get more than most. I hope all of my virgins are big in the chest like I have seen in American magazines. That is the only good thing about the infidels, their women have big chests and they smell very sweet, like roses."

Zahid smiled into the wan moon. "I hope my virgins—" The sound of approaching music took his full attention.

"I hear it, my brother. I did not know the infidel army attacked to country western music."

"The person doing the singing is the one they call 'Willie Nelson,' of that I am certain. No one else sounds like he does."

Aswad grabbed his Kalashnikov assault rifle. "There is a vehicle coming, but it is only a small, red Jeep. I do not think this is an attack."

"No, but we should maybe kill them anyway, just to be on the safe side."

"Not yet, Aswad. There is no reason to betray our position if the music-playing Jeep holds only kids out running around, like we know the young infidels do."

"I do not believe these are kids, my brother. I think Allah has chosen to send a greeting to welcome us to Heaven before we are dead."

Both al-Qaeda members stood transfixed at the shiny red Jeep that had come to a stop only dozens of feet away to the tune of "Angel Flying Too Close to the Ground." From the driver's seat the most beautiful girl they had ever seen climbed out to stand in the silvery moonlight. To their amazement the dark-haired lady wore almost no clothes save a pair of skimpy red panties and push-up bra, along with a pair of western cowboy boots.

Zahid said, lowering his weapon. "Now, my brother, that is exactly how I want *my* virgins to look."

"She *is* very big in the chest," Aswad mumbled. "I wish for the same . . ." He could no longer speak when the lovely lady began dancing alluringly, taut breasts quivering in the pale light, lithe fingers teasingly urging them to come close.

"My brother, we must . . ." Zahid gave a slight gasp and grew silent.

Aswad paid his companion's sudden muteness no mind. He kept his full attention on the sexy dancing girl, which he did for several seconds until a hand clamped hard over his mouth. At the same instant he felt a sharp burst of pain at the base of his skull. After that, Aswad felt nothing at all.

Esther Munson's stern face appeared at the passenger window of Samantha's Jeep Liberty. She climbed out to stand in the quiet desert night, where she smiled briefly at the bodies of the newly deceased terrorists.

"Well, *that* was easy money," Esther said. "Eight more of the sons o' bitches, we can go home, get some rest, and plan a nice, peaceful vacation."

Samantha felt uncomfortable being nearly naked in front of Sidney and Michael, then realized there was no reason. Both men were more concerned with cleaning blood from their silver ice picks than looking at her. She went to the Jeep and took out a black shirt and pants, along with a ski mask Esther had given her before they left the bed and breakfast.

"We mustn't allow ourselves to become complacent, Mother," Sidney said while Samantha quickly dressed herself. "That dreadful nuclear bomb still has to be dealt with, which may prove to be rather much of a challenge, even to all of our considerable talents."

Esther tapped out a Marlboro from rote before noticing both her son's and Michael's stern looks of disapproval. She tossed both the lone cigarette, along with the entire pack, into a patch of sagebrush. Even the tiniest of flames can disclose one's position. A hint of smoke, perfume, or aftershave lotion had caused the demise of many hit-people in their pursuit of profitable prey. Esther Munson had not survived to a ripe old age in what was likely the most hazardous occupation on earth by forgetting to pay attention to details. It was just that these days she needed a reminder.

"I wasn't gonna light the damn thing," Esther snorted.

"Of course you weren't, Mother," Sidney said with a tiny, dismissive wave after returning the silver ice pick to its leather holder. He turned to face to the south, where they knew the truck containing the nuclear bomb was, along with, hopefully, all of the remaining terrorists. "Approximately how far away is our target?"

Michael Herod studied the black GPS he held in his right hand for a brief moment. "No more than a thousand meters directly south of our present position." He clicked a switch and pocketed the device. "My friend, they are so close I am certain they heard Samantha's Jeep. The desert is well noted for carrying sound long distances."

Esther gave another snort, this one of impatience. "Well, like General Pershing said; 'Heaven, Hell, or Hoboken by Christmas.' Let's quit lollygaggin' and start skirtin' around to flank those bastards. They know we're *here*, it's time to get our butts over *there*."

Samantha fastened the wide belt containing items she had never known existed around her waist. Then she pulled the black ski mask over her head, as had the others, grabbed a heavy, black duffle bag that held the ingredients to nightmares, then strode off across the shadowy desert, taking up the rear position behind Esther.

Briefly, Samantha allowed herself to ponder why the gods had decided to use her as a pawn in such a ghastly game. With a start she realized that all soldiers going into battle undoubtedly felt the same. There were cold-blooded killers ahead who wanted to kill millions of innocent people simply because they were Americans. They were the same as a disease or some rabid animal, and had to be stopped—killed—at any cost.

Samantha's green eyes steeled with determination. She placed a hand on the unfamiliar yet deadly weapon in a leather holster on her belt. The steel was smooth and cold. Like a surgeon's scalpel, it could be used to cut out disease. In a few brief minutes, she would get her chance to start excising from American soil some bastards who desperately needed killing.

CHAPTER FORTY-SEVEN

As they had planned earlier, when the four hit-people got to within sight of the truck that held the nuclear weapon, Esther and Samantha split off, taking an easternly path, while both Sidney and Michael headed northwest to make a circular route that would bring them to where they could flank the terrorists.

After Sidney and Michael had disappeared into the shadowy brush of the desert night, Esther checked her watch, which was dull black, just like the clothes and ski masks they wore.

"Five minutes, thirty-two seconds, then we whack 'em," Esther said, her voice somewhat muddled by the tight mask that nearly covered her mouth.

Samantha made a quick check of her own watch. "We're coordinated."

The night vision glasses that had come out of the hidden room in the bed and breakfast were as remarkable as most of the other items. By all outward appearances, they were natty, aviator-style sunglasses with dull gray metal rims. To anyone wearing them, however, even the darkest of night shadows were lit up as if a powerful flashlight was shining wherever the users turned their gaze.

But the excellent night vision was only a partial benefit. Samantha pressed a tiny, almost hidden raised button on the right earpiece. Instantly the glasses began to magnify like binoculars. The longer the button was touched, the higher the power of magnification, while the illumination remained just as bright and intense as before.

After a few seconds Samantha said quietly, her voice strained with tension. "I see it. I can actually see the bomb. And there are two men wearing turbans bent over it—my God, I think they're working on it!"

Esther had already focused her glasses onto the site. "What a mess. Look at all those damn busted watermelons. The bastards took the sideboards off the truck and just tossed them overboard. Hell of a sticky mess we'll have'ta wade through. A little care on their part and we wouldn't get dirty. Nobody ever thinks about the cleanup afterward."

"There might not *be* a later if that bomb goes off."

"Nah," Esther gave a dismissive sigh. "We'll handle it, always have. A bomb's a bomb. A nuclear one won't kill ya any deader then a single stick of dynamite. Don't let the atomic part spook ya any, Samantha. I've been disarming bombs long before you were born. There's nothin' to it."

Somehow, Samantha doubted that disarming a Russian nuclear warhead would be a breeze, but this wasn't a good time to show doubt. Few people had ever *seen* an atomic bomb, yet there was one—long, sleek, and silver—on the back of an old flatbed truck surrounded by piles of busted watermelons that had been thrown aside to uncover the lethal weapon.

The bomb was much smaller than most people would suspect. The device was cylindrical, flat on one end and tapering gracefully to a point on the other, giving it a total length of just over two meters, or six feet. Yet from the briefings Samantha had learned that the "yield" or explosive force of this particular bomb was much larger than both of the two nuclear bombs that had devastated Nagasaki and Hiroshima, Japan, in 1945, ushering in the atomic age.

General Hawk had described the effects of a bomb this size detonating in a major U.S. city with all the emotion of an investment banker going over pork belly futures. "The area around ground zero, a circle of approximately a half-mile across, will be totally destroyed by heat as great as that of the sun. Depending on what particular city that is attacked and the placement of the weapon, we estimate from one hundred thousand to a half-million dead from the initial blast. Radiation and resulting fires, collapsing buildings from the wind storms, civil disorder, etc., will account for possibly two to two and one-half million more casualties within days. Then we move on to long-term and collateral damage."

Samantha did not want to go over the figures again. These were not numbers, they were living, breathing human beings. How any sane person could ever *build* such a terrible weapon of mass destruction, let alone actually use it, was beyond her understanding.

Yet, Hiroshima and Nagasaki were all too real. Proof nuclear weapons *will* be used. And there, only a mere thousand feet away, was one that, by the grace of God, hadn't made it to wherever the terrorists had planned to detonate it. With any good luck, they along with every living thing in Tombstone might dodge the proverbial bullet. And it was all up to the four of them. There was no one else to come to the rescue if circumstances turned against them. No one at all.

"Surprise is our best ally," Esther's voice shook Samantha from her dark reverie. "Those lunatics are expecting a full-out military assault, helicopters and all that shit. When the boys get in position, we'll nail 'em in a crossfire they won't expect." She patted the long black weapon cradled in her lap. The device looked more like a banjo with a shoulder stock than the rapid-fire poison dart gun that it actually was. "Bet those terrorist bastards have never even *heard* of one of these babies before."

Samantha nodded in agreement while keeping her gaze with the magnifying glasses focused on the truck. Her head was still swimming from the briefings she had just gone through about weapons she never dreamed existed. The silent, rapid-fire dart rifles like the one Esther lovingly held were unbelievably deadly. Working with the Centers for Disease Control and Prevention in Atlanta, the CIA had developed a super-powerful, fast-acting strain of botulism. An encapsulated covering on long, silver needles exposed and activated the botulism bacillus when it was fired. The effects of being hit were instantaneous; it shut down the entire nervous system, which stopped all muscle action such as the beating of one's heart. A single dart striking any part of the body killed very quickly, with no chance of survival. The director had said the person hit doesn't even get time to get off a decent scream before they're incapacitated.

The air rifle itself was another marvel. The banjo-like protuberance held three hundred and fifty of the botulism darts that could be fired either singly or fully automatic. Highly compressed carbon dioxide gas propelled the darts silently and accurately for a distance of up to a thousand meters, over half a mile. And the truck with the bomb was but a third of that distance from their position.

"Take a gander at the guy wearing that red baseball cap at the far end of the truck," Esther said, fingering her night vision glasses for a closeup look. "That's Husam al Din or I'm a monkey's uncle."

Samantha took a moment to make certain the man was the one on the picture they had been shown. It was. "That's him, Esther. The only one out there on our 'don't kill' list."

"Thoughtful of him to wear a red hat."

"I think there's something wrong there," Samantha said.

Esther snorted, "There's *always* something wrong, girl. What the hell is it? Information like that's really nice to know in testy situations like this."

"We were told by both the CIA and military we would be

facing ten terrorists. Sidney and Michael have killed two, but I count ten on that truck and standing guard. That comes up to an even dozen by my calculations."

Esther gave a snort and grasped for the pocket that usually held her cigarettes. Her eyes could be seen to draw tight behind the ski mask when she remembered she had tossed them away earlier. Didn't matter, couldn't smoke one anyway.

"Never, Samantha, I mean *never*," Esther said emphatically, "trust military intelligence. That's an oxymoron if there ever was one. Give three well-trained intelligence officers the task of counting up their own fingers and toes and you'll get three different answers. Actually, in this business you can't trust anyone. Live longer if you don't."

"I trust *you*."

Esther's eyes fluttered to become oddly kind. "You can, dearie, trust me, Michael, and of course Sidney. Just remember, the curve drops off real fast from there."

Samantha focused her glasses to a higher power. "I'm thinking the boys might be getting close to being in position."

"Let's ask." Esther touched a long red fingernail to a small microphone looped around her right ear. "Tango two, this is tango one. What's your twenty?"

"You're talking in code?" Samantha asked. "There's no one else out there except Sidney and Michael."

"Force of habit, usually you can't be too careful, girl. Not every time. You don't always have a government-issued scrambled cell phone. Never want to ruin the surprise party. That's the edge we depend on."

"I see . . . I guess I still have a lot to learn."

"You're gonna do just fine . . ." Esther cocked her head to her earpiece and listened for a moment. "The boys are in position to the left of and behind the end of the truck. Now we can pepper the hell out of those bastards without worrying about a stray dart hitting someone who doesn't deserve it."

Samantha grabbed up her own dart rifle. It was light as a feather; she had been told it was made out of nearly indestructible polycarbonate plastic. For all the world it both felt and looked like one of those big water guns kids used to playfully shoot each other on hot summer days at pool parties. Only this gun was unimaginably deadly, along with being totally quiet and giving off no betraying flash of muzzle fire as did conventional firearms. Another delightful attribute of the botulism poison that covered the needle-like darts was the fact that they had been engineered to become completely harmless less than thirty seconds after being fired and exposed to air. This gave a real measure of comfort when it came time to move in where the bomb was and possibly stepping on a dart or pricking a finger moving a corpse about. Samantha had to acknowledge the weapons they had gave them a wonderful edge over the bad guys, whatever the actual number of them turned out to be.

Esther listened intently to her earpiece. "You're got it son, we're coordinated . . ." She checked her watch. "Yep, that's when we hit the bastards. You did notice the bearded prick wearing the red baseball cap and make him as the one we let get away."

Esther's nod acknowledged that Sidney and Michael were apprised and everything was ready for the assault.

Samantha felt a flock of butterflies milling about in her belly when she checked her watch. "It's time to dance. I only wish I had nerves of steel like you."

Esther gave a knowing look as well as she could from behind the black ski mask. "Everybody but idiots gets scared, girl. But you won't have time to fret for long. Get your rifle focused in to take down the guards on the ground. I'll perforate the pricks on the back end of the truck at the count of three."

Samantha's butterflies grew as big as turkey vultures when

Esther pointed the dart gun and placed her magnifying night vision glasses to the special aperture.

"One," Esther said ominously.

CHAPTER FORTY-EIGHT

The second Esther Munson reached the count of three, the butterflies in Samantha's stomach grew still. She had read the most common memory of people who survive fierce combat is that events happened too fast to allow them time to feel fear.

It turned out those people were right.

As they had planned, Samantha unleashed a stream of tiny, silver darts at the two guards on the ground close by the trailer. The black weapon in her hands gave a low hiss like a provoked, venomous snake, but that was all. There was no recoil, no blasting of gunpowder, yet the two targets in her eyepiece danced wildly about for a few fleeting moments in a disjointed manner as if they were wooden puppets whose strings had become tangled. Then the pair toppled over, still jerking crazily. A quick glance to the truck showed all of the terrorists had been hit by darts, save the one wearing the red cap who jumped into a pile of broken watermelons, slid about, then regained his footing and charged off across the desert.

"The bastard!" Esther yelled. She pulled out a pistol and began firing shots at the fleeing man. A second volley from the south put the al-Qaeda terrorist Husam al Din running in a more northerly direction.

"Now that's a good boy," Esther said, standing and pulling off the ski mask. "Some people simply need guidance on occasion." She gave a thin smile. "Looks like the bad guys have stopped jerking around. Let's go take a gander at a nuclear bomb. Always wondered what one of those things looked like up close."

"I hope it's doing nothing but lying there," Samantha said as the butterflies erupted in her stomach. "The way those men were bent over working on it is worrisome."

Esther gave a dismissive snort, then keyed the ear radio to talk to Sidney, making sure the barrage of poisonous needles had indeed eliminated any immediate danger to their approach. The purple-haired hit-lady gave Samantha an affirmative nod.

A few minutes later, the now still bodies of the terrorists had been removed from the back of the flatbed truck. After the much-needed pathway had been cleared, Sidney, Michael, and the two women stood alongside the cylindrical device that was fastened to the bed of truck with sturdy steel straps. It was obvious the bomb was meant to stay there, and nothing short of a welder's cutting torch would free it.

Moving the atomic bomb, however, wasn't really of concern at this moment. A cover plate had been removed from the top-side of the weapon exposing a complicated panel of switches and digital readouts. The largest of these LED displays showed a series of numbers that kept flashing eerily green in the yellow moonlight. The numbers read 10:28, a second later 10:27, then 10:26.

"The damn thing's ticking," Esther said hoarsely. "I hate it when things like this happen. The bastards armed it!"

CHAPTER FORTY-NINE

Michael Herod squinted at the ominous, flashing digital readout that was ticking down in faster seconds than are usually experienced by the average person. The hit-man turned his gaze to Sidney and gave a tight grin. "Well, Ollie, here's another fine mess you've gotten us into."

Samantha suppressed a sigh. She realized that in times of extreme stress, humor is often necessary to keep one's sanity and focus. The blind, unreasoning fear that kept yelling at her from some recess of her mind had to be kept at bay. The urge to scream like a wounded mountain lion and run off in any direction would do her no good. Even if she gave in to her basic instincts, should the bomb detonate the radius of destruction would be so great that running away was not an option. There was only one choice to be made: do her job, coldly and objectively.

"I'll set out the lights," Samantha said, reaching for the duffel bag she had set beside a small pile of unbroken watermelons.

"Let me see," Sidney said in an even tone of voice. "I do believe I placed the disarming instructions that General Hawk gave me here in this pocket . . . yes, how fortunate. Now, I believe we'll have need of the tool kit."

Esther gave Michael a sharp poke to the ribs with an elbow. "Wake up, Michael. You've got that bag. Do your daydreaming later, for Pete's sake."

Michael gave a slight yelp of pain, then bent over to fish out a small canvas bag, which unrolled for about three feet to display an array of common along with some quite strange tools.

The lights Samantha turned on were very bright halogen, powered by long-life alkaline batteries—not that the part about them lasting a long time really mattered. A few moments later, the entire work area, along with the nuclear bomb, was bathed in enough light to easily work by.

"Nice not having any blood to slip around in," Esther commented. "Modern weapons are so nice and tidy, makes the cleanup easy."

Sidney Munson intently studied the weapon's manual that had the pages coated with thick plastic to make them both waterproof along with not flapping around in the wind. After a moment he said, "Ummm . . . does that number by the big flashing light look like a Mark VI or Mark XI? I really can't tell for sure in this light, but I believe we need to make certain."

"Damn Roman numerals, anyway," Esther pulled a pair of her usual cat's-eye glasses from her belt, put them on, and bent low over the bomb. "It looks like a Mark six, son. Now get on with the disarmin', if you don't mind."

"That sounds like a solid idea to me," Samantha added.

"Okay," Sidney said, turning pages. "Ah, here we are. Michael, we will need the number six Phillips screwdriver, the one made out of non-sparking metal with a magnetic head."

Deftly as a surgical nurse with many years of experience, Michael withdrew the tool and placed it firmly in Sidney's hand.

"Samantha," Sidney said. "Please be a dear and put that one light up near the nose cone so I can get a better look at the panel I'm going to remove."

Samantha had the light repositioned in a second. She was quite surprised to find that her hands were steady as rocks. Momentarily, she reflected back on the fact that only weeks earlier, even watching a movie where a bomb squad was attempting to disarm a ticking explosive device would have caused her a case of nerves. Now, if anything went wrong the Grim Reaper would have to work overtime to collect up all of the dead. She thought again on how strangely calm she felt. Everyone else seemed the same. Calm and professional. Maybe, just maybe, the Grim Reaper might be able to sleep in tomorrow morning.

Sidney Munson had the large panel that was directly below the open one unfastened in short order. He tossed the metal covering onto a pile of broken watermelons, then took a small, metallic flashlight from his pocket and shined the beam into the dark recesses of the nuclear weapon.

The digital readout flashed 6:10 when Michael and Sidney, who were hunched over the bomb began jointly studying the manual. Esther and Samantha stayed to one side, ready to help at a moment's notice. There was only the one opening, nothing else to do but let the two men focus their talents where they were desperately needed and hope for the best.

A time left of 4:59 flashed brightly on the readout when Sidney and Michael looked up from their work. Suddenly in the distance, Samantha's shiny red Jeep Liberty roared off, leaving a dark trail of dust flying in the night as it raced madly away.

Sidney clucked his tongue. "That Husam al Din isn't the sharpest knife in the drawer. I thought he'd be on his way well before now." He gave Samantha a questioning glance. "You left keys in the ignition like we discussed?"

"Of course I did. How's the disarming going is a much more pressing question."

"Ummm. . . ." Sidney looked from the page of the manual they had been studying to the bomb, then turned again to the page. "I am afraid we might have a bit of a problem."

Esther elbowed Michael aside, eliciting a cry of pain from the larger man. "Sonny, this is not how I taught you to disarm a goddam bomb." She grabbed the manual from Sidney's hands. A moment later Esther was sizing up the situation.

A time of 3:10 flickered across the readout.

"The bastards!" Esther fumed. "The dim-witted, lamebrained idiots who wouldn't make latrine cleaners in civilian life went and gave us the wrong gawd-damned book to work with. This bomb is a Mark VII. The manual doesn't cover the model we're dealing with. Can you believe this shit!"

Sidney took a deep breath. "Yes, Mother, I am afraid that appears to be the case. I believe we must now rely on our experience and skill to stop this nasty device from exploding and making a really big hole where our delightful home and the city of Tombstone stands."

Samantha interjected, "It'll only be there for—ah, two minutes and thirty-eight seconds. I suggest we all *focus* here."

"I concur with Sam," Michael said quickly. "The lady makes a valid point about hurrying. We can all have a nice, relaxing drink and a leisurely visit once this bad business is behind us."

Esther Munson slid her pink cat's-eye glasses up on her nose and stuck her head nearly into the open panel. "Some fricking Russian wire salesman hit the jackpot. There's more wires in here than you'd find in a Home Depot, for Christ sakes. Whatever happened to the good old days; red, green, or black were all the wires a decent bomb held. Nowadays everythin' is so blasted *complicated.*"

Sidney said in a calm voice, even though the countdown was now down to under two minutes, "All you need to do, Mother, is cut the correct wire and this sticky problem will go away."

"Glad to know I didn't raise an idiot," Esther pulled her head from the opening. "Give me the wire cutters, I think I've figured it out, only so many ways to detonate a bomb."

"Different wording would be more comforting," Samantha said.

"Keep thinking positive thoughts," Esther grabbed up the red-handled wire cutters with a bony hand. "Everybody knows you always cut the green wire."

A moment later, the sharp snapping of the cutters indicated Esther had made her decision.

Instantly, a loud wail, much like that of a tiny siren, split the still desert night air.

Everyone's eyes became glued to the digital readout that had begun spinning rapidly, to begin lining up zeros.

"I do believe Mother, that was *not* the correct wire to cut," Sidney said, oddly calm.

Esther Munson gave a snort. "Well, shit—!"

Then the digital readout displayed a line of all zeros.

CHAPTER FIFTY

Nothing happened. Everyone marveled they were still alive.

The four hit-people stood staring in frozen silence at the zeros lined up on the readout of the nuclear bomb. It was as if the entire Sonoran desert was holding its breath along with them. Not a single night bird nor a distant coyote ventured a peep that might trigger an unbelievably huge explosion.

After a long moment, Esther said in a whisper, "Well hell, now it looks like cutting the green wire *did* do the trick. For a brief moment there, I thought I mighta made a mistake."

In the distance, far to the south, a lone coyote ventured a mournful cry to the yellow moon. Everyone gave a nervous twitch when the eerie glow of the digital readout on the bomb grew dim and flickered out.

"See," Esther said, louder, "it *was* the green wire that needed cutting, just like I thought."

Sidney gave a dry swallow. "Possibly, Mother, but I am beginning to get a distinct feeling there might be another factor at work here."

"Hey," Samantha said softly. "I'm just glad that we, along with everyone in Tombstone, are still alive. Whatever kept that thing from blowing up, I like it."

Esther cocked her head at the bomb, then snorted, "I see your point, son."

Michael said, "Considering both the CIA *and* the military are involved, anything is possible."

Samantha blinked and turned to Esther. "What are they referring to? You disarmed the bomb when you cut the green wire. *Didn't* you?"

"We'll know for certain here in a few minutes." For a moment, it appeared Esther was so angry that she was going to kick the bomb, then changed her mind. "Sidney, get that damn General Hawk on the phone and tell him the coast is clear. If what I think happened turns out to be true, I'm liable to whack that son of a bitch myself and not even charge for the privilege."

Michael placed a comforting hand on Samantha's shoulder. "When Esther gets mad enough to offer to kill someone for free, she's *really* pissed off."

"I don't understand," Samantha said.

While Sidney talked into his cell phone, Esther looked at her watch. "The helicopters will be here in less than ten minutes. They've been staying well out of the blast zone just in case they were mistaken. The bastards!"

"Now Mother," Sidney said as he returned his phone to its holster. "Think about all the nice money we will be paid. Whacking General Hawk, while I'm sure it would be rather pleasurable for you, will only serve to prevent us from receiving our just rewards."

Samantha stood numbly staring at the apparently dead weapon of mass destruction, wondering what was really going on. A few minutes later the sound of beating helicopter rotors drawing close told her she wouldn't have long to wait to find out the answer to her questions.

CHAPTER FIFTY-ONE

Samantha kept watching Esther out of the corner of her eye. The purple-haired hit-lady was puffing furiously on a cigarette, fingering the pistol in a holster at her side while Air Force General Frank Hawk rather brusquely answered their questions. They stood in a clearing not far from the bomb while dozens of uniformed men scurried about picking up bodies, tossing them along with every poison dart they could find into an idling helicopter. A separate crew from a solid black helicopter with no windows except for the pilot's windshield were working to remove the weapon of mass destruction from the back of the truck.

Samantha didn't think Esther would actually pull her gun and shoot the four-star general, but the more the military man explained, the more likely the event could occur. Samantha thought she might add a slug or two of her own, should the opportunity arise.

"So what you are saying, General," Sidney's calm voice intoned, "is that there never was any chance of that nasty atomic bomb actually blowing up. It would have been kind of you to let us know this tidbit of information earlier."

"We are never certain of the veracity of our intel," General Hawk said. "Black-market weapons dealers are notoriously untrustworthy." He watched a body being bagged. "As these al-Qaeda terrorists learned the hard way."

"So you let us handle the matter while you were someplace

nice and safe if things went bad," Esther growled at the general.

"Proper military tactics, Mrs. Munson. Always expose the fewest numbers of troops to hazard as possible." He grinned. "You people handled the job quite admirably. I also note the slightly larger body count will give a nice addition to the amount we will be depositing in your Swiss bank account."

"A well-deserved bonus," Sidney said. "I must say we are quite happy the information you had about the nuclear bomb's trigger being removed before it was sold to those awful terrorists turned out to be accurate."

General Hawk shrugged. "The Russians aren't stupid. The dealer had a few million dollars of his own money invested in the United States. Bad for business if the stock markets took a nose-dive due to a nuclear bomb blowing up in our country."

Esther lit another Marlboro from the one she had been smoking. "And I suppose the bastard sold the nuclear trigger to another group. One that doesn't have a bomb to use it on."

"We are assured that is the case," Hawk said. "More profit that way. But without a trigger, this particular weapon is harmless, so we'll load it up and safely dispose of it. The scene here, once it has been sanitized, will be turned over to local law enforcement where the entire incident will be treated as a drug deal gone sour, no one got killed who . . ."

"General sir." A man wearing captain's bars interrupted them, then gave a snappy salute. "We have a problem."

"You may speak freely, Captain. These are trusted operatives who are privy to most of our secret information."

Esther's snort of disbelief stayed the officer's words for a brief moment before he said, "We've found two civilian bodies."

General Hawk gave a sweeping glance to the hit-people. "Let's go check this out, you might know them."

Michael Herod placed his fists to his lips as he bent over to inspect the bloody corpses. "You are certainly correct, Esther, these unfortunate individuals are indeed Rodney Page and Wab Smith."

Esther faced the general. "They're Tombstone Minutemen. Page was the leader of the local chapter."

"I maintain, always have," Hawk said, "that civilians should leave matters of law enforcement to the professionals."

Samantha said, "I'd say they might agree with you if they weren't dead."

Esther gave Samantha a skewed expression of satisfaction. The young lady had performed magnificently. It was obvious she could handle the most trying of circumstances and still keep a sense of humor. It was *so* gratifying to finally have some help she could depend on.

"We'll leave them here where they fell," General Hawk declared. "The law will use their deaths to persuade others to leave guarding the borders to professionals. They'll be simple casualties of what happens when people run across armed drug dealers."

"That is always such a sad sight," Esther said, giving the corpses a final glance before turning to leave.

General Hawk said soothingly as he joined her side while walking back to where the general's private helicopter sat idling, "I'm sorry for the loss. You must have known them well."

Esther took a long puff on her cigarette, gave a slight cough, and said, "Oh, they were total jerks. I was referring to the fact their bodies are worthless. In our line of work, that's always a sad situation."

General Frank Hawk's gray eyebrows lowered for a scant moment. He would never feel even slightly comfortable in the presence of professional hit-people, especially Esther Munson. It was time to move on.

"Let's get in my helicopter and go to your bed and breakfast,"

Hawk said. "I believe we have unfinished business yet to attend to."

"Yeah," Esther said, speaking loudly to be overheard over the noise of the spinning rotor blades, "and another nice, fat bonus check from Uncle Sam."

Moments later the wind from the rising helicopter blew a covering of tumbleweeds and dirt over the lifeless bodies of Rodney Page and his deputy, Wab Smith, as it rose into a jeweled sky.

Chapter Fifty-Two

Tex Birdsong awoke to the sound of a funeral dirge, complete with matching, though terribly loud, drum rolls. He opened one eye, grimaced with pain, and swore a vow to never, ever drink tequila again.

The retired longshoreman lay in bed for a few minutes to let the mournful music clear out of his throbbing skull, then made a dash to the bathroom. *Tequila,* he decided, *was Mexico's revenge for us taking a big chunk of their country.*

After a long while, Tex ventured into the kitchen, hoping his wife was in both a pleasant and quiet mood. He blinked at the bright orange sunrise that was washing over the desert from the east, then turned a red-eyed gaze to the coffee pot.

"Morning, hon." Fern's cheerful voice came across like fingernails scraping down a chalkboard. "Take a chair, I'll get your coffee, then fix you a nice breakfast of bacon and eggs over easy, just the way you like them."

Tex knew full well any food in his stomach wouldn't stay there long. "Just coffee," he grumbled, stumbling to his usual chair at the head of the table after taking a moment to turn on the radio. The local news would be coming on, and he didn't want to miss that. A man needed to stay informed.

"You must've had fun with the boys last night, I didn't hear you come in," Fern said as she filled her husband's big china cup to the brim. "I went to bed early, but those blasted military helicopters kept waking me up, must have been from Fort Huachuca on some sort of night training mission."

"I didn't hear 'em," Tex mumbled. For the past year they had slept in separate bedrooms, which suited him just fine. He couldn't even remember how he got home last night, let alone when. A helicopter could have followed him the entire way and he wouldn't have noticed.

Fern started to say something when both her and Tex's attention were taken by the radio announcer's urgent voice telling of a drug bust just south of Tombstone last night that had resulted in the shooting deaths of local Tombstone Minutemen, Rodney Page and Wab Smith. The announcer added that none of the drug dealers had been apprehended.

"Why that's *terrible*," Fern's sharp loudness started Tex's head to throbbing again. "Those men are friends of yours, aren't they?"

"They were good, American boys. I was hoping to meet them last night and offer my services, but they weren't at the bar."

"From the newscast, those men must have been killed trying to keep those awful drug dealers out of our country."

"I was gonna join the Minutemen, damnit," Tex roared, causing a sharp pain to strike behind his right eye with the force of a lightning bolt. "I tried before, but I was told I'm too old. Last night I was prepared to argue the point."

"I'm glad you didn't, hon. The law's prepared to handle patrolling the border. That's dangerous work these days. Besides, I need you."

Tex raised an eyebrow slowly to minimize the pain. "I'm worthless, Fern. I can't work, lost most of our pension money because I trusted the crooks that ran the union. We're old and broke, there's not a damn thing I can do about it. And it's my fault."

Fern stepped close and ran a soft hand up and down Tex's stubble-bearded cheeks, just like she used to do many years ago.

"You're the only one worrying, you old poop. We have a nice home that's paid for, Social Security, and each other. What more can we ask for?"

Tex Birdsong reflected back on last night. If he had gone to town earlier, hooked up with the Minutemen, his name could be on the radio, too. And for some odd reason, he once again felt comfortable being with his wife.

"You know dear," Tex said. "Maybe I have been too bitter lately. I think we should drive to Sierra Vista later, pick up some garden seeds. I always used to enjoy growing things."

"I'd like that," Fern said before her reply was drowned out by the beating of helicopter rotors.

"I'll be glad when they get through with whatever it is they're doing," Fern said once it had quieted down enough for her to talk.

Tex rubbed his throbbing temples. "You can say that again," then he looked up and added, "dear."

CHAPTER FIFTY-THREE

Esther Munson blew a smoke ring toward the ceiling of the room. After a moment, she pointed a bony finger to a flashing light on one of three huge plasma screens that graced the wall in front of them.

"That son of a bitch's been in that restaurant long enough to vote in local elections." Esther fumed to CIA Director Burr who, along with General Hawk, Michael, Sidney, and Samantha, were gathered in the "situation room" of the Sunset Bed and Breakfast.

"Husam al Din," Director Burr said, "is a trained terrorist. He's trying to make certain he's not being followed."

Sidney took a small sip of green tea. "And I am most certain he is in a quandary as to why that nasty atomic bomb didn't blow up. The device was ticking when he found Samantha's Jeep with the keys in the ignition, just like we'd hoped he would."

General Hawk turned to Sidney. "How big is the charge of C4 in that Jeep?. I keep forgetting."

"One kilo—or two point two pounds. The plastic explosive is in the form of a brick and lies directly above the vehicle's fuel tank, as does the GPS device, which is keeping us informed of the target's current location."

Samantha gave Sidney a frosty gaze. "I really liked that Jeep. I've had it almost long enough for the oil to need changing."

"You can afford to replace it with anything on wheels," the director said curtly. "Let's just hope our plan works, and soon.

We're all edgy and tired from being up all night."

"Thinking we were trying to disarm a nuclear bomb kept me wide awake," Esther said, shooting the Air Force general a look that would clabber milk. "Woulda been nice to know the only way that bomb could hurt someone was if it rolled on their foot."

Director Burr spoke up abruptly, trying to avoid any more yelling sessions between Hawk and Esther that were becoming more testier by the hour. "You and your people performed admirably, Esther, that matter is closed. I will hear no more on it. The task at hand now is to stay with the sole surviving terrorist. We have to stay focused, people."

Michael Herod said, "I must say, the chap is taking an inordinate amount of time before crossing into Mexico. My first guess was that he would be stopped for speeding, but he seems to be lollygagging for some reason."

"We know from ground surveillance that he made several calls from a public telephone using a credit card," General Hawk said. "Translators tell me he called his superiors for instructions. I suppose they're trying to decide what to do themselves."

Sidney steepled his hands and grinned evilly. "I feel pretty certain that the hiring of a hit-man to whack a certain Russian black-market arms dealer is among the topics being discussed."

"That much is a given, son," Esther said agreeably. "What I want is for that bearded prick with ears to get moving. I'm not as young as I used to be, need my rest."

"The sun is coming up," Director Burr said. "General, send the GPS coordinates of our target to NORAD."

"This will only take a minute," General Hawk punched numbers into his wireless laptop. "There, that ought to do it."

Every eye in the room turned to focus on the flat plasma screen that had just lit up. A moment later the screen gave a perfectly clear bird's-eye view of Bisbee, Arizona.

"Now, we'll do a little tweaking," Frank Hawk said as the streets became clear and steadily closer. "The satellite is in perfect position, just as it should be."

Director Burr said to no one in particular, "If someone is sitting on a park bench reading a newspaper, we cannot only see them, but read the paper with them. God, I love high tech."

Esther Munson said, "The mark's been in that same damn restaurant for three frickin' hours. Too bad that satellite you're so proud of can't set his pants on fire."

"We're working on that," Burr said without a trace of humor.

"Hey, he's finally moving," Samantha said, pointing to a man wearing a red hat leaving the restaurant. "Decent of him to keep wearing the same cap. I wonder what it says, I can make out lettering of some kind."

General Hawk fingered the keyboard on his laptop. "This will only take a sec."

Sidney gave a small laugh when he pointed a dainty finger at the screen. "How appropriate can that be?"

"I was right, he *is* a dickhead," Esther said.

"The man has a sense of irony that makes killing him and people like him a pleasure," Samantha said, drawing stares from everyone.

Then they returned to keeping an eye on the screen and watched as Husam al Din, wearing a red baseball cap with an American flag sewn on it, along with the words *9/11 We'll Never Forget,* climbed into the Jeep Liberty and drove off, heading south toward Mexico.

CHAPTER FIFTY-FOUR

Esther Munson crushed out her cigarette into an already overflowing crystal ashtray. She gave the flickering panel screen in the center another sneer, then began ripping open a fresh pack of Marlboros with her long, sharp fingernails.

Sidney acknowledged his mother's impatience by clucking his tongue while giving a diminutive wave with his right hand. "I must say, that terrorist chap moves like his shoes are made out of lead."

"Husam al Din is simply being cautious," CIA Director Burr said. "The man must take care that he is not being followed. I am also rather certain he is not too keen on meeting up with his comrades in arms. Not having that very expensive nuclear bomb go off like they were all expecting doesn't bode well for his future. After all, he *was* the man in charge of the operation."

"Pay raises, along with any retirement packages, are probably out," Samantha said. Her newfound sense of humor failed to cause even a raised eyebrow.

General Hawk realized the fire in his handmade Cuban cigar had gone out. He took a worn looking Zippo lighter that his father had carried in World War II from his uniform jacket and carefully relit the cigar. After replacing the sentimental lighter into his pocket, he laced his fingers behind his head, leaned back, and continued staring at the screen. Being in the military for nearly forty years had given him an almost natural ability to do nothing for hours on end.

Samantha gave Esther's carton of Marlboros a greedy look. If she was ever going to take up the habit, now would be the time. She had every needed excuse. Compared to dealing with nuclear bombs, fanatical terrorists, deadly weapons, skilled hit-people and the U.S. military, smoking a few cigarettes seemed like a really harmless thing to do. Almost petty, actually. Add in the fact that Esther had been puffing like a steam train for decades with no noticeable side effects was another incentive.

Director Burr gave a huge sneeze followed by a string of smaller ones. Shakespeare darted from the CIA man's open briefcase where he had been taking a relaxing nap. The cat then jumped on General Hawk's lap, who began stroking the feline's fur.

Michael Herod said, "It does appear the director has an allergy when it comes to cats. Pity, Shakespeare is such an adorable pet."

"I have always admired cats," the general's petting had started Shakespeare to purring loud enough to be heard throughout the situation room. "They are such able and efficient little killers."

"Cats gib me the sneezes is all," the director sniffed. "I didn't know the thing was ebven in the room."

"And you didn't have even one tiny little sniffle until you set eyes on him," Esther said from a cloud of smoke. "Allergic to cats, my fanny pack."

Michael Herod motioned to the middle plasma screen. He was more than a little pleased to interrupt another building fuss between Esther and the director of the CIA. "Our mark is moving."

"Well, it's about time," Samantha said. "I was ready to drive down there and give the bastard an incentive to cross the border, like start shooting at him."

Director Burr wiped his eyes with a Kleenex then studied the screen. "My guess of him crossing the border at Naco was correct. There are fewer law enforcement personnel there."

"Doesn't matter to us," General Hawk shrugged while giving Shakespeare a back rub. "With that handy little GPS device hidden over the gas tank we can keep tabs on him wherever he goes."

"It's the kilo of plastic explosives keeping it company that I'm looking forward to deploying," the director said, his voice strong once again. He turned to Sidney. "I must say, you people worked very quickly to install that package. My compliments on your expediency."

Samantha gave Sidney a glare that would wilt lettuce. Before she could say anything, Esther spoke up. "That's why we get the big bucks. We get the job done."

General Hawk began petting Shakespeare's ears, causing the cat to nuzzle his chin. "Director Burr, my old friend." He gave Samantha's voluptuous yet trim figure an admiring look. "Don't you think a wealthy nation like ours could show its gratitude to the little lady who has so unselfishly donated her brand new Jeep vehicle to our operation a nice additional bonus for her service to the country?"

"I was already planning on that, General. But for now let's stay focused on the task at hand. I believe the game is afoot."

"I directed U.S. Customs to work with the Mexicans," Burr said. "Make the crossing seem downright ordinary. It looks like everything is proceeding as planned."

Several minutes later Samantha's red Jeep Liberty, which they could zoom in on close enough to see that Husam al Din had removed his cap to occasionally run shaky fingers through his short, black hair, came to the junction of highway 2 where the road splits to either Cananea or Agua Prieta.

"The mark is obviously quite nervous," Michael Herod said. "I believe the director's surmise that he's wading in deep shit with his own people is accurate."

Samantha said, "Add in the fact that his ass is only a foot or two away from a big charge of plastic explosives, the man's going to suffer some big-time hurt before too much longer."

Shakespeare gave the general a big nuzzle when Hawk said, in a satisfied tone, "We can only hope that enough of his friends attend the party to justify the cost of the explosion. The more bad guys we blow up at one time, the merrier the occasion, I always say." He gave the tomcat a squeeze. "Blow 'em to Hell, eh big guy?"

"Now that's strange," Director Burr said somberly, his eyes glued to the screen.

Esther snorted, "Damn raghead terrorists. Can't predict either them or the frickin' weather."

Every eye in the room was fixed on the center flat screen when a large two-ton, ten-wheeler military truck with a canvas covering over the rear bed pulled up behind the now parked red Jeep. What held everyone's concern was the fact that the truck had markings saying it belonged to the Mexican Army. It came complete with at least three uniformed soldiers packing automatic weapons.

CHAPTER FIFTY-FIVE

"Well, isn't this just a fine kettle of fish," Samantha said with a shrug. She turned to the CIA director. "Does anything you guys plan ever work out the way it's supposed to? First we were supposed to be facing ten terrorists, turned out to be twelve. Then the manual for the friggin' atomic bomb was for a different model than the one we recovered. I swear . . ."

General Hawk continued petting Shakespeare, who had joined in staring at the television screen. "My dear, much of our intel comes from sources that are unreliable at best. We are constantly striving to update and improve our screening abilities. But it seems we always wind up having to rely on those at the front to know the facts . . ."

"That's why they pay us the big bucks," Esther said abruptly. "At this particular moment in time, I think we'd better see what the hell the Mexican Army's doing stopping our mark. They shouldn't be doing that."

The CIA director had moved to the far corner of the room for privacy. He kept waving an arm about in exasperation while growling into a cell phone. After a few moments he turned to his companions. "All of the Mexican commanders say they don't know a thing about what's going on, claim that truck's not even theirs."

"I believe they quite possibly are telling the truth, sir," Sidney said, pointing a dainty finger at the television. "I suggest you come over here and observe the events with us, they are becoming, ummm, *interesting.*"

"I'm zooming in on the soldier's boots," the general said, edging the cat aside to work his laptop easier.

"And what's that going to tell us?" Director Burr asked in an exasperated tone. "This is no time to go off on some tangent."

"Those men are not soldiers," Hawk declared. "Not in any army I'm aware of. Polishing and shining your boots is drilled into every soldier starting in basic training. Why, look at those men—they're wearing shoes, not boots, and they're all in need of shining. The Mexican commanders are quite correct about these men not being in the army."

Sidney lowered an eyebrow. "Husam al Din is getting out of the Jeep and going to meet with them."

"And he doesn't look like a happy camper," Esther added.

"I think we can understand why he was lollygagging," Michael said.

Samantha watched as the one soldier with the most medals and stars on his uniform approached Husam. "I wish we could hear what they're saying."

"Next year, if we're lucky," Director Burr said.

"I don't need to hear a word to figure out there's a pissing match going on." Esther said. "I'm bettin' them so-called soldiers are al-Qaeda."

"Give the lady a toaster," the general said. "Face recognition technology has just confirmed the man facing Husam al Din is none other than Abdul bin Said. He's one of the top ten al-Qaeda leaders."

Director Burr shrugged. "I thought the last we knew, he was in Pakistan."

"Pay attention, gentlemen," Sidney Munson said in an urgent tone. "I do believe this meeting is about to come to a bad end."

All five in the situation room, including Shakespeare, watched intently as two of the uniformed "soldiers" roughly grabbed each of Husam al Din's arms and twisted them to force the terrorist to the ground. Abdul bin Said pulled his sidearm, cocked it, and calmly fired a single round into the back of Husam's head. The terrorist shivered as if he was cold for a brief moment before growing eternally still.

Esther said, "Samantha was right about him not having to worry about retirement."

"The price of failure among terrorists," General Hawk said, giving Shakespeare a back rub. "Everyone is expendable in their particular code of honor. Vicious and unpredictable people there, kitty."

Director Burr said, "All they respect—aside from their misguided religious fever—is force. The greater the force, the greater their respect."

The uniformed men picked up the limp body of Husam al Din, carried it to the rear of the Army truck, and roughly tossed it inside.

"Now that's a good boy," Esther said with a genuine smile when Abdul bin Said walked over to the red Jeep Liberty and climbed into the driver's seat.

"Oh, I like this scenario," Sidney said in agreement.

A few minutes later the big diesel truck followed Samantha's Jeep along the paved highway leading toward the town of Cananea, Mexico. To any who happened on the procession, there was nothing to make one think it was anything other than a tourist vehicle ahead of a truck belonging to the Mexican Army. Certainly nothing appeared amiss.

Esther Munson lit a fresh cigarette and sighed. "There's a valuable dead mark in the back of that damn truck who'll never be worth a plug nickel to anyone. That's a mighty sad situation to my way of thinking."

The director of the CIA rubbed his hands together gleefully. "Now Esther, don't go getting down in the dumps. It was due to your people's skill and diligence that Abdul bin Said's radical ass is sitting over two pounds of high explosives."

Esther's quizzical expression was answered when General Hawk added. "That man has a twenty-million-dollar reward on his head, dead or alive."

Samantha again surprised everyone when she grinned evilly and pointed to her red Jeep on the television screen. "I think there's been enough said."

Chapter Fifty-Six

"Now there's a smart new twist," Director Burr said in an oddly admiring tone of voice. "I didn't know the al-Qaeda bunch to be so intelligently devious."

Every eye in the room was fixed on the plasma screen that showed Samantha's Jeep, followed close by the Mexican Army ten-wheeler truck, turning from the main highway onto a dirt road that appeared to be blocked by a pile of boulders the size of washing machines.

Abdul bin Said and a companion hopped from the Jeep and tossed the fake rocks aside as if they were made of cardboard— which they actually were.

Sidney Munson took a moment to explain, "People use those hollow, imitation boulders to hide satellite dishes when either some homeowners' association won't allow them or the owners simply don't care for the way they look."

"I gotta couple of friends who're making a good living whackin' members of homeowners' associations," Esther added, but she was totally ignored.

"Those bastards really went out of their way to hide that road," General Hawk said. "Look what they did, no wonder our surveillance never picked this up."

A few feet past where the heap of fake boulders had been, a couple of very large fallen logs lay across the road. As easily as the rocks, the counterfeit trees were moved aside, then both vehicles drove past the barricade and stopped. A moment later the rocks had been replaced, the logs were back in position, and two uniformed soldiers with gas-powered leaf blowers were back down the road removing all evidence of tire tracks. When they were finished and back inside the big truck, the narrow dirt road that wound its way up a craggy canyon appeared unused for many years and totally impassable, even to the most determined off-roaders.

General Hawk said, "Now we know where they hid that nuclear bomb." He gave a scathing glare at the director of the CIA. "We were *told* by those who were *supposed* to know to look on the other side of Mexico."

"If it's the same outfit who goes around passing out 'how to disarm this bomb' manuals," Samantha said, keeping her eyes glued to the television screen, "that are for bombs other than the one ticking in front of you, I can easily see that happening. Actually, I'm surprised they got the right country."

"That's enough nitpicking," Director Burr grumbled while drumming his fingers on a table. "I have already addressed all of the problems we at the CIA are forced to endure from bad intel. We are targeting high value targets here. Let's focus, gentlemen." He smiled thinly first at Samantha, then at Esther, "And ladies."

Sidney Munson touched fingers to his cheek. "As long as the Central Intelligence Agency remembers that the banks they write our checks on has the money to clear them, I believe, Mother, along with the rest of us, can forgive minor shortcomings."

"Yeah," Esther said, lighting a fresh cigarette. "But my blood pressure's still up over that episode with the nuclear bomb. I don't need this shit at my age."

"I do believe we are going to discover something big here," General Hawk said while scratching Shakespeare's ears. The big tom nuzzled his chin while the general's natty uniform was becoming covered with black cat hair, a fact that the military man seemed to ignore.

The Air Force general continued, "Al-Qaeda has had a major base of operations established somewhere in the Western Hemisphere for years—long before 9/11. The masterminds of the attacks on the Pentagon and World Trade Center are generally believed to be headquartered in Canada. I have a hunch that a lot of intelligence officers are going to have egg on their faces real shortly."

Samantha stepped over to grab up her cat. "Shakespeare, quit bothering the nice man, he's busy."

"Tut-tut, my dear, let the kitty be. Not only are they efficient and silent little killers, but they have an uncanny ability to sense danger from those who wish them harm." The general glanced sharply at James Burr, then returned his attention to the flickering television screen.

While the red Jeep and big "Army" truck slowly made their way up the narrow mountain road, Michael walked to the kitchen, where he quickly prepared a plate of imported cheeses and Italian ham, along with some quite excellent hard salami. He added a selection of both green and ripe olives, then filled another plate with assorted crackers and bread points. When he returned, he set them out on a table beside the television screens with a flourish. "Perhaps a few bottles of very good wine may be in order to join this fine repast. Especially since we should have good fortune to celebrate very soon."

"Things are going our way," the director said, his dark eyes pinpoints of concentration. "I can feel it in my bones."

"If they aren't the same bones that came up with that damn bomb manual," Esther said, "I'll tend to agree with you, especially with the price that Abdul bin Said asshole's got on his head."

"Ummm . . . Director, sir," Sidney said, tilting his head. "I trust our payment will not be contingent on having a body to identify. The explosion of the charge beneath the seat of Samantha's Jeep is so large it will leave only minute bits of human remains scattered over a considerable area."

Director Burr gave a dismissive wave of a hand while keeping his focus on the convoy. "Both the General and myself have confirmed the computer's face recognition program. All we'll need to see is the explosion."

General Hawk spoke loudly to be heard over Shakespeare's loud purring. "It's my fond hope that Abdul bin Said will have lots of company close by when we hold the barbecue."

"Well, *now* we know why satellite surveillance missed that nest of vipers," Michael said after taking a dainty bite of smoked ham.

Not another word was spoken as everyone in the situation room watched transfixed at what appeared to be a hole in the solid rock cliff of a huge, abandoned pit mine opened wide to allow the convoy to enter. The second the ten-wheeler truck had entered the mountain following Samantha's Jeep, the fake canvas once again covered a sheer rock face, making it appear solid.

"Clever boys," Director Burr said. "I'm impressed. They've utilized a pitwall working of the old Casa Cordova copper mine as a headquarters. The camouflage is absolutely first-rate, don't you concur, General?"

Hawk was busy punching buttons on his laptop while keeping Shakespeare at bay. "What's a pitwall, Jim?" The general surprised everyone with his showing a familiar addressing of the director.

"They are quite large tunnel-like excavations dug from the edges of open pit mines to extract areas of high-grade ore. Just like big caves, they often extend hundreds or even thousands of feet into the mountain. They are plenty big enough to hold a hundred trucks the size of the one we saw drive in there." After a moment the director added, "I grew up in a mining town, and used to work in a copper mine once."

"Unfortunately, I believe our al-Qaeda lovelies may be even smarter than we thought." General Hawk's voice was coarse with frustration. "We've lost the radio signal from Samantha's Jeep."

CHAPTER FIFTY-SEVEN

"Damn it to Hell!" Esther shouted. "That was a twenty-million-dollar mark we had in our sights! This is *not* shaping up to be a good day here, folks."

"I was hoping to turn a profit with that new Jeep of mine," Samantha added.

General Hawk's bushy eyebrows lowered as he furiously worked his laptop. "I can't believe this, we have lost complete contact. They must be using a shielding device of some sort. Every underground hideout has an antenna or two sticking out of the ground that we can normally utilize to eavesdrop on the bastards."

Sidney Munson eyed the general's laptop, then went over to the very large computer screen that covered nearly one entire wall of the situation room. He sat down and began working the keyboard.

Director Burr turned to Samantha. "My dear, the difficulties of obtaining reliable intelligence should be obvious by now. What the general is referring to is our ability to 'piggyback' on most any type of antenna. Even the deepest bunker must have communication capabilities. I honestly cannot understand the problem, nor how they are blocking us."

"The Air Force needs to update their computers," Sidney announced with glee. "*We* are running a Darby Model One Thousand processor, cutting-edge technology, and quite secret. The al-Qaeda people are probably using a strength-shifting module to disguise their communications to make them appear as background static. Quite commendable, I must say."

Michael Herod added, "Only an extremely powerful and expensive computer running the latest Darby processor has the capabilities to ferret out devious little tricks like that."

"I've never even *heard* of a Darby chip," Hawk said with exasperation in his voice.

"Before you leave, remind me, and I'll give you a brochure," Sidney said, punching keys.

From a fresh cloud of cigarette smoke Esther said, "Investing in technology is the way of the future. No farting around for us here in Tombstone."

Sidney stole everyone's attention when he asked, "Now that we have established contact with the GPS and our lovely little bomb, would anyone care to listen in on what the chaps inside that mountain are saying to each other?" He noticed the blank stares from the general and the director. "The cost of a microphone is relatively reasonable and often a very handy addition to a planted bomb, as it appears this one will be."

"We're worth every damn dime we get paid," Esther said firmly.

The director nodded. "For once, Esther, I completely agree with you." He turned to Sidney. "Can you put them on a speaker so we can all hear what's going on?"

Sidney gave one of his slight grins. "Of course. What is amazing is that they are communicating in English."

"Cocky bastards," Esther said. "I like that trait in a man. Makes 'em easy to whack."

Burr gave a snort that resembled Esther's usual response. "I can understand their reasoning; we have hundreds of translators working for us that can't speak English."

Samantha looked over at Michael. Both shook their heads sadly.

A crackle of static, then a voice speaking quite good English with only a hint of an accent came from Sidney's computer.

"—Abdul, it is good news that you have sent Husam to Allah. Failure cannot be tolerated."

"But sadly, the costly nuclear bomb has been lost. I do not understand why it did not explode as it should have."

"We are, ah, looking into the matter."

"The other bomb is here. Since this one came from North Korea, I believe it may be more *successful.*"

Everyone in the room felt a cold chill run down their spine. They listened ever more intently to the voices on the speakerphone.

"With this bomb you will take no chances, Abdul. In the name of God, I am asking you to personally place the device inside of your helicopter and fly it across the border into the infidel city of El Paso, Texas. I ask that you detonate it at a very low attitude. This will maximize the amount of radioactive fallout."

"I serve only Allah. So it shall be done, providing the infidels do not shoot down my helicopter."

"Surprise, Abdul, is our ally. You have painted the helicopter to make it appear as a Flight For Life medical response craft."

"It is done, Allah be praised. The soft Americans would always hesitate to shoot down a helicopter with those markings."

"Your sacrifice will be remembered in both word and song."

"All is in readiness. When shall we strike?"

"Delay gives the enemy opportunity. We know that all too well. Is the helicopter fueled and ready to fly?"

"Yes."

"How long will it take to place the bomb on board and ready it to detonate?"

"No more than half of one hour. We will have to take care all is clear and in readiness before wheeling it from the safety of our mountain sanctuary."

"Then proceed with all possible speed. We cannot risk another failure. There is no way to know when our communications might be intercepted."

"So it shall be done. Allah be praised."

"Allah be praised."

The speakers chopped off with a sharp popping sound like that of a falling guillotine blade.

Sidney clicked off the speakers. "I must say that was a very good investment we made when we purchased that quite expensive new Darby processor."

The director shook his head as if he had been struck by a fist. "We didn't have any intel on this situation. Nothing. Not a single goddamn clue."

Esther surprised the CIA man by placing a comforting hand on his shoulder. "All that ever matters is who wins. Thanks to my son's computer ability, the bad guys are going to lose this one."

Sidney beamed. "I always love catchin' 'em with their pants down."

General Hawk coughed to clear his mind. "Now that we have contact with the bomb in the Jeep, I assume we can detonate it any time we choose?"

"All it takes is a little flick of my finger," Sidney said gleefully.

"I have a plan." The general had a smile on his face now, and he had returned to giving Shakespeare a hearty back rub. "Let's give the bastards about twenty minutes, lots of time to arm that nuclear bomb they are getting ready to use against us."

"Will the plastic explosive in my Jeep be powerful enough to detonate that atomic bomb once it's armed?" Samantha asked the general.

"It will if it's close enough to that helicopter. I'm betting it will be."

"This could be exciting," Michael said cheerfully. "Anyone care for a nice glass of Napa Valley red wine while we await the appropriate time for Sidney to exercise his index finger?"

CHAPTER FIFTY-EIGHT

Sidney Munson rolled the crimson contents of his glass around to study the film of the wine. Then he took a testing sip and frowned slightly. "Michael, my friend, I am sorry to say this vintage is quite inferior quality. Perhaps our esteemed company would enjoy some of the scrumptious merlot wine we had shipped to us from that delightful vineyard near Lake Tapps in Washington. They may be pleasantly surprised, as were we, with the delicious quality of wine they make in that part of the country."

"Let's hold off on the wine tasting ceremony for a while," the director said, puffing on one of Esther's cigarettes. He thought he'd given up the habit years ago, but decided this was as good of an excuse as he'd ever find to start up again. "The way things have been going for me lately, I'll wait to see what happens before doing any celebrating. We didn't have a clue about al-Qaeda having a *second* nuclear bomb."

"It'll be a terrible disaster when one of those detonates in a big city." General Hawk drained his glass and held it up for a refill. "There are thousands upon thousands of nuclear weapons out there and millions of nuts who want to blow them up. It's only a matter of time until one of them gets lucky. The best we can hope for is to forestall that time for as long as we can and hope for an attack of sanity to strike this world."

Samantha gave Hawk a skewed expression. "I never expected to hear talk like that from a four-star general."

"We of the military simply do what we must to police the bullies. It is a sad fact of human nature that some people respect only a force greater than what they themselves can wield. The armed forces kills when it must, but don't believe for a moment we enjoy it. And only a madman would obliterate a city full of innocent people."

"Whackin' the bad guys first *is* a comfort," Esther said almost wistfully, watching the large metal wall clock that had leaden hands on it.

Samantha asked no one in particular, "If we cause a nuclear explosion, won't there be a huge amount of fallout that will kill a lot of people?"

Director Burr took a puff of his cigarette and said with a rare smile on his face, "No, my dear, there will not be any fallout. The fact that the terrorists chose to place their headquarters inside of an old mine will give us an underground blast. The extreme heat of a nuclear detonation is great enough to instantly melt rock into a liquid form in all directions. Consider now the fact that temperatures always decrease as distance from the source of the heat increases. This causes a wonderful encapsulating effect that seals off the radiation efficiently as anything could. In effect, the entire explosion becomes completely muted by a surrounding of impervious glass-like material. Only a few major seismic waves that can be attributed to an earthquake will occur. Well, that, along with a really big crater to explain away as being caused by old mine tunnels collapsing. A best-case scenario to a nuclear bomb exploding would be hard to come by."

Michael Herod said, "On that cheery note, I shall go open a few bottles of the delightful Lake Tapps merlot wine that Sidney mentioned to let them breathe. A hit-man must always be an optimist." He clucked his tongue and left without making a sound.

General Hawk chuckled when Sidney came and refilled his glass with what the military man thought was excellent wine. He'd never understood all the fussing over vintages, film, aroma, etc. The damn stuff either tasted good or it didn't. And that was that. "My daddy would roll over in his grave if he thought his son would ever be drinking at this hour of the day," General Hawk said after studying his glass for a moment.

Esther kept staring at the wall clock while beginning to drum her fingers nervously on a wood table. "Poor man likely died of too much stress. If he'd had a few drinks once in a while, your daddy might still be playing golf or whatever."

The general finished his small glass of wine in one gulp. "His name was Clarence, Major Clarence Hawk. He was killed in combat in Vietnam." He set the glass down, scooted Shakespeare aside, and stood. After a quick glance at his wristwatch to verify the time, he said, "Ladies and gentlemen, it's show time."

Samantha noticed Sidney wore the same tight grin on his face that seemed only to appear just before someone died. He walked over to where his personal computer was located on the far wall. After taking out a small silver key from a drawer, he unlocked a metal covering over a section of a second keyboard, flipped it open, then turned to Samantha.

"My dear," Sidney said, "since the vehicle we will be blowing up belongs to you, perhaps you might enjoy triggering the explosion."

"I think I'd like that," Samantha said as she came to stand by Sidney's side. "Thing's probably a lemon anyway, but it's hard to tell, since I've only got to drive it less than three thousand miles."

Sidney ignored her gibe and pointed a manicured fingernail at a red toggle switch. "Your honor Samantha, may you be the first lady in history to detonate a nuclear bomb."

Samantha's features began to mimic Sidney's as she touched the plastic toggle. "This is for 9/11, you sons of bitches." Then she flipped the switch using the middle finger of her right hand.

Chapter Fifty-Nine

A fiery orange sun was reaching its zenith over the rugged Sonoran desert. Sparse, fluffy white cumulus clouds floating randomly in the azure sky offered a fleeting, mocking respite of shade to the enduring dwellers of this harsh, unforgiving land.

Only the ever-present circling red-headed turkey vultures, seekers of the dead or dying, moved about in the oppressive and building furnace-like heat. In this true desert, only the most determined or desperate of creatures stirred more than absolutely necessary at midday.

On the rimrocks of a steep cliff overlooking the long abandoned open pit Casa Cordova copper mine, a herd of nimble-hoofed mountain sheep stood surveying the distant site with dull but wanting eyes. Perhaps, they thought as best they could, given their limited cognitive abilities, that food might be available in that direction. If not food, then possibly water might be found trapped among the boulders in the bottom of the huge hole. The hardy mountain sheep could go for days with little but an occasional bite of stunted, drying grass or leaves from a scrub tree to satiate its hunger. Water, however, was necessary to have on a regular basis, especially in the torrid heat of summer. And the animals vaguely remembered water being available before in the jumble of rocks below them.

First came the patient observation of the always hunted. No matter how severe the pangs of hunger or the drive to drink even a mouthful of foul water, eons of evolution had instilled in the species the ability to freeze every muscle in its body, while blending in with the surrounding country, for long, agonizing minutes to survey every nook and cranny of the far land it intended to visit for any hint of danger.

Nothing seemed amiss to the wary animals, yet they waited and watched. The smell of humans was on the slight breeze. It was an old scent, but heady—the scent of danger wafted on the hot wind, keeping them at bay to study the area even closer.

After a long while, the lead ram, a battle-scarred veteran of many fights with mountain lions and often others of his kind, began pawing the ground nervously. For some reason the beast could not fathom, it sensed a menace that could not be identified, yet it was present, deadly, and coming closer by the second. A single whinny of warning to the herd was all the ram could sound before the very ground beneath his hooves began to shake, crumble loose, and tumble down the cliff to crash into the valley below.

Had the mountain sheep ever seen the ocean, they could have compared the movement of solid rock and earth to a huge wave approaching their position. The sheep, however, had no way to make such an observation. Sheer terror gave them the survival impetus of flight. The venerable old ram could have saved his warning grunts. Unbidden, the flock turned from the cliff to run blindly away from both the strange wave of rock that came their way, but also the terrible rumble that now accompanied it. The noise grew louder than the most violent of thunderstorms any of their species had ever endured.

The rolling, earthen wave caught up with the mountain sheep before they had gone a thousand feet. Having no sure footing, the animals were batted about haphazardly, rolling as if swatted by some giant unseen hand. Then, as quickly as it had struck, it was over. The wave of earth moved on, but it was growing smaller. The din of thunder diminished to fade away on the torrid breeze.

After a while, the wide-eyed and terrified animals regrouped. They were battered, bleeding slightly from minor cuts, yet none were badly hurt. The old ram had no conception of what had happened, but years of survival had taught him a valuable lesson. He pawed the dry earth, kicking up a small cloud of dust, then snorted loudly. Without a moment's hesitation, the ram began to lead his shaken herd in the opposite direction of the old mine. Food and water could be found in kinder, more hospitable places than the one they were leaving behind. That much the battle-scarred old mountain sheep knew with certainty.

CHAPTER SIXTY

"NORAD confirms a nuclear detonation." General Hawk snapped his cell phone closed and looked over at the somewhat ashen-faced director of the CIA. "It appears to be a very large explosion of at least one hundred kilotons. Thank God the event happened underground in a remote area of Mexico."

Esther Munson blew a smoke ring at the panel television screen that showed a satellite image of the area around the Casa Cordova mine. "Those NORAD boys are sharper than a sack full of razor blades. They must be watching the same channel we get here in Tombstone."

Sidney, Michael, and Samantha stood slightly behind Esther, partly out of respect, but mostly to stay out of her ever-present cloud of smoke. They were all transfixed by the events they were observing. A huge circle had actually washed out in solid rock from the old copper mine. Clouds of dust now hovered over the newly formed crater that looked to be nearly a half-mile across, like a sheltering cover. But by now the explosion was over, and all they could see besides shifting dark dust clouds was an occasional animal or bird getting out of the area as fast as it could.

Director Burr grabbed up his silver cell phone with a somewhat shaky hand. The CIA man realized all too well the terrible damage that nuclear bomb would have wrought had it exploded in El Paso, Texas, as the terrorists had intended. *Except for the diligent service of these hired professional killers, there'd be well over a million people dead or dying now. The economy would be in shambles. Luck and God stay on our side. This country needs both now more than we ever have.*

The director announced to no one in particular, "I'm calling headquarters in Quantico to make certain the U.S. Geological Survey in Golden announces the shock wave from that bomb to be an earthquake. We've lucked out so far, with a little more of the same, this entire incident can be swept under the rug, the world can continue watching football and basketball games and planning their next vacation. No one but a select few will ever know just how close this bullet came to striking our country."

"There've been other close calls," General Hawk said firmly, turning to look at the director. "Some that even you will never know about, Jim. The United States is a target-rich environment. The price of being soft in this hard world is terrible to comprehend, yet we who defend our country have to not only deal with the bad guys, but also some of our own citizens who have traded their backbones for money and comfort."

"Mostly lawyers," Esther commented. "Be tough to make a living in our business without 'em though, that's for sure."

Samantha started to say something, but the general held out a warning hand as he checked his wristwatch, then he glared at the screen on his laptop. "It might be a good idea to find something to hang on to because . . ."

An empty wineglass on a table began to dance about, as this was the first announcement that the shock wave from the explosion had arrived in Tombstone. There was a deep, growling sound, much like that of a provoked bear. A very *big*, provoked bear. The floor shook slightly beneath their feet, a few loose odds and ends rattled onto the floor. Then suddenly as it had begun, silence returned to the desert.

"That wasn't as bad as I'd feared," the general said with obvious relief.

Esther gave a dismissive snort. "I've suffered through more monumental farts than that."

General Hawk kept his eyes glued to his laptop. "The explosion was approximately seventy-five miles south of here and, to the best of our preliminary information, possibly as deep as a quarter-mile. All of the news is good, radiation monitors show no leakage from any unexpected vents which makes the encapsulation most likely total. We're working with the Mexican military to do a ground check as soon as possible."

"The Mexicans will cooperate," Director Burr affirmed. "As long as we don't do something stupid to embarrass them. An earthquake of moderate size striking the desert of Sonora and old abandoned copper mine workings collapsing from the shock and leaving a big crater is nothing much to explain, so long as there are no leaks."

Samantha tilted her head in thought. "I suppose in this case, the truth *would* be disastrous."

Michael Herod came into the situation room. He was pleased that his fancy dessert tray had survived the jolting. "Oh my yes, a nuclear explosion not far from our border along with that really nasty, though delightfully inoperative one we first dealt with are terrible things. Why, the stock market would take a disastrous turn should any hint of what has happened lately were to be found out by the news media."

"Damn stock market's nothing but gamblin' where they don't even give out free drinks," Esther said, eyeing the bottles of wine Michael had brought with him. "Normally I only drink white wine. The way these last couple of days have gone, I'll make an exception and go for some merlot."

"There are only slightly more carbohydrates in a nice red wine, Mother," Sidney said cheerfully. "Besides that, a few extra pounds would do you good."

"Is it really over?" Samantha asked no one in particular.

"Aside from Rodney and Wab, nobody but the bad guys got killed. That's a miracle."

Esther said, "The only reason nobody ever whacked Rodney Page or Wab Smith was 'cause they were worthless. But let's not forget the border patrol agents who were killed. They were some of the good guys."

"Yeah," Samantha said with a hint of sadness. "It seems to only strike home when it's someone you know."

"Keep in mind, my dear," Sidney said cheerfully as he helped set out wineglasses. "That a lot more villains than heroes died this day. Being on the side of winners is always cause to celebrate, especially when the deceased are far more valuable and less trouble in their present condition."

The CIA director stood and stretched. "My, but it has been a trying experience. I'm so tired I feel I could sleep for a week."

"Don't forget to put in our claims first," Esther said to him firmly. "People die in bed all the time, ya know."

"Yes Esther, I'll take care of the matter while in the helicopter on my return trip to Fort Huachuca."

General Hawk grinned when Michael filled his wineglass. "I'll make certain to also check our intelligence sources and to see if possibly some others with bounties on their turbans might have been in that mine." He beamed at Samantha. "And, of course, we will tack on a substantial bonus for the loss of your Jeep." He shot a glare at the director, who had begun picking through the snack tray. "*Won't* we, Jim?"

The director delicately placed an anchovy on a point of organic white bread. He glanced over at Samantha, who had begun to glare at him with a cold expression that took him aback. "I will authorize an additional million dollars." He shrugged. "A few dozen toilet seats will cover that and not raise a eyebrow in Washington."

Samantha simply gave a nod of agreement and said, "That'll

take care of the matter." Which verified the man's impression that she had been spending too much time around Esther.

Esther grabbed up a glass of merlot, a rare smile on her overly painted face. "My, my, let's see now, twenty-five mill for starters, then add twenty million for Abdul bin Said, a million for destroying Samantha's Jeep, two hundred grand a head for the bad guys with the first bomb. I must say we will need a calculator to add up our fees for this episode." She took a large gulp, then grinned evilly at the CIA director. "Not to mention the tidy *bonus* we're certainly due, especially considering that fiasco with the wrong damn bomb manual. That sort of thing is what lawyers call culpable negligence, which gets expensive in a hurry."

Director Burr didn't hesitate to answer. "We wouldn't have dodged this bullet without your services. When you access your Swiss and Bahamas accounts in a couple of days, I have no doubt you'll be *very* pleased."

"It is always a good idea to support your local hit-people," Michael said, chipping ice from a block with his silver pick. "Money and lots of it works wonders at keeping us *all* happy and, ah, *healthy.*"

General Hawk was unsuccessfully trying to interest Shakespeare in an anchovy. "We will enjoy a brief social time, then the director and I must be on our way. I'm sure we will be seeing each other again, but hopefully not soon."

"I agree we need a break," Esther said, refilling her glass. "After the first atomic bomb disarming went like it did, my digestion will be off for weeks."

Sidney held up his glass. "I propose a toast to the newest member of our team—Samantha."

A clinking of glasses, then after a few cheery words, along with more wine, the government men were off to the tune of helicopter blades beating in the still desert air.

Every resident of the Sunset Bed and Breakfast watched their departure save Shakespeare. The black tomcat was too busy batting an anchovy about the situation room to be bothered with decorum.

CHAPTER SIXTY-ONE

For the next three days, all of the residents of the imposing Sunset Bed and Breakfast stayed indoors. There was simply *so* much to do. During this busy time with no visitors to worry over, the thick bulletproof door to the situation room remained open.

Samantha came and went whenever she pleased without question. It was quite obvious to the lovely young lady that she'd become an accepted and trusted ally of a family of professional killers.

Well, ACCEPTED, anyway, Samantha was careful to remind herself. In the brotherhood and sisterhood of hit-people, at least those who seriously planned on collecting their retirement, the word "trust" held a more fluid and venturesome meaning than the one found in your average dictionary. A wary attitude was conducive to good health, as Esther had ingrained in her.

After a late lunch on the third day, a scrumptious feast Michael was so proud of that consisted of farm-raised quail breasts in a cream poppy seed Alfredo sauce along with a medley of organic vegetables, Esther had become perturbed that the CIA had not yet transferred their earnings into the various accounts that had been established for that purpose.

Finishing her third glass of white wine, Esther lit a cigarette and stomped off into the situation room, saying she was going to get their money. Samantha decided to tag along, which left Sidney and Michael to handle the cleanup of the table and kitchen. Not that they ever complained of that task, however, it was just that she was curious just how Esther was going to handle the matter. Being around the purple-haired old hit-lady was *always* interesting.

While Esther looked up a number in a black leatherbound book, Samantha made a mental bet that Director Jim Burr was going to hear epithets usually reserved for Marine Corps boot camps. She could not have been more wrong.

"Why hello—Jim," Esther said into the receiver, her voice dripping with sweetness. "My son and I were just going over our Christmas card list. I need to verify that your home address is still 1027 Valley Road in that delightful town of Pimmit Hills, Virginia. And you live there with your lovely wife Emma?"

A moment of stone silence, then Esther's voice became as cold as a wind coming from across blue ice. "Oh, by the way, Jim, we have yet to be paid for—yes, I'm certain you *have* been busy. I look forward to it. Thank you, *Jim.*"

Esther hung up the phone with a smile on her face while taking a long puff on a Marlboro. Without a word she went out to help in the kitchen.

Within a half-hour Sidney's powerful computer had verified that a great deal of money had just been deposited in several different-numbered bank accounts.

"You have to be able to communicate in this business," Esther said to Samantha with a satisfied wink. "In a language the bastards can understand."

"Ah yes," Sidney remarked, keeping his eyes on the computer screen. "Sweet. The promised bonus was in the endearing amount of ten million euros. The entire sum is in Switzerland. The balance of our money is scattered about in mostly offshore banks, untraceable and untaxable, just the way hard work *should* be paid for."

Samantha gave a stern look, which Sidney took note of. "And

our little lady also received a tidy million dollars for her lovely Jeep." He pressed a few keys. "There, that placed a hundred grand into your new 'sanitized' Sierra Vista bank account. I believe a fun shopping spree to purchase a nice suitable replacement vehicle for our little lady is in order."

Esther tapped a cigarette from a fresh pack. "Hummers are good, but so big they're a pain in the ass to park."

"You know," Michael said, tilting his head. "I have been thinking we could do with hiring a driver. Someone who is local so we can keep an eye on them and, of course, dumb."

"That is very observant, my friend," Sidney remarked. "Business has become so stressful of late and one of us should always remain here to fulfill the many tasks required of us and keep snoops at bay who aren't valuable enough to warrant whacking."

"A driver could take Esther shopping in Tucson," Michael said. "There is such a delightful organic produce store on Speedway. And we must remember the wonderful ethnic stores where one finds many items *so* hard to come by. I could make a list, and I am sure Esther would enjoy the trip."

Sidney turned from the computer and grinned evilly at his mother. "And I am certain the other drivers will appreciate her being a passenger." He looked at Samantha. "You have become much too valuable, I am afraid the hiring of a chauffeur may present us with a daunting task."

"Maybe not," Samantha said. "I have noticed an older man who looks to be retired and bored living at the first house on the right as we enter town. He would be close enough to keep an eye on."

Sidney nodded. "Why yes. The gentleman's name is Tex Birdsong." He punched a few keys on his computer. "Let's see, a retired longshoreman, wife is Fern, good driving record and health. The chap has mainly Social Security to live on along with a big hospital bill from being bitten by a rattlesnake. A moderate salary of say two thousand dollars a month should make him both happy and trusting."

Esther snorted from a fresh cloud of smoke. "Being a retired longshoreman helps. Squeeze all the dumb out of one of them and all you have left is a baseball cap sitting on an empty pair of shoes."

Michael clucked his tongue. "But they are such rough-and-tumble fellows. I suggest we approach him straightaway with the offer. I am sure he would be quite protective of Esther."

Samantha coughed. The image of Esther, who carried a pistol in her hairdo along with an assortment of hatpins, needing protection was ludicrous. Most everyone needed protection from *her*. "I believe this will work out fine. That way I can drive my new vehicle home." She glared at Sidney. "I'd appreciate you *not* putting any bombs in this one. At least not without telling me first."

"My dear, you have my word when I tell you we will never resort to such measures again." Sidney clucked his tongue. "Working with us is *far* too profitable to mess up and we have gone to a very great deal of time and expense to give you a totally new identity."

"Except for her pretty red Jeep," Michael said thoughtfully. "We didn't get around to changing the serial number." He gave a thin chuckle. "Not that it matters now, there isn't even an atom left to identify."

Samantha kept staring at Sidney's computer screen. "You seem to have files on everyone in Tombstone. After all that's happened, I can't help but wonder who is trustworthy and who isn't."

"Healthy attitude, my dear," Sidney said. "And, of course, we do have files on most residents of our fair town, at least those of note. We can pull up the others instantly should the need arise.

The Internet has rendered privacy but a fiction."

Samantha felt more at ease than at any time since her arrival in Tombstone. "First off, I am wondering about Minnet Page and Lucas Levy. I'd like to know if I can keep them as my friends."

"Certainly, my dear," Sidney said, turning to face her. "We have throroughly checked them out and they are exactly as they appear except for the fact that sweet Minnet will soon have a very significant check coming her way."

"Rodney's life insurance for a million bucks," Esther said. "When they got divorced, I told her to keep it in force, helped her make the payments. I like Minnet too much to see her in poverty. Besides, Rodney wouldn't have been around much longer, somebody woulda' whacked him. Those terrorists simply hurried his demise, allowed me to be thrifty."

"And Lucas is simply a retired postal worker who happens to be a failure at being a vintner." Michael said. "He has built up a quite . . . interesting gourmet vinegar works, I must say. We find his unique products often, ah, useful."

Esther finished her third or fourth glass of white wine; at this time of day it didn't matter anyway. "Let's have a party this weekend, invite the both of them. It's been a stressful time, that damn atomic bomb episode still has my guts messed up. A celebration is just what we all need."

"Mother, you are absolutely correct," Sidney punched a few computer keys. "Our next 'customers' aren't due until next Wednesday. And they appear, strangely enough, not to be law-yers."

"That'll be a refreshing change," Samantha said.

Sidney continued, "We will be disposing of a married couple, both are televangelists. Seems they are raising considerable sums of money, which are funneled overseas for the drug trade. The lovely man and wife believe they will be meeting a substantial donor here at the Sunset House."

"Never whacked a preacher before," Esther said. "But I guess they're same as politicians or lawyers. Thinnin' out the species is probably a sound idea."

"My, my," Michael said, turning to eye the kitchen. "I do believe the shadow is over the yardarm. May I suggest a pitcher of Tombstone Blues to be in order? We simply have *so* much to celebrate."

Esther said, "Anyone in my way will suffer pain."

Samantha smiled as she turned to follow Esther. "There's a risk no one should take."

With a slight laugh the four hit-people left the situation room together. As they entered the parlor, their footsteps blended and their shadows melted into one when they sat down at the table to enjoy a nice, frosty drink called Tombstone Blues.

ABOUT THE AUTHOR

Born in the shadow of Pike's Peak, **Ken Hodgson** has enjoyed various interesting careers. He has worked in a state mental hospital, been a gold and uranium miner, worked as a professional prospector, and owned an air compressor business. He has written hundreds of short stories and articles along with over a dozen published novels in various genres. Ken is an active member of Mystery Writers of America and International Thriller Writers. He lives on a small ranch in northern New Mexico with his wife and prime editor, Rita, along with two totally spoiled cats, Sasha and Ulysses.